DUSK AT THE GROVE

DUSK AT THE GROVE

By

SAMUEL ROGERS

BOSTON
LITTLE, BROWN, AND COMPANY
1934

Samuel Rogers

To

C. A. R. AND A. R.

CONTENTS

PART I

June 1909

June 1909

Now, Luly Waring thought, the real journey has begun. They had been traveling since quarter past seven, after a breakfast at six, but the ride to Philadelphia was so short, as the train rushed by the local stations at which the later trains always stopped, that from the moment you left North Chester you could picture its whole course in your mind, like the path of a rocket; and afterwards you hardly remembered it: that morning ride seemed to belong to a different journey. The ride to New York was nearly three times as long, but that too seemed still like a prelude, at least to her and, she imagined, to Mark; for the children it must have the endlessness of this final stretch, but if so, with their books and their drawing, their walks up and down the train, they were better than most children would be. Perhaps the journey really began on the ferry, with the smell of smoke across water, the sound of whistles, and the children chasing each other through the crowds; though this year it was not so confusing: Linda had stayed close to her father for the first time, subdued by the sky line of New York and the smell of the river; Dicky, since he could not coax her away, had not gone far alone, and Brad was content to stand by the rail and talk with Thornton Ellis about the ships they were passing. Yes,

that was when it really began, she thought, as she leaned
her head against the back of her chair and cleared her
throat, which was not quite so sore as it had been, and
closed her eyes and, listening, felt through all her body
the joggling rush of the train; and yet she could remember now that even boarding the train in Philadelphia she had had the sense that the journey was starting; even in North Chester leaving the Rectory in Mr.
Shephard's cab, even then, at the time, she had felt that
she was off, that the vine-covered Rectory, given by the
early sun the look of unbelievable cleanness and fresh-
ness that architects give their drawings, had become a
strange house the instant the door was closed, a house in
which they would not be living for three months, in
which possibly they would never be living again. Many
days are like that, she thought, and certainly years are
like that: as you go along you keep having the sense that
you are starting, that they are still ahead of you; what has
gone before seems like nothing of consequence, until all
at once you realize that this new start is not the first
but the last: it is already the beginning of the ending.
The long train to Wickford Junction was exactly that,
for the trip across the bay was a part of the end. Once
you were on the little white steamer sailing between the
lighthouses and the islands you felt that you had arrived,
that the journey was over; you could begin to rest.

Luly opened her eyes. She could see walls of scorched
brick full of windows, some of them with plants on
the sills or bedding hung out; she could look up streets
crowded with children, strewn with papers, cluttered
with all kinds of things that you could n't remember
from block to block; there was a mattress spread on the
balcony of a fire escape; clotheslines were stretched be-

tween house backs over yards that were nothing but dirt
and cinders, except here and there for an ailanthus tree,
so grimy-looking that its shadow seemed more alive
than its own leaves and branches.

What a contrast to the trees at the Grove, she thought:
I long to be there and yet it seems almost not right to
be there, spending the summer with the children in that
heavenly dreamlike place, when there is so much to be
done. The engine whistled, and the sound seemed to
be coming from inside her head and from the ends of the
world, to be hurrying her down long dimly-lighted slopes
to things, everywhere, that she could not quite remember. Its sound rang in her ears until at last it was absorbed by the rush of the train; and the walls outside
slipped by with greater speed and smoothness, as if these
hurrying walls which she saw and this rushing which she
at once felt and heard were two groups of instruments
in an orchestra, brasses and strings, each of them following the swifter and swifter beat of the conductor's
arm.

But for Mark this gathering speed meant only that
each block they passed was one more proof of his lack
of moral courage or his false pride. If Luly had been
in his study yesterday afternoon he might have handed
her the letter without comment; as it was he had slipped
it back in the envelope, put it in his pocket, and continued
arranging his desk drawers; but as he looked through the
mass of old letters, tearing them up or sorting them into
piles on his blotting pad, he knew it would be easy for
him to tremble; it would be easy to empty all the drawers into the fireplace, to leave the house with Luly packing upstairs, with the children rushing about in their
excitement at going, and walk out of town as fast as he

could, so that no one would be near him to look at him
or talk to him for the rest of the afternoon. This is
ridiculous, he thought; nobody promised me in so many
words that I was going to have the parish, and Luly will
not mind except for my sake. When I think of the
nagging silly wives of some of my clerical friends I
really don't see how the poor men keep their sanity; perhaps God deliberately arranges it to test their virtue,
but if so, I must say I think He's rather unsportsman-
like. Ministers' wives are either fools or nonentities or
saints: of course Luly's a saint, but without the unpleasant qualities that so often go with saintliness. He gazed
at her in the seat ahead of him, her chair turned, like his,
to the window: the first time he saw her, he remembered,
he had thought her nose and mouth were too large but
that her eyes were very beautiful; he had thought she
looked distinguished and passionate, slightly Italian; he had
been rather scared of her as he was of most young women
when he was a young man; she must look almost the
same to-day, he thought, except that she's heavier; she
would have been magnificent in the rectory of Saint
James's, and now I suppose we'll be staying in North
Chester for years and years — perhaps for the rest of our
lives.

Luly, glancing from the window to Mark, saw that
he was scowling. Mark loved to state that "a good traveler" never fussed and that only a man could be a good
traveler; yet Mark was apt to be snappish by the time
they reached the long train, partly because he must feel
self-conscious traveling with three children, two violins,
and a cat. When she tried to make him admit that on
the train at least he had never caught her fussing, "My
dear, you're an excellent traveler for a woman," was

all he would grant, partly teasing her, of course, but partly in earnest. Perhaps now he felt guilty because he had not sent for the doctor yesterday. She had been slightly feverish; she was sure enough of it to refuse to take her temperature; if Dr. Grosvenor had called he might have said that she could not travel to-day, and she knew Mark hated to turn back tickets almost as much as he hated asking directions. But he need n't be distressed, she thought; nothing would have induced me to let Dr. Grosvenor look at my throat.

She turned again to the window, to those streets and fire escapes, to those reddish walls with green or liver-colored trimmings: there are rooms behind those walls, she thought, and people in those rooms, but for me the houses have no thickness; even the walls are not solid; I cannot imagine that they endure; it would seem that they must dissolve like the smoke the instant they pass out of sight; and yet it is n't as if I did not know what those rooms are: I may actually have been in some of those rooms, but that was so long ago — how long? — was it fifteen years? Nearly twenty years, before I knew that Mark existed, before the children did exist — so long that those years and the people who filled them seem to have no more substance than the houses. There was Maggie Sullivan, whose parents would not see her in the hospital when she died having her baby, and the Dugan family in their one room, with the grandfather who played the violin, and how many children? Four or five, their heads swarming with lice: I remember the time I had getting the nits out of my own hair. And then there were the orchestra concerts those winters: I remember standing in line for an hour and then climbing hundreds of steps like the endless stairways in a dream;

7

how could I do it and not get tired? And the greasy whitish poodle at the boarding house with pink rims to his eyes and a scaly nose like the skin on a vulture's neck. Through an open window a young woman in a green shirtwaist stared upward scowling into the sun at the train, a dark woman, handsome, Italian or Jewish; it was a pleasant face in spite of the scowl. Luly turned her head to keep looking at that dark face. Why did I hope that woman saw me, she wondered; for her this train and all the people in it must be as unreal, as momentary, as those walls and back yards and fire escapes are for me; she has gone and I have gone, for each other we no longer exist, and yet I would have liked to know her; I wonder why.

"I heard yesterday from Budlong about Saint James's," Mark said.

She knew from his tone, with the same forced quality in its naturalness that you saw about his eyes and mouth when he sat for his photograph, that he had not received the call.

"What did he have to say?" she asked.

"They don't want me," he said shortly.

She knew how he had hated to speak of it: his straight brows were carefully not frowning, his lips were pressed together; he looked like a student who had just been told that he had failed an examination. His air of candor, his slimness and straightness, which sometimes made him look triumphant, as if he were a young god whom the world could not touch, made him now seem all the more to be pitied and the action of the vestry of Saint James's all the more callous.

"It seems to me that 's rather odd of them," she said, "after the way they talked."

8

"Oh, they did n't commit themselves."

"No, but they certainly gave the impression that you 'd hear from them. They certainly liked you."

"Oh, people are apt to like me," he said, "except the few that hate me. They like me but they don't want me."

"You know that 's absurd, Mark," she said. "Did Mr. Budlong give any reason? Have they chosen anyone else?"

"They 're considering Mendenhall in Downingtown. No, he gave no special reason."

Like a qualm of nausea the humiliation that he had felt yesterday came over him once more as he recalled the "tactful" tone of the letter. This won't be easy, Budlong must have thought as he began; how can I word it so that he will know he 's definitely out of the running and yet not hurt his feelings? He must have felt pleased with himself as he signed his name: that 's a neat job, he must have thought; perhaps he had read it to his wife for her approval, and then of course he had tried to forget about it. I have had to write such letters, Mark thought: to men who have wanted to use my pulpit to preach on some absurd topic, to people who have wanted money for some crazy scheme or other; you don't for a moment consider doing what they want and yet you sort of hate to turn them down. You pity them and you feel a little contemptuous; it 's a relief not to have to think of them.

"I 'm sure I know why," Luly said, "and it 's precisely the same reason they did n't take you at Trinity. It 's because you look so young, Mark. You look more like twenty-five than forty-three. There 's a demand for young men just starting, but they know you must

9

be too old to be considered as a promising youth, and yet you look too young for them to believe that you can have much experience." And then of course Mark gets so nervous, she thought, when he suspects that there are delegates from another parish listening to him; he does n't do himself justice; he becomes more and more involved, he repeats himself, and his voice grows harsh and strained: if only they would come quietly into the church without his seeing them! He would be equal to anything, she thought; he is a man that no amount of success would spoil, but he will not push himself, will not make a move. Perhaps it was wrong of me to feel such relief at the prospect of going to Philadelphia; no one need be wasted anywhere: you could work all your life in North Chester and there would still be things to do; but you cannot entirely overlook such a difference in salary when you have three children. We could have gone abroad before Mark took possession of his new parish; there are so many things that ought to be done at the Grove. . . . If only Mark won't be too discouraged, won't feel that he is not a success! I 'm thankful that he 'll have two weeks at the Grove now, she thought; we must do a lot of walking and reading. If it were not for the children, I would certainly go back with him.

The children meanwhile (and Thornton Ellis, who, though he was just fifteen, a few months older than Brad, could hardly be thought of as a child) were enjoying their table d'hôte luncheon in the dining car: five courses, all you could eat for a dollar. There had been a threat of a row at first because Linda could not decide what she wanted and made Brad keep scratching out the orders on the slip, and even had sent back her chilled fruit because it contained a piece of pineapple, which she did n't like. This had embarrassed Brad and Dicky very much, but now it was all forgotten.

Linda had to keep reminding herself to go on with her creamed chicken, which she really loved as soon as the waiter promised her that the spots in the gravy were not pepper; she kept looking at the telegraph poles; if she was n't eating she would have felt like counting them: each one that goes by, she thought, means that we're exactly so much nearer the Grove: I wonder if they last all the way from here to Wickford Junction: I wonder how many there would be — fifty thousand, or ten million perhaps?

The waiter, a nice colored man, was taking away her chicken. "Be sure not to put any mayonnaise on the salad," she told him with a smile, and he promised that he would remember. It's funny, she thought, different people like such different things, and it's not always just the taste: I love to hear a knife cutting green peppers, but I hate the taste of them. Do they taste just the same to other people, I wonder, and do they like it, or do they taste different? I'd hate to like green peppers and tapioca, but if I liked them, I suppose I would like liking them.

She began listening to Dicky as he told Thornton about the moving picture they had seen as a reward the day after their recital. "If Brad and Linda had n't been there," Dicky was saying, very cunning with his red hair and his bright blue eyes, "I guess I'd have wasted a couple of cents because I would n't have looked at half of it. It was too exciting. The dog kept jumping at the man . . ."

"He kept trying to bite the man's foot," Linda ex-

11

plained. She knew she remembered the picture better than Dicky.

"Biting his trousers, you mean," Dicky said.

She paid no attention to Dicky, but leaned towards Thornton, trying to catch his eye.

"And then the man locked him in a door," she said.

"In a door?" Dicky asked. "What's that?"

"Well, in a room."

"In a *closet*," Dicky said.

It was rude of Dicky to interrupt. "Well then," she explained again, "they locked him in."

"*They?*" Dicky asked. "Who's *they?* There was just one man."

"But the dog got out of a window," Linda said quickly, "and ran around behind, and the man picked up a chair and tried to kill him, because he was afraid, the big coward."

"He was not afraid," Dicky said. "He just wanted to kill him, that's all . . . and every time Linda starts a new . . . after a comma, she says, 'and er — er — er.'"

"Dicky, *please* be quiet!" Linda felt that all was ruined. Dicky was being as mean as he could. "*Please!* I wish Dicky wouldn't keep interrupting." Dicky was grinning at her fiercely; he was about to speak. "Sh-s-s-sh," she said loudly into his face.

"Sh-s-sh yourself," Dicky said, and suddenly his face turned red, his eyes grew small; she felt that her "sh-s-s-sh" had been too fierce, like a snake squirting poison.

"Shut up, you damn fool," Dicky said. He was crying and Linda felt like crying too, but instead she smiled at Thornton. "Dicky's so cryable, isn't he?" she said.

Brad felt that the whole car was listening and watching. "Now suppose we have no more of this," he said.

12

"You're enough to make a person throw up — acting like this when you're on your way to the Grove."

We *are* on our way to the Grove, he thought; all day he had kept thinking of it, then forgetting it, then thinking of it again.

"They're all right," Thornton said soothingly. "Cheer up, Linda, girl. You better get at that pear, Dick, old scout, or that waiter, that friend of Linda's there, will be taking it away."

Brad felt a little jealous of Thornton's smooth grown-up voice, not really put on but not quite natural; Brad felt superior to it but he sort of respected it: it did make him feel young. He would not want Thornton to know that he still loved to get valentines and counted them just as carefully as Linda and Dicky, and that he liked to play with Dicky's electric train. On the other hand Thornton thought medical books were dull except for the pictures, and that was just morbid curiosity; he might have a tuxedo to wear to dances, but he was not old enough to be interested in science. I'm kind of sorry Thornton's coming to the Grove, Brad thought, but it's only for three weeks, and I'd rather have him at the start than at the end; Thornton did not belong to the Grove or to Rhode Island; he belonged to Philadelphia and school, but everything was so wonderful at the Grove that it didn't matter. Joel would be coming down this evening, to-night, in just a few hours; he would be sorry to see Thornton, but Thornton's being there, Brad knew, would make Joel and himself feel closer together, more alike. Brad remembered how Joel and he had laughed together last summer after Thornton had brought home a blackfish from the point, where he had gone fishing with a most elegant rod, and said he had caught it;

13

and then the next day when they were all together on the beach a Portugee came up to Thornton and asked him for the money to pay for the fish he bought yesterday. That was the kind of thing Thornton would do — something really childish. Joel and he might not be so slick but they both of them would be too proud to do a thing like that; each of them knew the other would n't do it, just as each of them knew so many things the other would n't do or would n't not do. I 'm lucky to have a friend like Joel, Brad thought; I 'm sure he 'll be my best friend as long as I live. In his mind Brad could see Joel only a few hours away with no night between; he could see the whole summer, weeks and weeks of it: Joel and he swimming before breakfast, walking on the ledges, all of them playing kick-the-can after dark — everything different from everything anywhere else because it was at the Grove.

"Can we have second helps of ice cream?" Dicky asked.

"I 'm sure if I ask the waiter he 'll bring you a second help," Linda said.

"No, you don't," Dicky said. "Not for me." Catch him letting Linda get jawing again to that waiter; she never would stop. He wiped his mouth and slid off his chair into the aisle.

"Where are you going?" Brad asked.

"Back to the folks," he said. "Where do you think I 'm going?"

"Look out," Brad said. "Be careful between cars."

"Not for you I won't," Dicky said. "What do you think I are, anyway?"

It must be nearly half over, Luly thought. She was pleased with her idea of having the children go into the

dining car first, and then Mark and herself: it had been
very peaceful at the little table opposite Mark, even though
she was n't at all hungry and had not dared not order the
regular lunch for fear Mark would say she was "sulky."
It was easier every year traveling with the children; surprising how much difference a year could make. She had
rather dreaded having Thornton along as being one more
person to look out for, but it really meant one less because Brad was completely off her hands. She was fond
of Thornton, partly because he had such an awful mother,
a fast selfish woman; it was much to his credit he
had not been ruined; he is one of those boys, she thought,
who can't help being plausible, but I think also that
now he 's truthful, which plausible people very seldom
are. It might be a risk to have Brad thrown so much
with a slightly older boy coming from such a background,
but you had to take risks, and after all if you did n't
trust your children, whom would you trust? Now that
we 're staying in North Chester, she thought, it will mean
still using principal to pay for the music lessons and for
Brad's school, but I 'm sure it 's worth it. She looked
at Brad: he was too thin; he did n't have much color, but
he always put on weight at the Grove, all three of them
did; and he was far more self-reliant than he used to be.
She remembered how once at the beach when he was
about Dicky's age or a little younger, he had refused to
put his head under water until at last she had waded in
above her knees without even pausing to take off her shoes
and stockings and ducked him herself: an episode she
was quite proud of because it was such a proof that she
did not spoil them.

Linda was the most difficult, because she was a girl,
and girls, Luly felt, were always more difficult than boys,

15

DUSK AT THE GROVE

and because she had a tendency just now to be self-conscious: poor little thing, she was hardly to blame when she was so very charming to look at, with such gracious ways, and when everyone looked at her and paid her compliments. Luly turned now to glance at her across the aisle: with bent head, drawing a picture on her pad. She had a lovely clear skin, fine smooth features like Mark's, with eyebrows raised towards the temples; and, in spite of her dark eyes, her dark straight hair, parted and drawn over her ears like a Russian dancer's, a face that when she was interested or pleased became radiant so that at such moments you thought of her as golden. Linda's the only one of the three who is really beautiful, Luly thought, and in a way I'm sorry to have such a beautiful daughter, though I couldn't bear to think of Linda's being different; Brad is nice-looking, but his nose and mouth are too big to be handsome, like mine, and Dicky with his red hair and small round nose and sticking-out ears is really rather ugly, I imagine, though I love his face and love to watch it. She remembered how on a walk with Mark and Dicky last spring she had missed him at a turn of the road and stopped to call, but could get no answer; she had felt a little worried and suggested going back to look for him; then Mark had seen a small figure running as fast as it could a quarter of a mile away on another road and they had walked slowly so that they would meet him where the roads came together, and he had trotted up to them, panting, smiling but very tired, delighted to have surprised them. "Why, Dicky," she asked, "how did you happen to do it?" "Oh, just because I did," he said. "I thought I would." And after that for a time Dicky had loved to keep disappear-

16

ing and then surprising them by turning up where he was not expected.

"Papa," Dicky asked now, "is a snapping turtle a mammal or an insect?"

"It 's neither," Mark said. "It 's a reptile."

Mark leaned sideways to see what Dicky was writing: on the top of his pad he had printed the words — WILD ANIMALS I HAVE COUGHT.

"Would it be worth putting down insects?" Dicky asked. "No, they 're too easy to catch. But it would be worth putting down a snapping turtle, don't you think?"

"Why not?" Mark said.

You never know what Dicky will say or do, Mark thought: as a matter of fact I don't suppose you know what any child will do — and with most grown people you know only too well; I wonder when they change; I wonder what spoils them. I suppose I know just about what I 'll be doing for the rest of my life, though you never can be perfectly sure: there might be an accident on this train and we would all be killed. I was a fool to have set my heart on Saint James's; a consolation now is to think that if I had got it I probably would n't have liked it as much as I thought; there would be disadvantages living in a big city; it might have been interesting to pass from Saint James's to some bishopric, but I probably would have stuck at Saint James's for the rest of my life, and if that 's the case I would just as lief be in North Chester — that is, if we don't end in the poorhouse. But there is a lot of the Old Man in me, he thought; I 'm afraid I 'm not intellectually humble; perhaps God means it for the best to leave me in North

17

Chester: it ought to be hard to be too conceited when you spend most of your life in one small-town parish. Sometimes it is rather hard not to think of God as a trifle meddlesome, like some well-meaning elderly relation who has your good at heart and insists that you do all sorts of unpleasant things. I suppose I'd be considered frivolous or profane, he thought, but I'm sure God has enough detachment not to mind profanity, whatever people say; the thing Christ seemed to mind more than anything else was smugness, and He knew what He was about. When I think of smugness so glibly, I'm probably being smug myself, though I think of smugness as a quality of rather fat people with pouchy faces. No, I'm not smug; what I'm doing now is whistling to keep up my courage, to make me forget how I felt when I read Budlong's letter.

The children at any rate should have interesting lives, he thought. Brad should make a fine doctor; he's intelligent and sympathetic, there is no reason why he should not be distinguished; Linda and Dicky perhaps have more of a spark, they are more erratic; it would n't surprise me if one of them should turn out some kind of genius, though I rather hope not; I prefer geniuses after they are dead. Why is it, I wonder, that I'm not sorry neither Brad nor Dicky wants to be a clergyman? Is it because I have failed? But who is the judge of failure? Besides, what I should think of is the actual good I do, if any: life is such a muddle; life is so difficult; and is that why I'm tempted to hide my head and try to make it easy? The Lord said, "Whom shall I send, and who will go for us?" and I said, "Here am I; send me." Yes, Isaiah knew the thrill and I too have known it; but I was young, the world was before me; nothing made a

18

thing seem so easy as the knowledge that it was difficult.
Will I know it again? You should act without it as if
you always felt it: that would be true Christianity.

"What is Rhode Island?" Dicky asked.

"It 's a state, like Pennsylvania."

"Are countries in states or states in countries?"

"States are in countries," he said.

"What state are we in now?" Dicky asked.

"We 're in Connecticut."

"I 'm making a list of the states I 've been in," Dicky
said.

I 've always been traveling on this train, Luly was
thinking. She could see pictures against her eyelids: girls
crowded into the Rectory parlor, the Junior Auxiliary
playing games; girls of all kinds, and often the tough-
est were the nicest if you kept at them long enough and
did n't seem meddling — that black-haired Martha Farron,
for instance, and Pearl Maxcy and Reba Weissmuller; she
could see them all eating ice cream, with chairs packed
around the edges of the room and Linda passing cake,
having a beautiful time, a perfect hostess. Yes, no one
could say there was not enough to do in North Chester.
"Mrs. Waring, you 're just the parish dump," someone had
told her; and one of the women in the Mothers' Meeting
had said to someone who repeated it to her: "I like Mrs.
Waring. She 's so common"; and after the Strawberry
Festival at the Negro Episcopal Church, Mrs. Tyndall,
the pastor's wife, had written her: "We all felt with you
just as if you were a colored lady." Remarks of this
sort probably made her happiest, unless it was praise of
the children; sometimes she would repeat them, trying
to pretend to herself that it was just because they were
amusing, but afterwards she would feel uncomfortable

and guilty because she knew that really she had been showing off. I'm afraid some of the husbands would have
been glad to see me go, she thought — I'm afraid I
must seem like a dragon to some of them; and she recalled
how Mrs. Fahnestock, the bishop's wife, had told Mark how
"strong-minded" she looked. Mrs. Fahnestock was not
famous for her tact, but Luly had never quite forgiven
her. The women who came to the Mothers' Meeting
and the Guild had husbands of all kinds: nice hard-work-
ing ones for whom you could be devoutly thankful;
nice ones who worked when they were sober but who
were rarely sober; and a small number of nearly every
kind of not nice ones, who took drugs or beat their
wives or stole things and were sent to prison or ordered
their daughters on to the streets or even, in one or two
cases, made love to them; but there are not many such
holy terrors, she thought; most of them are very pleasant
men and remarkably polite when you think how sometimes I lay down the law. She remembered how she had
talked to Mr. James O'Donohue, whose wife, poor woman,
had had nine children in eleven years and who showed no
signs of stopping although she had nearly had a break-
down when she learned of her tenth pregnancy. "It's
outrageous," Luly had said, "to make Maggie go through
all that," and he at first had looked down, and then,
gathering courage, had given her a mischievous and
wholly charming smile. "I know, ma'am," he said,
"that's very true. But it's the poor man's one diversion,
ma'am." Perhaps she should have reminded him that he
seemed to find plenty of diversion in North Chester's
various saloons, but she could not bear to. But all that
was very long ago; it seemed at least twenty years ago —
like the rooms in New York.

20

Linda stopped trying to draw because the train joggled so and made her spoil all her faces. A lovely breeze came in the window, an afternoon breeze: to-morrow at this time, she thought, we 'll probably all be having lemonade under the tulip tree. There were marshy fields outside the window of the loveliest brightest green, like the too green fields you put in pictures; but these fields were all rippling, never still, — how could you paint that? — and little ponds sparkled among them; there must be turtles in those ponds; and along the top of the fields was a blue line of water, very quiet, with a few sails; you could not see them move but they must be moving; the breeze was coming from that water over the fields and ponds. Is it the sea? she wondered. She looked across at Mother and Father; she would like to ask them but she could see only the backs of their chairs; they might be asleep and she was too comfortable to stir. On a train your seat would get awfully uncomfortable so you felt you could not bear it any longer, and then it would get comfortable and then it might get uncomfortable; you never knew when it would change. Those boats out there look as if they 'd be very happy, she thought, as if you would love to be on them; when I close my eyes I can almost think I am on one of them, especially when I feel the breeze moving my hair; it would be very peaceful, she thought, and bright, like some kind of story; but last summer on Mr. Conway's boat I was seasick and hot; I did n't like it, and then the houses on shore looked beautiful in their trees, they looked like heaven; the Grove with its white columns between the trees, so small and neat and far away, looked just like a house in heaven. It 's more pleasant to think there is a heaven because you could n't just go to sleep for always, but I should think different people

21

would like different heavens. I would n't like mine if it was not at the Grove. When I was small I used to think that sometime I'd know all the people in the world: I thought that would be my job; perhaps that was when I was Dicky's age (I wonder if Dicky thinks that now) but I may have been smaller. It's hard to remember what you were like when you were smaller. It's hard to remember the time when you can just begin to remember.

Mark loved the breeze playing over his forehead from across the aisle; he loved just now the rush of the train: he could think he was on the train from Liverpool to Chester twenty years ago. When will I go to England again? he wondered, not unhappily, because just now he could almost think he was there; just now he did not want the journey to be over. He could see his first cathedral after dinner at that hotel, his first English hotel, and the walk on the walls with the young Englishman he had met on the train. Mark had caught his eye, they had smiled at each other, begun talking; Mark had seen him only for that one afternoon and evening and all the next day, and yet he felt that for that time they had loved each other. Where was he now? Was he alive? Mark had not thought of him for years and now he could see his face distinctly; it was as if you had fallen asleep on that train twenty years ago and now after twenty years were waking on that same train.

That sketchbook, Linda thought suddenly, that I buried in the stone wall: I must look for it the first thing after breakfast to-morrow morning. Every now and then in North Chester she would think of it between the stones and wonder if it was there; it would be strange if it was not because no one could possibly find it unless the wall fell down, but it seemed almost stranger, like

22

magic, to think that it was: it would be like bringing a piece of last year over into this summer; it was a sort of secret thing connecting the years. If I drew one more picture in it every year, she thought, and then buried it in the wall again, all the summers would be connected. I guess I'll do that, because last winter I loved to think it was in the wall, when I could believe it was there — and then if I died no one would ever find it.

"*Westerly!*" shouted the conductor.

"It's Westerly," Brad said, getting up from his chair. "Now we're in Rhode Island. Linda, Dicky, we're in Rhode Island. Ought n't we to begin getting ready?"

"There's no hurry," Father said. "Just remember, each of you, what you have to carry. Luly, are you awake? We're at Westerly."

Oh dear, Linda thought; they never start getting ready in time; I'm sure we'll be left or some of the bags will be left, and if I ask them to hurry, Papa may get cross and tell me not to be nervous. Oh, I just hate it when people won't get ready!

Brad looked at the wooden houses and the fields as the train gathered speed; now it was passing a pond beneath the railroad embankment with yellow cow lilies on the water and a swamp behind. This is all in Rhode Island, he thought; and as soon as you were in Rhode Island you were nearly at the Grove. This was the border region where things started changing.

"Ought we to begin to get ready?" Luly asked.

"We don't have to do a thing till we reach Kingston," Mark said, "but I thought I'd better wake you if you were asleep."

"I was n't asleep," she told him.

"Is your throat better?"

23

"It's much better," she said. "I knew it would be."

I do feel a little tired, she thought, but I'm sure I won't as soon as we are on the boat. It would be calm and cool to-night, with this breeze that would grow fresher and fresher as they sailed through the islands and down the bay to Newport. She had always loved coming into the harbor, with the sailors from the warships standing up in the stern of their swift little launches, and the white yachts and the gray shabby wharves, all the masts and the steeples, and the ends of the old houses through the trees: the windows will be flashing, she thought, but the sky over them will be pink and quiet; and then we'll have the drive behind the beaches and by the time we turn in to the Grove it will be nearly dark and there will be lights in the house, shining through the trees, shining on the piazza columns.

"This is Kingston," Mark said. "I suppose now . . ."

Yes, she thought, we are almost there now; and really it hasn't seemed long.

24

PART II

June 1919

I

LINDA stopped by the clump of boxwood halfway down the garden, put her flowers on the grass, and stood up very straight, her arms close to her sides. I must remember not to slouch, she thought, though naturally you keep your shoulders forward when you're stooping for flowers every minute: it might be good to practise walking with a jar of water on my head the way the Italian peasants do, — it gives them a most beautiful carriage, they say, — except that I'd probably start thinking about something and forget the water and spill it all over me, and break the jar.

In her shadow, in the shadow of the boxwood, the blades of grass, the leaves and petals of the flowers, had a frosty bloom from the rain before breakfast, but you could not see it in the sunlight. It will be a lovely day, she thought, but you hardly know what kind of day yet; days have a color of their own, except the ones that you're too lazy to notice, that slip by as if they had never been; it is partly the way they look and the way they feel, and partly what happens, and of course it is always partly where you are; days at the Grove are never quite like the days in North Chester, just as my days are never quite like the days of anyone else. To the south, beyond the hedge and above the fields, the water was milky

27

blue, cut into different regions, farther and farther away, by darker bands; it looked as if it would be impossible for a ship to cross from one to another: each of those bands, the cornflower-blue ones and the lighter milky ones, might be the ocean at a different hour of the day, which magically, this morning, you were allowed to see for once at the same time, before a breeze ruffling the whole surface from beach to horizon brought them all back to the present hour and minute. Thousands of miles away, straight southward across that water, would be South America; to the west there were three thousand miles of land beyond the trees of the Grove. It will be warm later, she thought, very hot in the cities. I wonder if anyone now, looking up between hot walls through sticky air, is thinking of cool places in the country and imagining a garden like this; I wonder if any girl is standing on the shore of the Pacific Ocean and thinking that the land is stretching eastward three thousand miles to another sea, and wondering whether someone, like me, is wondering about her. Linda smiled to herself: there's not much sense to that, she thought, is there? — but if you can think of that other person thousands of miles away thinking of you, — not you of course, she does not know you exist, but someone like you, — then it makes the place you are in exciting, a place where anything might happen, and it makes yourself seem different, a far-away, imagined person that might do anything.

In a few more days, she thought, and to-day is one of them whatever it turns out to be, Thornton will be back, but I cannot imagine him back any more than I can imagine, really, our being married; I could imagine a beautiful young man like Thornton coming back from the war to marry a girl like me who might be in that boat out there beyond Sachuest in that strip of darker blue, but not Thornton, really, coming back to me, really, the me that is here, now, in this garden. A second ago, for just an instant, anything might have happened, but as soon as I noticed it, it vanished. Just now I cannot imagine anything happening except being simply here and picking a few more flowers and then going back to the house to put them in water.

Luly Waring had hurried down the path from the house to tell Linda the good news, but Linda looked so thoughtful, so withdrawn, as she stood with bent head in the middle of the garden, that Luly could not bear to call her. As you looked at her standing there you could almost feel how light, how poised, she must be feeling, like a dancer resting for an instant as the music stops, ready to be carried on, to enter the new rhythm, the moment it starts again. When I watch her, Luly thought, I can remember sometimes how it felt to move and breathe when I was a girl as slender as she is, though I was a little awkward, taller than Linda and apt to be conscious of my height. Linda's brows were drawn together, her lips almost pouting, but not really: no one could look more discontented and annoyed than Linda when she really sulked — one instant as if she were going to cry, the next as if she were going to attack you; but then, as you watched, you could see her make up her mind not to sulk (especially if you had refused to sympathize; and that's the way, Luly thought, she must be treated) and her face would instantly clear, with every feature slightly changed to suit this new moment: a face all serenity and charm, only remembering what it had been through the hint that its new pleasantness was so very ingratiating as a kind of bribe to make you forget. This ought to be one of the happiest days of her life, Luly thought fondly; I'm sure it is the happiest of mine: to have them back safe, Dicky and Brad, and Thornton too, all of them here at the Grove; it is the day I was hoping and praying for and that often I thought would never come; it seemed surely as if one of them would be killed; I had made up my mind for it, I had tried to prepare myself; if only for the last two years I could have known that this day was coming!

She stepped forward into the garden.

"Linda," she called. "I have a surprise for you."

Startled, Linda raised her head and then smiled. It was pleasant when you thought you were alone, when you felt that no one was seeing you or forming pictures of you, when the ends of your thoughts spreading in all directions were being absorbed by the sky and the earth (her thoughts just now weaving among the damp flower stems, sliding over the bands of the water, spreading themselves to catch the warmth that was slowly falling through the haze from the upper air), it was very pleasant to find that someone friendly was near you, had been near you for a minute or more perhaps without your knowing it; it made you feel that they had come very close, closer than usually you could let them come no matter how much you wanted to, as if they had seen your thoughts moving, free and quivering and unashamed, like the soft fringes of a sea anemone that are quickly drawn in and disappear at the slightest touch.

Mother was smiling. It was a smile that came and went on her lips, behind her eyes: it was the expression that made her look youngest. When she smiles in that

30

uncertain way, Linda thought, filled with happiness but not quite daring to show it, about to tell some good news to the family or to give a present, and not quite sure that they will like it as much as she hopes (of course the surprise is that Thornton's ship has landed), then I can almost imagine how she must have looked to Father when he first knew her. You noticed it all the more because sometimes, since the boys were away, her face would become fixed and empty and sad; the corners of her mouth, her cheeks, would droop, as if her thoughts and feelings were too tired to come quite through to the surface of her skin: just the expression that showed in most of the proofs she had taken last Christmas to get a picture to send to the boys, proofs that she had simply hated. "They make me look so large and soft," she said; "I won't allow you to have them, and the one Mark likes is the worst of all" — and after that Linda had loved to tease her by saying that the underneath of her chin felt like a toad's stomach.

But even now as she came smiling down the path, with the trees behind her, Linda could not quite imagine her as a girl, as someone expecting her lover home from the war, for instance, or someone going on a wedding trip (on Mother's wedding trip, she would tell you proudly, nobody suspected she was a bride because Father was reading to her Lecky's *History of Morals*): more and more as she came nearer, you could not think of her except as a mother with children, except as your own mother; and yet, Linda thought, Mother did not marry until she was well over thirty; she is older than Father, though we have never been able to find out exactly how much: she had lived more than half her life before she was married. Linda had a distant image of a young girl with

31

Italian eyes and a lovely half-pouting face, who spent her winters in Savannah and danced all night with young men, and played Chopin nocturnes, and rode the most frisky horses (that was ages ago, before Grandfather lost his money); and another image of a serious young woman who taught piano lessons for hours a day in New York to help support her mother and keep the Grove from being sold, who did settlement work in tenements and hospitals and prisons ("I saw some awful things," she would tell Linda, "some things I 'll not forget. Oh, you would revel in some of them," she would say teasingly, "but nothing would induce me to tell you, because you can think of enough horrors for yourself"); but she could not really make these two young women into the same person, and neither one, not even the second one, could she quite fit on to Mother.

"What is your surprise?" she asked. "I bet I can guess."

"Perhaps you can," Mother said, "but I very much doubt it."

Linda hesitated: should she guess some absurd thing, but not quite so absurd that Mother would know she was not serious? But Mother was looking so happy that she could not bear to tease her.

"Thornton's ship has come in," she said. "I told you I could guess, did n't I?"

"Yes, you did," Mother said, "but as it happens, you did n't guess right."

Linda frowned, really surprised now, eager to hear the news.

"At least you did n't guess enough," Mother went on. "You did n't guess the most important thing."

"Tell me," Linda said. "What is it? I can see it 's awfully nice."

32

"You better think it's nice." Mother's eyes were beaming; tender, almost mischievous eyes, unable to contain their delight. "Thornton and Dicky are arriving here to-day. They may even get here by lunch time. It depends on what ferry they catch."

"Thornton and Dicky to-day! But I did n't know Thornton could land before to-day, and how did Dicky get here? I thought he was at Saint Aignan, and I did n't know they 'd release him. How did you find out, Mother? Are you sure he said to-day?"

"If you give me a chance," Mother said, "I can tell you very easily. In the first place I'm sure it's to-day because I 've been talking to Dicky by long distance, and I was just as amazed as you are."

So this was to be a day of excitement, a day that you could not quite see for a minute or two, because everything was hurriedly being changed, water and garden and sky, to go with it: lights were being switched on and off, scenery being withdrawn or slid into place; that was at least what you felt, but from the first it had been intended; the day had known it, had kept it slyly just beyond the horizon, just beneath the petals of the flowers, scattered so thinly, so subtly, that you just could not feel it, or could not know that you were feeling it, in the warmth and coolness of the air. If you had been clever, you thought now, you should have guessed; you should have been prepared for this sudden swift movement which, after it had happened, in only a few minutes, would fit neatly into the day; but days were like puzzles or mystery stories that, once you were shown how they came out, and always you were shown in time, made you feel very stupid at not having guessed before — though you rarely did guess.

"But did Dicky come back on the same boat with Thornton?" she asked.

"He did," Mother said. "Thornton looked him up in camp at Saint Aignan and spoke to someone high up that he knew and got him shipped back immediately. If it had n't been for Thornton, Dicky said, he might have been lying around there with some other casuals for weeks. I 'm sure I 'll be everlastingly grateful to Thornton. They landed yesterday morning and Thornton saw General Burnett at once and Dicky was let out that same evening. They rushed everything through. I 'm very much afraid that Thornton used his pull for all it was worth. Dicky says it 's all pull getting things done in the army; it seems outrageous, does n't it?"

Mother smiled with only the faintest pretense of condemnation, the way she smiled when Brad or Dicky made some not too improper remark, the kind that if it had been someone else she would have hated. "Thornton called Earl," she went on. "He drove the car to New York and they started this morning at some unholy hour. Dicky wanted to surprise us, but Thornton thought that someone might not be here or there might be guests or something, so he telephoned from New Haven, and I 'm thankful he did, because Brad 's arranged to stay over till to-morrow night. He talked to Mr. Norton in Chicago and explained the situation, and he was just as nice as he can be. I 've always liked Mr. Norton. He has such a kind face."

"Then we 'll all be here to-night," Linda said.

"Yes, we 'll all be here. It will be like before the war."

Not like before the war, Linda thought, that 's one thing we can be sure of; we were all so young before

34

the war — at least it seems so now, of course it did n't then: perhaps Mother is right; perhaps in a few years we will seem even younger now than it seems now that we were before the war; but I 'm sure there will be a difference; I 'm sure that nothing, not even part of a minute, will be quite the same.

"I thought I 'd put on my new gray voile," Mother said with a question in her voice, "the one I got from Miss Gilpin. I thought I remembered that was the one you liked."

"You look perfectly charming in your voile," Linda said, smiling. If you could not see Mother as a young girl, you could sometimes, just for a moment, see her as a child: she loved pretty clothes, more and more, it seemed, as if now that she was growing old she was beginning to care for the things she had liked when she was young and then for years had not had time for; and she 's not much surer of what clothes to get than a child, Linda thought; sometimes she gets sweet things, but now and then they are terribly dowdy; it 's just as well that I 've trained her to consult me; poor Mother, she feels now almost guilty when she chooses things herself. Linda could remember times when Mother had called her into her room and taken down boxes from the shelf in her closet and then, timid, triumphant, and ashamed, had shown her hats or dresses she had recently bought. Sometimes, even if she did not like them, Linda would pretend to be enthusiastic, because after all if they were bought there was nothing more to be done unless they could be exchanged; but sometimes she would say, she would get a cruel pleasure in saying, just what she thought; she could hardly help it sometimes because Mother as she showed them seemed so eager and uncertain, so very

easily hurt, and you knew that what you said would disappoint her so much that you could not resist using that
power.

"Perhaps I 'd better not put it on till this afternoon,"
Mother said, "because then it will look fresher for supper
and I don't suppose really they can get here before lunch.
I besought Dicky not to drive too fast and to keep Thornton from doing it, but of course those boys . . . when
they get in a car . . ."

Again there was pride in her voice: she hated to think
now that they might be speeding; but once they were
safely arrived, she would love to think and to tell that
Dicky had averaged fifty miles an hour to get to the
Grove. "It was perfectly outrageous," she would say.
"There 's not a particle of excuse for driving so fast. It
would have served them right if they 'd had a bad smash-
up," but all the time, in her heart, making it another
reason for loving Dicky.

"I suppose we ought to ask Ellen down to supper,"
Linda said.

For the first time since she recognized Dicky's voice
over the telephone, Luly felt a drop in her happiness: if
Ellen were there it would be a different evening from the
one she had imagined.

"I think it would seem strange not to have Ellen,"
Linda said. "I bet you Dicky will want her."

"Do you think so?" Luly asked. "His first night?"

It would seem that Dicky might be content with the
family for this first evening at home. Luly felt suddenly
cold: was Dicky engaged? Had he told Linda? Dicky
was so featherbrained about girls, so irresponsible. She
always felt embarrassed now speaking to Mrs. Manship
after Dicky had been so attentive to Joyce and then

36

dropped her completely (which was fortunate, though he might have shown more tact).

"Do you think there's anything between Dicky and Ellen?" she asked. "Anything serious?"

"Mother!" Linda exclaimed. "You look so woebegone. After all, Dicky's only nineteen and he'd hardly think of getting married at that age, I hope."

"I know — but you can't tell about Dicky. In some of his letters he's sent her most affectionate messages, but I think that was partly because he knows I don't regard her with enthusiasm."

"I would n't worry," Linda said gayly. "You know Dicky, Mother. Remember Minnie Watercress?"

"That was different," Mother said, but remembering it she felt relieved. Dicky had written her quite seriously from camp that he was engaged to the daughter of a saloon keeper whom he had met at a dance hall. The girl's name, he wrote, was Minnie Watercress, and of course she would have known he was teasing her if she had read the name correctly, though everyone pretended to believe that she had. No, she was n't quite such a fool as that.

"If you really don't want Ellen," Linda said, "I would n't ask her. I don't think you have to."

Luly looked at her gratefully, but no doubt she was right: much better have Ellen than disappoint Dicky; and the best way to encourage a love affair was to try to stop it; but she would be relieved when Dicky, though not for a few years, let us hope, found some really unselfish, interesting girl for a wife. Brad you could be sure of; Brad would not lose his head for a pretty face with nothing behind it; poor Brad, she could not bear for him to be going to Chicago to-morrow (though

37

that was better than to-day), to the heat and drudgery
of a bond house in a huge office building.

"I think I will ask Ellen," she said. "I think you
were right, Linda."

Linda watched Mother walk out through the boxwood,
leaving her alone once more, in this so different garden.
I can almost see it now, she thought, almost see the day;
the garden belongs to it entirely. The sun had grown
brighter, the haze thicker, so that everything, except what
you were looking at directly, glistened as if you saw it
through the outermost edges of a fountain; the gaudiest
colors, scarlet and rose, magenta and blue, each seemed
more brightly itself, yet each seemed filled with all the
rest; Linda could imagine them making music that you
just could not hear but only remember having heard,
the instant it was gone, music that reminded you of dis-
cordant *arpeggios* struck swiftly and softly on a harp.
I can see all the outside of the day, she thought; I can
feel it moving: in a moment I'll be getting quantities
of flowers and then I'll think up special schemes for each
room, though nobody will notice them unless I speak of
them myself; and of course on a day like this I won't be
practising; and they will be arriving, Dicky and Thornton
— we won't be even sure that we will not find them when
we come back from the rock; and this afternoon perhaps we'll go walking, and there will be long intimate
conversations, and to-night there will be sonatas, and
everyone will be very happy and keep remembering questions they want to ask. I can see all of it except the
very centre; all of it except Thornton coming back, my
lover come back from the war to marry me. If it were
not for Father and Mother, I would be married to Thorn-

38

ton now; I would be expecting my husband. How out-
raged I was, she remembered, and then how miserable,
and yet after all I'm sure they were right; I am glad
now that I'm not married to Thornton. I'm afraid
Mother and Father are often right, oftener than you are
apt to think: when you are very young you feel they
can never be wrong, and then, as if in revenge, when you
begin to grow up, it seems as if they could never be right,
or, if they are right, not for the same reasons; it is easy
sometimes to feel like brushing them aside like that young
girl in *The Master Builder*. What fun, she thought, if
I could ever act that part: to stand at the end watching
him climb the steeple, to stand very still, yet so full of
excitement — excitement just showing in your hands,
your still tense arms, in your eyes as you kept staring upward — that all the people in the theatre would be staring
at you, breathless as you were breathless, feeling yourself with him as he climbed, listening to the harps in the
air, and when he came crashing down not seeing it, because you could still imagine him climbing and climbing.

Why should it be hard to picture Thornton? she wondered, because I have always been in love with him from
the time when I was fourteen or fifteen. It was easy
to think of Thornton at that time, so kind and so supple,
so much older than she: teaching her to ride, coaching her
in tennis, much more patient than either Dicky or Brad;
always calm when she grew excited, treating her of course
like a child, not suspecting how she felt, but with always
a protecting warmth in his voice as if it were gently,
calmly stroking her. She remembered how she used to
play for hours everything she knew best when Thornton
was visiting, in the hope he might be hearing her from
some other room, though Thornton was not musical.

She had thought of him as many things: as a Blakean angel, as a young man on a coin, a coin of very soft smooth metal; he was a person who did everything easily, without the slightest strain, without raising his voice; there were lots of things of course that he could not do at all, but you could n't imagine him trying to do any of those; you could hardly imagine him really noticing them, though he would always admit they were there and talk of them in his good-natured voice and say he wished he could do them. But the Thornton who was hard to remember, at least to remember as having any possible connection with *now*, with *to-day*, was the ardent young man of that last visit early in June, just over two years ago, before he went to camp, who told her he loved her and thought he must have been in love with her for more than a year; it was all that time that was hard to remember, or hard to attach to anything before or afterwards: their long rides together until, when they reached some lonely field, they would get off their horses and lie in the grass with his arms about her; their kisses and their plans for being married; and then the strained scenes with Mother and Father, and the awfulness of everyone going to war. It was as soon as he left, she thought, that time stopped suddenly: it floated twinkling away, and then what? That was what you could not remember, the bridge you could not find. The first thing you knew you had been getting his letters, reassuring letters that sounded like his everyday voice, affectionate, but almost the kind of letters he might have written if none of this had happened, except that he loved to make plans for what they would do when they were married, where they would go, the kind of house they would live in, the kind of dogs and horses they would keep. And to-day he is coming back, she

40

thought; I am very happy, but I cannot see my happiness clearly because there is so much excitement and surprise between, and the kind of being afraid, you don't know of what, that comes with excitement: it's like trying to look at a thing under water on the sand when you are swimming; one moment you can see it quite clearly through the side of a ripple and then you can't see it at all; its shape keeps changing and even its size, and you can't imagine what it is — a tangle of seaweed, or some rather frightening fish, because with all the ripples you can think of it as moving, or possibly something that fell overboard from a ship.   But it's foolish, she thought, to try too hard to picture what the rest of a day will be like, because you have only to wait, quite still, and it is bound to come: I could just keep standing on the grass by this boxwood, as the sun moves over the long curved line of the ocean, until, when you look westward through the trees, you see that bluish misty light that floats between their trunks in the afternoon — I could just keep standing here, not moving, not thinking, I could pretend to be asleep or enchanted, and before I knew it, Thornton would be coming through the boxwood to call my name, or wake me with a kiss.

II

"I GUESS there's no doubt you've got me," Mark said: this would be forty-one games for Brad as against only nineteen for him, and presumably this would be the last chance to-day, with Thornton and Dicky arriving. "You wouldn't like to start another right off?" he asked.

"It's after eleven," Brad said; "Linda will be lugging me over to the rock in a few minutes."

"It's just as well," Mark said. "The score is humiliating enough as it is without my tempting Providence, and you'll want a long swim your last morning, I suppose."

"Yes, that's what I was thinking. God damn it, when I think of leaving here to go to that stinking city . . ."

"Brad, if my neighbor, the Reverend Charles M. Baxter, could hear you, he'd think I had very blasphemous children and I'm afraid he'd be right, and I'm very much afraid he might assume it was a case of a tree bearing fruit according to its kind."

"You know what he can do," Brad said. "Any time."

"There are a number of things he thinks he can do," Mark said.

With an old-fashioned stub pen (he never would use a fountain pen: they're messy, he would say, and you never can be sure they'll work) he put down, in figures

42

neat as Chinese calligraphy, the final score: as far as chess is concerned, he thought, you would say Brad had received grace, while I'm a poor sinner steering my course by the flickering light of my own intellectual pride. "You're not sorry you're going in with Mr. Norton, are you?" he asked.

Brad scowled. If anyone had told me, ten years ago, Mark thought, that one of my sons would go into business instead of entering a profession, I would have felt very sorry, but the more I think of it the more I feel I was prejudiced: as a young man I was far too squeamish and intellectual; doubtless I was an awful prig, though I like to think I was not without charm. Now I've lost my charm and my beauty; I'm beginning to grow plump; I'm probably growing even a little vulgar, as a result, I suppose, of contact with Brad and Dicky and the unregenerate in North Chester; but I think on the whole I am happier, now that the boys are safely home, and I'm sure I'm more sensible; whether I'm more godly or not only God can decide; certainly I should think He would find a man like Mr. Norton far more congenial than the Reverend Charles M. Baxter.

"I might as well go in with Mr. Norton as do anything else," Brad said.

"Of course," Mark said, "I suppose you must expect it to be dull at first. Most things are. But Mr. Norton is an exceptional man; he's especially interested in you; he's not taking you in as a favor to us, you know. He told me he considered you a first-rate investment." Brad still scowled, lifting one of his eyebrows ironically, as his fingers played with the white queen. "You can't get many of the first-rate things in life with money," Mark went on, "but I hope you'll be fortunate enough to get

43

those anyway; but money can bring you most of the second- and third-rate things, and they're important too — at least they're mighty convenient. I could never have educated you children on my salary, not even with your mother's income, what little there was left of it. I've used principal right along for your school and your music lessons and everything that I thought would give you a good start, and I don't regret it for a moment; but there won't be much when I die, except my insurance for your mother, if she survives me; and you'll probably want to marry — you'll be having children, you'll want to be able to do things for them. I honestly don't think you'll be making a mistake, Brad, unless there is something else you definitely want to do. No man's happy if there's a thing he'd like best to do, and he has to do something else."

"There's nothing special I want to do," Brad said.

"Of course we always thought you'd be a doctor, a surgeon. I think your mother still is slightly disappointed. It's a long training, and it's expensive, but we could have managed it. If you should find you hate working in a bond house and feel after all you want to be a doctor, we could still manage it, especially now that Linda will be off our hands." Mark thought of the misery of his few weeks in the law school before he gave it up: the sense of safety still tremulous, of gulfs avoided, when at last, after reluctance, after struggle, he had decided to enter the ministry; it was a question then, he thought, of being the vilest, the most loathly of sinners or perhaps a saint and hero; I am certainly neither hero nor saint, and the pit of damnation that haunted me was an illusion of my youth and innocence, but I'm glad on the whole I did not study law. There are plenty of fools in the ministry, but a

44

rather low proportion of knaves, I think; even Charles M. Baxter is hardly a knave, though I'd prefer to deal with your average knave any day in the year.

"I know I'll never want to be a surgeon," Brad said, "or any kind of doctor."

A doctor, Brad thought — how could I be a doctor? The thought had struck him first on the home-coming transport, late one night as he stood guard at one of the hatchways near the bow of the ship; there was moonlight through fog, and the water smelled as it does in mid-ocean, fresh and empty and endless, with not a trace of the smell of seaweed or fish, the various sharp nice smells that were in the air at Newport and that you thought of as being the smell of the sea when really they were smells of the shore. While the war lasted you did not think of afterwards; at least you did not worry about what you would be because you were not sure that you would be alive; even after the armistice what you thought of was getting home, that was the only thing that mattered; but now on the way home you thought suddenly of what you were going to do. How can I be a doctor? he thought in panic; how can I ever perform an operation? He remembered the operations that Doc Anderson had let him visit: he had never turned faint; he had watched the gloved fingers with earnestness and fascination and tried to remember details that might be useful; this is part of my training, he had said to himself, I'm beginning to collect experience; and now as he stood on the cold deck listening to the fog-horn, he felt that perhaps that could not be. I don't remember a thing, he thought; it would mean repeating all my pre-medic work at college; I wouldn't be on my own feet for years. Probably he did not have the right to take so much time and money from Father unless he were perfectly sure he would be a success, and how could you be sure? Your hand might slip and your first patient bleed to death on the table: of course an accident of that sort was not likely, but you might easily flunk out of medical school after a few years when it was too late to go in with Mr. Norton. With him you would be self-supporting from the start: it was a damn good job for a beginner and you were lucky to get it; there was not the least doubt of that — and yet sometimes he caught himself wishing that the family had not known Mr. Norton, that there was not any job in sight. Then things would be different.

But I'm a fool, he thought, to be moping on a day like this; don't expect anything for the next few years, and then every good time you have will be that much velvet. I'll have two weeks here next summer; in a few years I may be having a month, and if I do half decently I ought to be able to retire by the time I'm forty-five. You're not old then, and I could live here if I wanted to from May to October; I could get a first-rate tree surgeon to fix up all the trees; I could do no end of things. I'm not like Joel, he thought; Joel's an impractical idealist; he's getting socialistic, but I don't suppose it will last, and you can't blame him for feeling a bit sore when he never got overseas and spent a year and a half helping run a venereal camp in Iowa.

"You know, Brad, I think we're getting out of the woods," Father said, "with you going in with Mr. Norton: with reasonable luck you'll be a rich man or at least comfortably off, far more comfortably than I have ever been — and with Linda marrying Thornton. Of course the place goes to the three of you. I'm not sure that it's wise to leave a thing jointly to a family, but it's what your

46

mother wants and I suppose it 's the fairest. On the whole I 'm very much pleased with Thornton."

"You know, he has a lot to him," Brad said. "I did n't use to think so," and it gave Brad pleasure now to speak of his earlier opinion as if mentioning it were a kind of guarantee, to himself and to others, of the genuineness of his new attitude. "I certainly will be glad to see him, and gosh, Parson, it 's funny to think that Dicky will be here in a few hours, is n't it?"

"Yes it is," Father said, "and getting him out of the army that way is just the kind of thing Thornton can do. You know, Brad, Linda 's not exactly extravagant, but she 's born to be wealthy, I think. Some people are. I 'm not and neither is your mother, though she is much more than she thinks. And yet Linda is the kind of girl who might take it into her head to marry some penniless freak. If she did she 'd regret it, but then it would be too late. Of course in a way Linda 's a freak herself; probably Dicky is, and perhaps I am; but if we are we 're nice freaks, we 're not the messy long-haired kind. Your mother is n't of course, and you 're not. Linda 's the most beautiful, and perhaps Dicky 's the most original, but you 're the most dependable. Yes, you 're very satisfactory, Brad, but still you 're all pretty satisfactory so far. Your mother worries about Dicky and Ellen, but still she 'll worry about girls until you 're both married and then she 'll begin to worry about her grandchildren. It 's a Bradford trait."

"Dicky would never fall for Ellen," Brad said. "She 's too obvious."

He smiled now, realizing more and more that Dicky was arriving, that he himself had another whole day at the Grove instead of being this minute on the train to Chicago.

47

Hell, it was n't so bad to be landing a good job with a first-rate boss, a man like Mr. Norton, a man with whom you had all kinds of a drag. Years don't take long, he thought; I was almost four years at college and it seems like no time. Who knows what I 'll be making in four years? Who knows what will happen now that *la guerre est finie?*

"Did I tell you about the absent-minded man?" he asked.

"If it's improper I don't want to hear it," Mark said, but Brad told it none the less.

"You used to be so chaste in your language, Brad," Mark said plaintively. "You used to be my one thoroughly decent child. Linda was never obscene exactly, but she wrote obscene poems; she was indecent in a highbrow way, and Dicky was indecent in a lowbrow way. Of course Dicky never had a shred of shame, but I used to think you had. Do you suppose the war has demoralized you?"

III

LINDA stopped at the cliff's edge, among the bay, to wait for Joel. She had hurried over the hill through the fields, she had been hurrying with her flowers, in the hope that her artfully increased speed had tricked time itself into moving faster. But as usual the effect was just the opposite; you could not trick time in that way any more than you could help the old car up hills by stiffening your body and straining forward in your seat as if you were pushing: the day was moving over the field, over the darkly glinting bayberry and the goldenrod, at best no faster than Joel; or perhaps she had outstripped it further: she might have to wait, slowly reliving her snatched moments, until Brad, who was climbing the fence back by the road, arrived with Ellen. If it is partly like the day before Christmas, she thought, it is partly like the day before my appendix was removed (I should think Thornton would hate to find that horrid scar on my stomach, though of course he knows it must be there). Oh dear, she thought, it won't be so bad on the rock because we will be moving and the water will be swaying and flashing, each flash part of a second, but lunch will be endless; everyone will feel he has to eat but no one will be hungry, or Brad will ask for a second helping of soup just as Maud is about to begin changing plates; and I'll want to be

49

getting up from table and looking at a magazine or a book, but I won't want to either, because I like meals as a rule to be orderly, and if I get up there's no way to stop Brad from getting up, and I hate, I just hate, to have the boys keep getting up and coming back; the nuisance is, she thought, that there are always so many things you like to do that you hate to have other people do; I'm sure no one really minds my getting up from table the way I mind having Brad and Dicky — but of course it would do no good to say that. Linda almost blushed at the thought of how ashamed she would be if anyone, if Joel, for example, joining her at last with his deliberate walk and just now rather morose expression, should be able to read her mind.

"You ought to look gay," she said to him, "with Dicky and Thornton coming back, but you don't. You look cross."

"Why should I look gay," he asked, "if I don't feel gay?"

"Well, I mean you ought to feel gay, of course."

"I'll be glad to see Dicky and Thornton," he said, "but I don't know that grinning or jumping about will help matters."

"I suppose you mean that I'm grinning and jumping about. Wouldn't you be happy if your fiancé were coming back after nearly two years?"

"Heaven preserve me from getting myself into such a situation," he said.

"Look out, Joel," she said. "When people talk that way it means they are about to get married."

"That's another one of those ridiculous fallacies," he said crossly. "I'm surprised that you should make such a trite remark, Linda. It's like saying that a person who threatens to commit suicide never does it. I've known two suicides and both of them said beforehand they might do it sometime."

"Not really?" she exclaimed. "Did you, Joel? Tell me about them."

She turned to look at him, balancing herself carefully, for she had reached the slightly dizzying corner where the dirt path through the grass and bay ended and you had to scramble down the last thirty feet over the steep crumbling face of the rock. In spite of his scowl he could not look really fierce: at best like someone acting the part of a ferocious character in a play. It was a shame, because Joel would love quite often to look savage and vitriolic, and yet he was doomed always to look gentle in spite of his thick eyebrows, his large handsome nose, his all-over bigness and squareness; if he had a little moustache and a pointed beard he would make you think of some of the nicest pictures of Shakespeare: you could think of the young Shakespeare with that red-brown coloring and those deep-set, rather veiled eyes.

"Of course I won't tell you," he said. "Watch yourself or you'll fall."

"Why not?" she asked.

"Because I see no sense in satisfying morbid curiosity."

"Oh, very well," she said, turning and picking her way down the cliff, trying not to touch her hands to the ground if she could help it. "I bet you just want to be mysterious, Joel. I don't believe you ever knew a suicide."

"All right," he said. "Let's agree that I never knew one. Oh, I'm sorry, Linda. Did that stone hit you?"

"No, but I'm covered with powdered rock. Now I suppose you are happy, Joel."

She half slid, half ran, down the last few feet of the path and jumped on to the beach of rounded stones that separated Castle Rock from the side of the cliff. Joel came after her, quite reckless, in a fog of slaty dust.

"When I spoke of a fiancé," he explained less crossly, "I did n't mean I might not sometime get married. I 'm not quite such a fool as to make statements of that kind: I meant I 'd never let myself be engaged. It strikes me as damn foolishness, in fact I think there 's something rather disgusting about it. You either marry or you don't. This being set apart business, this survival of tribal custom . . ."

"Joel," she exclaimed laughing, "you 're so funny! But I love you that way. I love you to be earnest and cross. It makes me feel as if I ought to stroke you gently and smooth down your hair."

Joel stooped, picked up a stone, gave it a sharp jerk with his arm, and watched it skip over the water. "Any time," he said, but she knew he was a little embarrassed. Joel 's a darling, she thought, one of the few people I could not do without; I must remember to ask him sometime about those suicides because I would really like to know: did they throw themselves off bridges or drink poison, I wonder, or shoot themselves? Do you suppose there was anything particularly horrible or strange? Sometime, when he has forgotten this, I 'll lead the conversation around to suicide and I 'm sure he will tell me. Or do you suppose, she thought suddenly, that they were good friends of his, people that he loved, so that it makes him very sad to think of their killing themselves? If that 's the case, I must seem cruel and flip. I could not bear to make Joel sad, she thought; I could not bear for him to think I was heartless.

"You might give me your hand, Brad," Ellen said, "with all this poison ivy. Next thing I'll lose my balance and fall into it."

"I thought you never took poison ivy," Brad said.

"Never take it!" she exclaimed. "If I get the least little bit I'm in perfect agony. . . . I swell up so that I look like nothing at all."

"Then I guess you've got a bad night coming," he said, "because I saw you brush some with your ankle a moment ago. But you said the other evening at table that you could sleep in it and it wouldn't hurt you."

"I couldn't have said that, Brad, because it's not true."

Now she's wondering whether she said it or not, he thought; it was fun to bring together two of her contradictory stories and make her choose which she preferred to stand by. She frowned at him; then looked away with a toss of her head, and stared shrinkingly down the last thirty feet of the path. Was she really scared? You never knew; she might not be nervous in the least, but pretending that she was, or she might be very nervous and trying to pretend she was not.

"You'd better watch your step," she said, "instead of paying so much attention to my ankles."

A typical reply for Ellen: sneaking out of a question by dragging in her ankles. "I'm crazy about them," he said. "Darn clever of you to guess it."

Brad smiled as she could not help looking down; someone was crazy about them, that was evident: pretty legs she had, but too soft and slender, almost like a child's legs, and her feet were too small.

"You're horrid," she told him, "but I suppose you think you're funny."

Now she must be narrowing her eyes, being brave; too

bad he could not see her face. As she started to climb down the rock, some small stones slipped from under her foot; she gasped, clutched at a branch; now she had stopped again.

"What's the matter?" he asked.

"Oh, nothing," she said. "I've twisted my ankle a little. I'll be all right."

"I suppose you want me to help you," he said. "I suppose that's the meaning of that graceful, helpless position."

"I wouldn't take your help if you were the last man on earth," she answered.

He watched her walk down the path in front of him, moving now with reasonable speed, pick her way across the stones (how she would love it if he offered to carry her, except that she would not believe that he really meant it), climb around the end of the rock, and arrange herself carefully, like a small cat, beside Linda.

As an epicure considers a wine list (he must make the most of everything these last few hours, enjoy them to the full), Brad wondered where he would choose to sit.

"Who's got a cigarette for me?" he asked, and bent forward to take one from Joel. Then he sat down opposite Ellen, leaned his head back against the rock, stretched out his legs, and between drooping eyelids stared upwards through a maze of swimming iridescent threads; I've got a swell burn this year, he thought, and I don't suppose it will last more than a week out there in Chicago. But that was something he must not think of: he must think of this bluish rock that he knew so well, where they had always swum and fished, each in his special place (there was Linda's place, and his own, and Joel's and Dicky's, he could see them without moving); think of the cliffs and the lighthouse . . . or why think at all, when you could feel the sun on your skin?

"I saw something in the paper this morning," Joel said, "that just suited me. I don't know when I've seen anything that pleased me so much."

"I can tell from his tone that it's something *dreadful*," Ellen exclaimed. "Linda, I don't think he ought to be allowed to tell it, do you?"

"What is it, Joel?"

Linda's voice was pleasant and polite; by polite Joel did not mean formal, but really gracious, doing its best to show the interest she did not feel so that he might be pleased and satisfied instead of being hurt. Nothing I say interests her, he thought. For the moment he felt that if he could have one wish it would be to say something that would make her look at him with half-startled eyes, her neck thrust slightly forward, her head held a little to the side as if she were straining her attention to catch a far-off sound: when she looked at you that way her eyes were very clear and glistening, the kind of eyes that young Eve might have had the first minute she opened them and looked around her at the trees of Paradise before she noticed Adam; eyes that made all other eyes seem as if they were covered with the film that shielded the eyes of birds when they stared at the sun (probably birds' eyes never had such a film); her lashes did not seem so much like a screen of protecting hairs as the finest, most sensitive feelers, themselves needing protection, charged and tingling with the overflow of her glance, feelers invisibly extending until they pricked the surface of your skin as with the finest needles. But although she looked straight at you, although you were seeing her with such sudden clearness, she hardly was seeing you: her eyes

55

were looking at something out of space that you could just not imagine; you could imagine not the slightest part of it, yet it seemed as if you were on the verge of imagining the whole, absolute and perfect, just as after awakening you sometimes felt a dream, which you did not even remember you had dreamed, for an instant about to explode softly in a puff of light and then, because you reached for it too eagerly, felt it float glimmering down and off forever. If your imagination once could catch what her eyes saw at those moments, you knew that you would have, intact in your mind, the essence of Linda, have it there to adore, to play with, to serve, but never to let go; and Linda would be captured with it, caught like the swan maiden when the prince stole her plumy cloak while she bathed in the spring and she could not fly away with her sisters. And yet, Joel thought, on the cliff when she asked me about the suicides, when something I said did interest her by a rare chance, I was too stubborn to tell her anything; I took a sadistic delight in not gratifying her interest; I swelled like a turkey gobbler with fatuous power. He could not resist now giving her a sidewise glance. Her hand next to him was drawing lines with a soft gray splinter on the rough face of the rock; the scratching sound made him slightly curl his toes and just failed to set his teeth on edge, but he liked it. He could see her profile against the sky; she had taken off her bathing cap; her hair swept smoothly down over her temple and ear as she had worn it as a little girl, except that then it was braided behind and now it was twisted into a small knot; her face was tilted upward, her eyes staring perhaps at the lighthouse. He loved the little dent beside her nostril; he loved the corner of her mouth like the tapering to a point of a flushed slender leaf. Remote she looked, but not entirely remote: her face now had the same pleasant politeness, the expectancy, of her voice, not at all perfunctory, not insincere, but not really within herself expectant. Joel smiled sardonically.

"It 's about a man and his wife," he said, "and the charming way they spent their fifth wedding anniversary. I was reminded of it coming down the path a minute ago. They drove into the country, down to some lonely beach for a picnic, but the poor husband forgot to put part of the lunch in the car — I think it was the coffee. You can imagine how most wives would behave under the circumstances. Well, this one acted in just that way until she drove the poor man nearly crazy; but this particular husband was still a man of spirit; you see they 'd only been married five years, and also he had a fine original mind — something of a genius, I imagine, though I believe he 's a retail druggist; but I suppose that 's about what happens to most geniuses. Well, his wife went in swimming but he would n't, and while she was in the water he got some poison ivy in a towel and rubbed it thoroughly all over the inside of her underwear. A few hours later she had a frightful case of poisoning, and swelled up all over, with a high temperature. Can't you imagine his suspense as he watched and waited to see how badly she 'd take it, and then how he 'd chuckle as he saw her begin to scratch and her skin getting red and the little blisters coming out! That must have been pure delight. But his wife was a stupid woman and now she 's suing him for assault."

"Pretty," Brad said, stretching his arms. "Very pretty! But how did she find out he did it?"

"I don't know that it said. Perhaps she saw from the joy in his eye that he must have done it, or perhaps he told her. In a case of that sort you would n't get the last drop of pleasure unless your victim realized you were responsible."

"Joel!" Ellen exclaimed. "I think that's positively indecent. And the gloating way you told it! Linda, if he ever should get engaged, though I can't imagine a girl's accepting him, I think we ought to warn her that she's marrying a monster." She drew up her knees and hugged them with her elbows, making herself as small as she could. "It scares me to have you near me," she said. "I don't think you're respectable."

"He'd love to be able to do a thing like that," Linda said, "or he loves to pretend that he could if he wanted to, but he never could and he knows it, don't you, Joel? Even if you hated and despised someone you could n't really hurt them. When you marry I hope you get a gentle, kind wife, because if she stuck pins in you I don't think you could do more than look reproachful or perhaps walk out of the room. And that's why you like to tell about such things so proudly and savagely, is n't it?"

She's right, he thought, I'm without spirit when it comes to action: too chivalrous, too nice a little gentle-man, the result of a polite emasculating social background. I'm like a big tame animal that goes around licking every-body's hand.

Linda got up without warning to herself. "I'm going in," she said.

"We don't need to go in yet," Brad said. "Lunch is always late."

That may be true, she thought, but I can't sit still any longer. She stepped across Joel's legs and carefully down the rock, wondering if anyone would follow her, hoping they would though not really caring, which was just as well because nobody did. She stopped by the pool between the two ledges to put on her bathing cap: it was a real pool this morning, not just an inlet, because of the low tide. The bottom was strewn with flat stones, gray, yellow, orange, when you looked at each one separately, but all stained a clear olive-green when you looked at them together, and smooth like the cross sections of the stones in the marble paper weight shaped like a book on the *étagère* in the parlor. Mother's father had brought it back from Italy, and it made her think, like so many objects in the parlor, the bronze dogs from Pompeii, the temple of Vesta, the black stone urns on the mantelpiece, of what the Grove must have been long ago: elegant and stately, with shiny horses in the barn, and a coachman in livery (his name was Matthew), and an air about it like the taste of hothouse grapes or the color of sunlight through wine (the wine that used to be served in the goblets that lived now on the top shelf in the milk room); and yet, she thought, when they looked back at the cliff from this rock it must have looked just the same as it does to-day, except that the junipers were not so large, or perhaps there were other junipers; if I closed my eyes quickly and opened them and then by magic were looking at the cliff on a morning fifty years ago, would I see a change? It would seem as if you'd have to feel it, feel something in the air, in the light, beneath the shine of the water. In a shadowed corner of the pool a purple-pink starfish was sprawled upon the stones, its arms nonchalantly twisted as if it had been slowly whirling; you could imagine it posed for her there to illustrate a figure in a dance; through her own body she could feel its position: her arms would be raised and swaying to the left, her neck twisted to follow them, her right leg bent at the knee, her left languidly trailing. If Joel and Brad and Ellen were not there she would try it now, but she could n't with anyone looking at her. A wave lapped the end of the pool, scattered its surface with bubbles, and made the stones and the starfish undulate. How delicious bubbles like that would feel along her arms and legs!

None the less, as she stood at the end of the low point staring down at the water, she did not at once dive in. Even on the warmest day there was a chill moment, as the water swallowed your arms and head and slid along your body, that you could not bear to think of; if you thought of it long enough you might stand there on the rock forever; and to-day she thought of it deliberately because the moments she stood there were moments gained from the day: you were using one trick of time to cheat another. She wrinkled her nostrils, tried to get a firm grip with her feet on the barnacles: for a moment she could feel exactly the way Ellen must feel as she stood on the rock and delicately cringed for the benefit of whoever was watching; Linda curled her upper lip, shrank together, trying to look like Ellen; but it was horrid to make fun of her, horrid to talk about her the way she sometimes did to Joel and Brad. I 'm sure Ellen is fonder of me than she is of anyone, she thought; I 'm sure she does n't talk about me, that I 'm the only one she does n't; when we 're alone together she has charming natural moments when she 's all affection and gayety, or again when she 's sad and sees quite clearly that many people do not like her, and wonders what she can do, and grows humble and beseeching like a small silky animal.

"Be careful where you dive," Joel shouted. "When the tide 's as low as this it 's easy to hit a rock."

60

She turned her head to frown at him. As if she did n't know all the rocks as well as he did! He was scrambling to his feet: now she must dive, because she was not going to wait for Joel.

It was over. She shook the water from her eyes, pulled herself with a few strokes away from the rock. Looking back, she saw Joel poised on the edge; Brad and Ellen were climbing along the rock behind him: so they were following her now even if they would not before (but that was a foolish thought, because they would be coming now anyway). Linda swam straight out towards the reef — a line of deep-sea fish or huge barnacled turtles with ridge-shaped backs; but I might as well wait for Joel, she thought, because I know that really he will be pleased if I do.

She moved her arms and legs just enough to keep afloat: in the water you ought to have many more joints, so you could sway limply with every ripple like seaweed, so that your arms and legs could move in stretchy curves like the arms of that starfish. The reflection of the cliff laced the water with green and gray and brown; the stains from the iron springs that oozed from the rock looked like smears of pollen, and the cedars, high up, with their dead-looking trunks and bluish leaves, turned the whole cliff into a Japanese screen.

But at the very top of the screen something was moving: figures against the sky, a deep sky like the zenith, caught for once at the rim of this cliff-horizon. Who can they be, she thought, coming down to our rock? There were two of them; they were waving: they were Thornton and Dicky. At this hour? How could they be?

"They 're here!" she shouted to Brad and Joel and Ellen. "Look, they 're coming over the cliff."

She waved back at them; Joel and Brad and Ellen all
waved. Thornton came hurrying ahead, but Dicky had
stopped where the path turned; he seemed to be looking
about him, taking in the view. Does Thornton know
which one I am? she wondered: I must make him see me,
here in the water, make him sure that this is I before the
rock covers him.

The rock had covered him. I 'll never know if he
really picked me out, she thought, because if I ask him of
course he will say he did.

Dicky looked all around him: northward up the channel, bluer and bluer, with a couple of nets on poles
stretching into it like bits of camouflage, bluer and bluer
until the land on each side joined together in a line of
blue or purple; Linda would know what color it was, he
did n't, but he knew it was as fresh and clean as the floor
of heaven. He looked straight eastward to Sakonnet:
those fields, some yellow, some green, some of them spotted
with houses and toy trees, they were just the same as he
remembered; how could anything be so exactly the way
you remembered it? There was the red barn, sort of
pinky gray from here, but you knew it was red; there
was the lane leading down to the water; there was the
spire of the Little Compton church, and there to the southeast beyond the line of the rocks stood the lighthouse,
with Sachuest, due south, pointing towards it like a long
slick blade. He looked down to the rock; the tide was
low this noon, you could see so much of the reef, and to
make it perfect there were the folks in swimming; just
as you 'd thought. Oh, how often you 'd thought of
swimming from that rock, and perhaps you never would
again, perhaps you 'd never get home, never get within

62

three thousand miles of this place. I'll swim out to the reef, he thought, and I'll lie on the rock; what the hell if I am late to lunch: there's no penalty, there are no bugles to call you, and there won't be to-morrow or next day or ever again; it's mighty monstrous to think of! Was it day before yesterday I was eating in the hold of that ship, eating that filthy slop from a stinking mess kit, and talking with Jerry about ice cream and chocolate and roast duck till we almost got crowned, with enough garbage on the table to make you puke, and how they did, for the first few days, cabaret service around that old barrel, high comedy acts while you ate! And Joel, down there, he was a first looey, just as Thornton was a captain, and I can call them whatever I like (but I bet they were both swell officers, a couple of the chosen few); and I can thumb my nose at any sergeant or any corporal, any man in the whole damn outfit: noncoms, they were the worst, doing nothing but creeping around camp and showing off — a strange species of animal. But why think of them now? Why do that honor to the bastards? It's like thinking of smutty jokes when you're in church.

When was it? he thought suddenly; last August it was at Coivrel: I was sitting in the sun before the dugout peeling potatoes, and there were birds singing from the orchard and those damn French flies were buzzing; but just then it sounded peaceful, and I got to thinking and dreaming (the warm sun, the birds and the flies buzzing, were the logical combination to make anyone dream); and I imagined myself at the Grove, in white pants and a shirt, and then getting up and going to the line back of the barn to get my towel and then going over the fields to the rock. I could see it all just as if it were happening; I'd have given a leg to have it come true, and now it has come true. Here's where I was going: I'm here now thinking of that dugout in the orchard, and that lazy buzz of the flies, and my fingers wet from the potatoes; it gives you a funny feeling to remember that time when you were thinking of here, three thousand miles away; because now it's here that is real, and it's there that is just a thought: I was peeling potatoes, the flies were buzzing, and yet I was walking over to the rock; and now I'm at the rock. It's as if you had a swell dream, too happy to be true, and you felt you were beginning to wake up, and then somebody said: You're crazy, you're awake already. Those flies buzzing and those clammy potatoes, the smell of orchard, and that tapping sound from the battery in the woods, that was the dream; all that damned army was the dream, and a merry dream it was, if you ask me, enough to make you die laughing if you did n't die smeared all over a gun like Whit, or pass out in a hospital barracks with a sweet hole in your guts, like poor Jimmy. But don't be afraid now: you're out of it, it won't come back; you're in heaven now till you die. The Grove is really there, just over the hill, and all the country's there: the swamp and the ledges, with their junipers and their dry moss, and herons flapping up from between them, and the view over the Second Beach, and the road winding up the hill towards Newport. I want to go everywhere, climb over every foot of cliff and every stone wall; I want to lie in the sand and roll in the grass; I want to sail out around the lighthouse just to see the other side of it. But I have all the time in the world, all the rest of the summer, all the rest of my life. I thought I'd get knocked for a goal over there, but I did n't. Christ the Lord was a good sport for once. I'm not asking anything more.

64

Linda watched Thornton raise his arms, balance himself, and dive; watched his hands, his head, appear through green swirling bubbles four or five yards in front of her.

"Hullo there," he said in the quiet voice of his letters. "You see I did what I promised. I said I'd come back and here I am."

"Hullo, Thornton," Linda said. "If it is you really. I can't be quite sure."

"It's me all right," he said, "for better or worse. What do you say we swim to the reef, Linda?"

She was glad he had not suggested kissing her then and there in the water: it would have been funny, even without people watching, like two trained seals performing a new trick. It has come, she thought, the waiting is over; but it came so soon that I'm not prepared for it; I can think of nothing but my surprise that I'm not still waiting. She pulled herself up on the reef, fixed herself carefully in a niche on top of the seaweed and the barnacles. What would Thornton do next? What would he say? She watched his legs beside hers: not thick legs covered with hairs like Joel's; not nervous thin legs like Dicky's or Brad's; but shapely impersonal legs, golden-white, stained green where they trailed into the water, with fronds of kelp licking about the ankles and shins to hide the feet. You could think of them as the legs of a statue, an Olympic athlete, which had lain for centuries under the sea and now were being revealed by this exceptionally low tide, though if they had lain under water so long they would not of course be smooth, but rough and dark like the reef against which they leaned.

Linda raised her eyes and looked back to the rock. Dicky had arrived at last: he was shaking hands with Brad and Ellen while Joel stood discreetly at a distance, smiling, a little self-conscious, as if he thought he should n't be there at all. Linda could not see Dicky's expression, but she was sure that both Brad and he felt just as self-conscious as Joel; she knew the way they were grinning, not quite sure what to do with the corners of their lips, not quite certain about meeting each other's eyes. Suddenly she felt that she could not bear not to be on the rock with Dicky; why had she allowed Thornton to drag her off here? And yet when he had suggested swimming to the reef it had not occurred to her to refuse, perhaps because Thornton's sudden appearance had made her mind feel at once so empty or so crowded, she hardly knew which, that she had grasped at whatever was nearest. Now she waved her arm, leaned forward, and shouted to Dicky. "Hullo there, Dicky, hullo! Come over here so I can see you."

Dicky turned sharply as he heard her voice, and now with the sunlight shining on his face she could see his grin, like the expression in a photograph that's almost satisfactory but not quite. "Hi there," he called back. "I'd be right over except I'm kind of scared of the captain."

"You'd better be," Thornton answered, and Linda felt all at once that Dicky was very near: there was no longer any hurry; she was glad now that she had come to the reef with Thornton so that before anything else she might break through this foolish sense of strangeness. There was something warm and pleasant about looking forward to Dicky when you knew he was there waiting, that he would n't escape, that he was looking forward to you just as surely.

But what about Thornton? she wondered. Will he kiss me now? Are we expected to make love? Even here on the reef it would not be easy; they might be dragged over backwards and come up with noses full of water and legs streaming blood from long tooth-like scratches, like that plump clergyman, a friend of Father's, who had insisted so jovially on swimming off the rock "with the young folks." Then she knew that there was no fear of such a thing. Thornton could be trusted never to put himself in a position that could appear ridiculous: not that he would stand on his dignity or anything so foolish as that, — you never thought of his being dignified, for dignity always ran the risk of being overturned, — but he would have an instinct for avoiding the possibly absurd; and if Fate and his enemies combined to trick him into something that for any other person would mean certain ridicule, even then he would be granted, without seeking them, a thousand little cadences of voice, little gracious deprecatory gestures, that would turn the joke against the contrivers of the plot: the amusing thing would not be Thornton ridiculous but the absurdity of the idea that he ever could be made ridiculous, though Thornton would smilingly protest that he felt an utter fool.

"Well, Linda?" he said at last.

"Well?" she replied.

She raised her eyes until she met his glance. You could think of his eyes as honey-colored; they seemed far more ingratiating with his golden-white skin and yellow hair than any blue eyes you could imagine. He is beautiful, she thought, but is he what I remembered? It was hard to say, hard to compare so many thoughts and images and dreams with one tangible person definitely bounded by the surface of his own skin.

"How did you get here so soon?" she asked.

"We hit about fifty except through towns," he said. "We were just going down the hill at Saunderstown when

the eleven o'clock ferry blew its whistle, but I kept toot-
ing like a fire engine, and she waited for us."

"But if Dicky telephoned from New Haven?" she said.

"New Haven?" He lifted his head and laughed.
"Gosh no. Dicky called from New London."

"Oh, I see," she said; and she smiled because she was
remembering once more that Dicky — actually Dicky —
was over there across that strip of blue water. She could
not see him now because he was hidden by the rock, but
if she called his name he would hear her voice.

"I'm very sorry," Brad said, "but I've come to the
conclusion that Ellen rates a ducking. That curl or
wave or whatever it is might pass on the Newport Beach,
but she can't get away with it here."

"Dicky," she called, "you're not going to let him, are
you?"

"Hell, no," he called back. "Hi, there, Brad, you lay
off that woman."

"I'm very sorry," Brad said, "but I resent that curl."

Dicky swam after him and caught his leg. They were
doing nobly, he felt; this struggle with Brad, half under
water, was almost the real thing, almost as if Brad and he
had been scrapping together for the last couple of weeks.
He swam deep down under Brad's kicking legs, opened his
eyes in the cold dull water: you could see a tangle of weeds
or a rock, and a light patch that might be sand; it all
looked wobbly, as if it were not really there, like the spots
that swam across your eyelids when your eyes were closed.

As he came up he looked for Ellen. She was out of
Brad's reach, in close to the rock. Pretty as a picture, she
was; Brad and Joel didn't appreciate her because they
were so used to seeing her, and besides they liked their

women to be sort of highbrow. Is she lovable? he wondered. But remember you're not in the army any longer; she's not one of those Red Cross dames, waiting to be kissed, hoping you'll go farther than you'd ever think of going with the likes of them: Roses of No Man's Land! Humph! where do they get that No Man stuff?

Ellen smiled at him as he swam near her, but her eyes looked startled. Brad had really scared her; he ought not to be so rough, the big goof; but Brad's all right, Dicky thought: he's just trying to kid himself, like all the rest of us, that this isn't a special occasion.

"Oh, thank you, Dicky," Ellen exclaimed. "I'm glad there's at least one man around here that has a little chivalry."

"I'm like a knight of old," he said. "I'm a regular Galahad."

"Now Dicky, don't you start in too. I hoped you wouldn't."

"What do you mean, 'start in'?" he asked. "I'm not starting anything that I know of."

"Oh yes you are," she said. "They all make fun of me, at least Joel and Brad do. Linda doesn't. She's the one person I can trust. They do nothing but tease me, and I don't mind for a little, but it does grow rather tiresome in the long run. I should think they could at least be more original."

"Go on," he said. "If they kid you it's because they think you're one of the family."

"They say I'm always acting, Dicky," she said. "That's the trouble. They won't believe anything I say. But how can you be natural when people are looking at you all the time and smiling to themselves at whatever you do, because they say it's affected?"

"You 're too sensitive," he said. "It 's just your imagination, Ellen. We all kidded each other, of course, but we never picked on you; we never picked on anyone."

"You can't tell me," she said. "That may have been true once, but it is n't any more . . . and, good heavens, you just have to listen to what Brad says. It 's all perfectly good-natured, I don't deny that for a minute; but you get them all looking at you and smiling, and then you try to be natural. You just try it!"

Ellen had grown fierce as she talked: she looked as if she might almost be going to cry. He never remembered she was so serious; she used to be a gay little thing, always laughing and playing tricks.

"I don't believe it for a minute," he said. "I mean I think you 're exaggerating, Ellen, but I 'll keep my eyes open. I 'd just as lief speak to Brad, and Joel too; give the word and I 'll speak to anyone you say."

"I would n't have you for anything in the world," she said. "Promise me you won't, Dicky."

"But if they keep riding you, Ellen, and you never let on . . ."

"If you ever breathed a word to them," she said, so fiercely that it startled him, "I 'd never forgive you. I mean it."

"Sure, I promise," he said. "But why, Ellen?"

"They 'd say I was just acting," she said. "I know them."

He smiled at her, her face floating so near him in the blue water, with one lock of wet hair streaming like a mouse's tail across her forehead.

"I think you go too far," he said. "Seems to me you 're the one that is n't giving them a chance."

"Perhaps *you* think I 'm acting?" she said. "Do you?"

She stared straight at him, her lips trembling, her eyes very wide open: she was all wrong, of course, but you'd never think she had so much spirit.

"Don't be ridiculous," he said. "You can't think that, Ellen."

"You *do* — you *do!*" she exclaimed. "I hoped you would n't."

She turned quickly, and swam out from the rock; he swam after her, but not too quickly: she would n't like it; he would give her a minute or two to calm down. Of course he would speak to some of them; Linda perhaps would be the best, and she could pass on the word. We'll go for a walk this afternoon, he thought, and I'll see if I can cheer her up with my feeble pranks; after listening to some of those Y.M.C.A. birds, I ought to be an expert on keeping them smiling, with chins high and stiff upper lips.

But why brood so romantically on suicide? Joel asked himself, as he sat on the rock and looked in disgust at his big toe, which he had scraped just now climbing out of the water: to kill oneself requires no thought; possibly determination kept unwavering for a short period, or perhaps simply a coincidence of mood and opportunity; the distressing and complicated question is how to live, how to live when you are driven by the urge for money — filthy lucre, and yet the key to freedom, if that is not another romantic illusion. Tea is in itself not undesirable, one could even invest it with a certain glamour; but the wiser thing is to see your money-grubbing as frankly that, like sweating or emptying your bowels: after all, had the position offered, it might have been cosmetics. I almost wish it were, to point the irony even more sharply.

He watched Brad swimming along under the base of the cliff. His thin brown arms rose and fell as if they were moved by machinery; his feet churned the smoothness of the water — blue and pale as you looked southward along the cliff, with a sheen that you could make either gray or mother-of-pearl, like the lining of a mussel shell. Poor chap, Joel thought, you can see him as trying to escape; it would not be surprising if he looked back over his shoulder and then climbed out on to the barnacles, scurried up the cliff, and hid among the bayberry and the junipers; but he can no more escape than a thin-legged young horse cantering about a field, and the knowledge, which the horse would not have, of what is coming does not help him, but only throws a chill over his last day of freedom. In a way it is worse for him than for me, because he had a clear alternative, something that he wished to do and could have done, whereas my alternative would be simply brooding over the poems I could never write; and yet, such is the adaptability of the human mind, he persuades himself, or almost persuades himself, that what he has chosen, what he has been driven into, is for the best. With most people I would regard that as merely stupid, but in Brad's case I see it as pathetic, perhaps even admirable. May it not be more self-respecting to identify yourself as closely as possible with whatever system of life you have chosen, with whatever class you belong to, even if it be the well-to-do, standardized American bourgeoisie? If you see your way of life as inevitable, take it for granted, perhaps there may be often around the edges a margin of spiritual freedom which no outsider can observe, because for him you are merely a representative of your class. And what do I, with all my fine resolves, actually accomplish? One has at moments the uncomfortable sense that the way I fondle the idea of a mystical (or mythical) integrity preserved within my spirit is not unlike the foolish pride in her virginity of a morbidly-minded spinster. At times, when I consider the tragedies that result from economic injustice, when I read of some particularly egregious blunder of our bourgeoisie, my thoughts veer sharply to the left; I dip into Marx; I flaunt copies of the *Masses* and the *Daily Worker* before people I think they will shock; I stupidly explode at dinner parties before the wealthier of my friends in communist tirades which they, with true instinct, refuse to take seriously; and yet any one of the Warings, Brad, Dick, or even Linda, would be happier, would be less out of place, in a soviet state, once it were thoroughly accepted, no longer an experiment or a revolutionary novelty, but merely a fact, than I could ever be.

Joel looked from Brad to Linda, out there on the reef beside Thornton, to Dicky swimming near the rock with Ellen, trying to show her the correct way to move her legs. Why am I so fond of that family? he wondered; is it simply because I have always known them, because I associate them with this region? Is it because I'm so very different from them? They are so slim and hairless, so swift-moving; their bones might be filled with air or quicksilver; you could think of them as birds, those gray gulls out there beyond the reef, and me as a chunky ground hog blinking at them from the entrance to my burrow; or, if we must all be the same species of animal, they would be greyhounds and I some mongrel shaggy mixture of Newfoundland and sheep dog; they move lightly over the rock, even Brad is light in his awkwardness, and I go stumbling along cutting my toes on the barnacles. And Ellen and Thornton are more like them than me, he thought, superficially at least. He scowled at Ellen in the water below him and caught her eye. She waved at him.

"You must n't watch me," she called. "Dicky 's giving me a lesson and I 'm too frightfully clumsy, as you can see."

No, she was n't clumsy, she could n't be: helpless, futile, yes, but not clumsy, and she knew it. It would be interesting to have that girl psychoanalyzed: you might discover anything from Volume I to VI of Havelock Ellis. It was odd how she looked at the same time so much younger and so much older than Linda, like a petulant child, with her big eyes and short upper lip, in whose face you could already see the "well-preserved" woman she would be twenty years from now; "ashen blonde" he supposed she would be called, though to do her justice she did n't look like a chorus girl or a movie star when she so easily might have. No, what her face suggested was the heroine of some minor novel of the late Victorian age, one of those sweet little women with fluffy hair and slender waists, who on the croquet ground or across the tea table repulsed admirers, while they wistfully thought of their soldier husbands in India; and like as not Dicky will fall in love with her, he thought, like as not he 'll marry her, or if not her someone no more intelligent. If Linda is marrying Thornton, what can you expect?

He looked again at the reef: Thornton was certainly smooth and slick, smoother than any of them; but it was the smoothness of well-oiled furniture at an exclusive men's club; or no, it was not something applied to the surface, it was all through him and yet it was not natural, or at least not the right kind; it was synthetic. You could think of Thornton as the highly successful product, protected by patent, of a superlaboratory, an automaton, like Frankenstein's monster but far more skillfully made, for the purpose of fascinating young girls, and endowed, unfortunately, with the power of sexual reproduction; and Linda, of such a different smoothness, like a leaf unfolding, like the breast of a gull, the curve of a wave, Linda would be infected with that synthetic product, it would fill her full, insidiously corroding like cancer or leprosy; she would give birth to little smooth mongrels, half real, half manufactured: bastards, because across such a gulf there could be no marriage. Is it his money? Joel thought. I cannot believe that. Is she just a damn fool? I'd like to tell her just what I think of her. Thank God he has the decency not to be mouthing her and handling her with the rest of us here to look on! I couldn't stand it if he did. I'd be sick at my stomach.

"You haven't told me you're glad to see me," Thornton said.

"And you haven't told me you're glad to see me, Thornton."

"I guess you can take that for granted," he said. "The one thing I'm scared of, Linda, is that you'll find out how crazy I am about you and then you'll know you can make me do anything you want. I might be in a bad way."

"Would you be afraid of what I'd make you do?" she asked.

"No," he said, "I guess not, not if you still liked me. Still, I might be at that. You can be pretty fierce when you feel like it."

"Suppose I wanted you to do something awful?" she asked. "Would you do it?"

"Try me," he said. "I'd rob a bank."

"Oh, it would n't be anything like that," she said.

What would it be? She was like a princess in a fairy tale inventing some difficult quest to prove her lover; now for the first time she realized why a princess might give even the most charming prince impossible tasks to perform: it was so she would have time to get used to him, time to catch up and know what to do. She stared once more into the water. Green matted beards sprouting from the reef were pulled back and forth just under the surface, and just above, in a fringe of brown rubbery leaves, points of violet blue slipped and gleamed, like drops of oil catching the sunlight. I might send him to the bottom of the sea, she thought, to bring back a branch of coral that would keep you young and beautiful as long as you lived; I might send him to China to bring back the nightingale that sings on the top story of an enchanted pagoda (these barnacles all around us, dried by the air, rough and pale like pumice, might be carvings on the wall of the oldest pagoda in the East, carvings so fine that you could hardly make them out thousands of years ago when they were new); but wherever I sent him, she thought, I 'm sure he would be back in a moment with the task magically performed, because it is hard to believe that he cannot do anything he wants to: that he could not send all the mermaids in the sea, all of them in love with him, poor things, to discover the coral, miles and miles under water, in the depths of the coldest cavern; that he could not with a lift of his arm send the whole race of birds to fly in circles around the tops of all the pagodas in China and coax away the nightingale.

"Well," he said, "what would it be?"

"I don't know," she said, still not looking at him. "You must give me time."

"I'll give you anything you want," he said. "And that goes from now. I mean it."

But it seemed as if the one thing she asked for he would not give her, for his arm, reaching out, touched her knee and held it firmly. Joel and the others were out of sight beyond the bulwark of the rock. I can't, she thought; I can't.

She thought of the young girls in the gardens of Eastern temples, sent there to offer themselves to the first stranger who desired them: this was a beautiful young stranger, more than she could have hoped for; his touch was perilous, exciting, but that made it all the more fearful. I can't, she thought; I must speak to him, to-day, I must talk to him, I must explain; I will not have an instant's peace until I explain; but I'll have to think, I'll have to decide what to explain.

He was leaning towards her. "Linda," he said, "you can't guess how I've been counting the days . . ."

She slipped into the water, struck out as fast as she could for the rock; but no matter how hard she tried, Thornton swam close beside her, nonchalant and gay as a young seal.

Brad, the last one, stopped a moment on the grassy rim above the cliff to look backward. The morning is over, he thought: we'll be taking a swim before supper, but the rock seems different then, just as nice but different, and it's usually too cool to do much lying around. I'll never forget this morning, though, he thought, with Thornton and Dicky surprising us; it will be a sort of anniversary. We'll remember it years and years from now when we are swimming off the rock; we'll think of it especially when the tide is very low; but it is higher already; you can see the difference, you can see only about half as much of the reef as you could at first.

He turned slowly, watched them walking back in single file along the path through the bayberry. Above them in the depths of the sky there shimmered a warm whiteness that reminded him of afternoon.

IV

IT was hot and bright here in the bushy meadows. You could imagine rainbows dissolved in the blue-black shadows of trees and rocks; you could imagine that the blue-white film of the sky was about to burst into flame. If it did it would sweep eastward across the ledges and Thornton and she would be consumed with the rest of the world, and nothing would matter.

"Thornton," Linda said, as they stepped through the gates into the woods, "I 've something to tell you."

The path was narrow; she pushed ahead of him, but his arm, tightening, held her back.

"What is it?" he asked.

"Thornton, you must n't make love to me yet."

"That 's a note," he said chuckling, his arm tighter than ever. "If I can't make love to my girl, who can I make love to?"

"Anybody you want," she said, "except me. Thornton, please, I ask you." Her voice rose sharply; she pulled away from him, and hurried on over the hummocks of the path.

"Can I make love to Ellen?" he asked.

"Thornton, I 'm serious," she said. "You must listen."

"I 'm listening," he said. "What is it?"

His voice, reasonable and considerate, just the voice

79

with which he had soothed her ever since she could remember when she grew excited, made her feel that she was very foolish, made her feel once more younger than he: it is Thornton, she thought, of course; what am I doing? Why am I running from Thornton? And yet she felt rather that this strange and beautiful young man was more and more taking on Thornton's mask; she could much more easily imagine herself liking his kisses than recognizing him: the fearful thing was that she knew she could hardly resist him (just his being there, so confident, so beautiful) even without recognition.

"I can't marry you, Thornton," she said. "At least not just yet."

"Don't you worry, Linda," he said. "As far as I'm concerned, I'd say put it to-morrow, or better still this afternoon. But that would be too much to hope for. It's entirely up to you when we get married."

"But you don't understand," she said, her tone rising again. "Why can't I make you understand? Probably I can't marry you for several years, and perhaps never. Thornton, we can't be engaged."

"I should think this is serious," he said. "Tell me about it. What's happened?" He spoke calmly, as if he were talking to a sick child; he's humoring me, she thought, and he has no right to; it makes me feel as if I were just being temperamental.

"Nothing's happened," she said crossly. "What do you mean, 'happened'?" And now, she thought, I'm quarreling; next thing I'll be screeching and stamping my foot, as if poor Thornton were to blame.

"You've told me we couldn't be engaged," he said, "but you haven't told me why."

"Because I don't know why," she said, and she felt like

bursting into tears. "Because . . . because I can't see you, Thornton . . . because you seem strange."

He did not answer for a moment. Then he said: "I guess that means that I don't measure up to what you expected. I don't know what I can do about that if you 've really made up your mind, but it 's sort of hard to get used to, hearing it so suddenly."

"No — no — no!" she said. "It does n't mean that. How can I be disappointed in you when I can't see you? And I have n't made up my mind about anything, that 's just the trouble. But how can I marry anyone that 's just mysterious?"

"If you married me," he said, "if you could bear to, that might help clear up the mystery. Had you thought of that?"

"But I could n't, Thornton. It might clear it up the wrong way."

"Yes," he said. "I suppose it might. For you. But of course it might not. For me there would n't be any mystery."

His quiet voice made her feel cruel and mean.

"But I do love you, Thornton," she said. "Of course I love you. It 's just perhaps that I don't love you enough. The trouble is that I don't know. Perhaps I 'll find that I love you more than ever . . . but I don't know . . . I can't tell."

"Linda . . . Darling . . ." His step was quicker; he was going to put his arm around her again. She ran a few steps along the path, then waited for him; how silly, how horrid, to be running away from Thornton. He was close behind her again, but he did not touch her except when his arm brushed her shoulder as he reached forward to push branches out of her way. When the path rose from the swamp and they stood once more in the sunlight, at the end of the ridge, she turned her head to look at him. His face was friendly and hurt, really hurt: not angry, not bearing a grudge. "Why don't we sit down here, Linda," he said, "and talk a bit? I have n't said more than half a dozen words to you since we got back and you have n't said a thing to me until just now. I wondered why you were so quiet, and I hoped it was because you were happy like me. Don't you think this is mostly because you're sort of scared of me, because you have n't seen me for so long? When I first saw you this morning, for a minute even you seemed a little strange. Is that beautiful girl there Linda, I thought, so calm and sure of herself? How did I ever have the nerve to call her down because she held her racket sloppily?"

No one could be fairer, more wistful; but she knew that she must not sit down with him, here among the cedars, in the brown moss and the dry pinkish grass, here where they had kissed each other so happily one afternoon two years ago, the day he first spoke of their being married. If only she could feel that way now! She almost could, and yet her just not feeling, her so nearly feeling, that special kind of happiness seemed to make far more difference than if she could not feel it at all.

"I want to walk up the ledge," she said. "It will be cooler and we can see the view."

She turned away so that she would not see his face if he looked too disappointed.

"All right," he said. "It certainly will be cooler up there."

She walked up the ledge; it might be the long thick tail, the spine, of some prehistoric dragon. She noticed the blue-green berries on the junipers; was it they that smelled so hot and bitter? Crickets or frogs were scraping below in the swamp, and now and then you could just hear an automobile passing on the road to Newport. I 'm getting nowhere, she thought; it 's like a dream when you have to keep walking and straining so you won't get pulled backward into something mysterious that you do not dare turn your head to look at. The tops of the trees, maples and cedars, by the foot of the ridge on their left, made a sunny wall against which she could see their shadows, Thornton's and hers, silently, smoothly hurrying: Thornton's never came nearer, never got farther away. . . . It must be much worse for him, she thought; it must be terrible for poor Thornton; if anyone did a thing like this to me, I would feel like dying; I would be so angry that I 'd want him to die; I must seem so treacherous and changeable — beneath contempt.

"One reason we can't be engaged, Thornton," she said, "is because I may want to be an actress."

"That 's nothing new, is it?" he asked. "You 've always loved acting, have n't you, Linda?"

"I know. But I may want to be a real actress, a professional."

"When did you decide this?" he asked. "This morning? After you saw me?"

"No," she said. "Of course not. Don't be silly, Thornton. But when I did see you, it made me think that I 'd have to do something, either marry you or do something else . . . and not just keep putting off; and if I did marry you, and then decided I had to be an actress, I know you would n't like it, would you? You 'd hate it."

Perhaps I really will be an actress, she thought; perhaps I 'll decide definitely, now, this minute; you always

83

have to decide everything sometime. When you are acting, the part is always there, that's the thing that is such a relief: Hedda or Lady Macbeth or Juliet; as you study their lines you know little by little how they feel, and then it's easy to feel it yourself. When they feel excited you can feel their excitement, but even when they are calm it's exciting for you to feel their kind of calm; and then if there is an audience all their excitement as they watched you would become yours, too, until you could hardly bear it, and yet it would be nothing but triumph, because you would be so sure; no, there is never any doubt of the feeling when you are Lady Macbeth or Juliet or Hedda, but when you are just yourself there seems to be doubt almost always; you never can be sure what your lines should be; you almost never can be sure what you are or what you mean.

"If you married me, Linda," he said, "of course you could do anything you pleased. Because I was your husband would n't mean I was your boss — I 'd like to see me try it; but I *would* feel very sorry to see you go on the stage professionally, and I 'd feel even sorrier if you were n't married to me than if you were, because you 'd have no one to look out for you."

"Why would you be sorry to see me on the stage, Thornton, if I was n't your wife? Because you think it 's not respectable? Not like being a trained nurse or a teacher?"

"Don't be foolish," he said. "It may be very fine to be a famous actress like Ethel Barrymore, though from what I hear even that must be a dog's life, but for one successful actress there are a thousand that don't get anywhere, and, believe me, the life of the average unsuccessful actress is about the dreariest and cheapest you could find."

84

"So you think I'd be no good, Thornton? That's not very nice of you."

"You might be a second Nazimova," he said, "and not get anywhere. You don't know what you'd be up against, Linda. It's ninety per cent luck even if you have the talent, and I guess you have it; I've no doubt you have talent: I think you could do anything you really wanted to, Linda. But nine out of the remaining ten per cent is pull, and having someone to back you."

"How do you know so much about actresses, Thornton?" she asked. "Do you know any? You haven't told me."

"I've met a few," he said. "I can't say I've been carried away by them, nor by the kind of life that lots of them lead — not all, of course, but a great many. They have to, to get on. That's just my point."

"What kind of life?" she asked.

"I guess you can imagine, can't you? Just promiscuous. Running about with all kinds of men."

"How do you know I wouldn't like that kind of life?" she asked. "Perhaps if I married you I'd have lots of lovers. I might drive you distracted."

"You can't scare me that way," he said.

"I imagine you've been very gay, Thornton, and that's why you talk so wisely to me."

"I'm not such a fool," he said, "but I've had enough friends who were to know what I'm talking about."

"Who were they?" she asked, smiling. "I'd like to know them."

"No you wouldn't," he said. "You wouldn't like them at all. You've got too much sense."

They had reached the open part of the ledge; the tree-tops now were below them; you could look eastward

across the reservoir and the Sakonnet River to the lighthouse, very white among its pink rocky islands; southward, straight along the ledge to the sea; and there, coming
to meet them, not a hundred yards away, were Ellen and
Dicky. Linda was delighted; she waved and called.

Thornton came close behind her. "This talk about
being an actress is beside the point," he said, "and you
know it, Linda, and I believe that 's why you brought it
up. All I ask is don't do anything yet. Don't break
the engagement. You say I seem strange. Wait a bit
till I don't seem strange, and then if you don't love me,
all right. You did love me once, Linda, or I would n't
be hoping, because you 're about ten times as clever as
I am, and you 're musical and artistic and a lot of other
things into the bargain."

"That has nothing to do with it," she said, "because
I 'm not clever, Thornton; or if I am it 's just that, just
a stupid kind of cleverness that prevents you from being
anything worth while; but I must tell Mother and Father
we 're not engaged, because otherwise I 'd feel so deceit-
ful, and I could n't bear for them to talk about plans
for our getting married when perhaps we won't be. You
won't mind if I tell them, will you, Thornton, and nobody else, until we can see what happens?"

"Tell them of course, if you want to, Linda."

"And you 're not angry with me?" she asked. "You
don't feel I 'm cheating you, Thornton, that I 'm just
making everything turn horrid and empty? Oh, I know
it can. I know the feeling."

"You can't expect me to feel like cheering," he said,
"but I 'm not angry, Linda. You could n't make me
angry if you tried."

Linda smiled very brightly to greet Dicky and Ellen,

because she knew that there were tears in her eyes; but at the same time she felt relieved and victorious: I have spoken to him, she thought; the worst is over; I won't feel that I'm being dragged along, that things are moving too quickly; and perhaps I'll find that I do want to marry him, that I have just been muddled and confused the way I so often am. To-night sometime I will speak to Mother and Father; I won't like that, but it will be much easier than speaking to Thornton, and then I will be quite free.

"How nice to meet you!" she said to Dicky and Ellen. "And now you must both turn around and walk back with Thornton and me to the end of the ledge."

"Sure," Dicky said. "That's just where we've come from, but never mind. How about it, Ellen?"

"You go," she said, "by all means. I'm going home. I've got a headache."

What was the matter with Ellen? Her face looked pale and tight; and she smiled the way she was apt to smile when she felt angry, with a kind of false meekness in her voice and dark stary eyes. Have they been quarreling too? she wondered: though Thornton and I have not been quarreling, because Thornton would not let me. What is happening to-day? Things seem so simple beforehand and often so perfect, and sometimes when you look back at them they seem that way too, but when they are happening they are nearly always complicated and far from perfect; any number of small things turn up that you had not expected, and people don't fit into your plans; the wisest thing would be not to have any plans, but I can't help having them, not only for me but for everybody else, and that is even worse. Dicky was standing at the edge of the rock, staring at the lighthouse, very jaunty and perhaps a little impatient. Dicky, too, was not quite the same as she remembered him: perhaps everyone was changed by the war, or perhaps it was that everyone seemed changed the first time you saw them after a long absence; Brad did not seem changed now, but perhaps at first he had and you had forgotten, just as in a day or two you might forget that Dicky had seemed different, or even Thornton; but now you felt a kind of toughness about Dicky, as if he were hardening into grooves that would not let him out to express, to feel, all the things he naturally could feel; as if he could not quite wait, this new Dicky, for his feeling to become clear and truly itself, but rather would force it, because he did not care, into the groove that happened to be nearest.

"I 'd just as lief go home," he said. "It 's all the same to me."

"You stay with Linda," Ellen said. "I 'm certainly not going to break up your walk."

"Thornton will go with you, Ellen," Linda said, "and I 'll keep Dicky, because I have n't really seen him yet."

"You keep them both," Ellen said. "I 'm going."

She walked quickly past them: this would never do.

"Thornton," Linda whispered sharply. Thornton gave her a look that reminded her of Frolic when he wanted to go with them on a picnic and thought they would not let him.

"Why don't we all go?" he asked.

"You 're not the only one that arrived to-day," Linda said. "Perhaps I have important secrets to tell Dicky."

Thornton smiled at Dicky. "What 's the good of being out of the army?" he asked, and ran after Ellen.

Linda was surprised that he seemed so gay; it was partly

of course because he must behave as if nothing had happened, but mostly because she was ordering him about, in spite of what she had been saying, as if they still belonged to each other. If we are really not engaged, she thought, I have no right to expect Thornton to do things; but I must try not to think of him now; the more I worry about him and ask myself questions the less I'll know what I think.

She turned to Dicky. "It's true," she said, "I haven't seen you, Dicky. You've been so busy with Ellen. I haven't had a chance."

Dicky shrugged his shoulders. "She beats me," he said.

"What's the matter, Dicky?"

"Oh, nothing," he said shortly. "Shall we be walking, Linda?"

He turned, and she walked along beside him.

"Would you be insulted," he asked suddenly, "if a boy tried to kiss you?"

She laughed. "Why, Dicky," she said, "do you go around kissing girls offhand?"

"I swear she didn't act as if she'd mind," Dicky said. "Good Lord, I hadn't thought of kissing her. I liked her too much to want to kiss her right off. There was no point in rushing things. I was perfectly content just to be here. I wasn't going to start anything. But I'll swear she acted as if she expected something; she was all right, I mean, but I got to feeling that she'd think I didn't like her, that she might feel insulted if I didn't start a move of some sort. If you think a girl wants you to kiss her, you've got to do something, haven't you?"

"Dicky," she exclaimed, "you're so funny! I'm sure I don't know the proper etiquette under the circumstances, but I wouldn't worry too much about Ellen."

"When I did kiss her," he said gruffly, "she sort of flopped in my arms. She got all limp and closed her eyes. I couldn't tell whether it was because she liked it so much or because she was scared or what. She strikes me as being darned high-strung, Ellen does. I didn't remember she used to be that way. I got scared myself, but I couldn't let her fall, could I? I had to hold her up till she opened her eyes, and then she acted as if I'd betrayed her. Gosh, the last thing I wanted to do was to hurt her feelings."

Oh, Ellen, Ellen, Linda thought, what are you up to now? Are you really in love with Dicky? I don't suppose you know how you do feel, but I cannot blame you for that. Is it all pretending? she wondered. But when Ellen pretends she does it so hard, and she's so ready to believe it herself, that it's just as bad as if it were real; and often it may be real, that's the trouble. Certainly her fondness for me is as real as anything; if there's pretending there it is not she, it is I. It is so hard, she thought, to know what to do, it is so embarrassing, when someone is much fonder of you than you are of her, especially when it's someone like Ellen that you cannot help laughing at now and then: because you always feel like a hypocrite when people talk about her if you pretend she's not sometimes funny or even absurd (it's as if you were trying to be noble and virtuous but really being sentimental); but if you laugh at her yourself and admit she's foolish, then you feel like a hypocrite, too, when she admires you and says she loves you and that you're her dearest friend. Always I feel guilty with her, she thought, because I'd so hate to be much fonder of people than they were of me; because it would be so humiliating, and it seems that if I were decent I ought to be just as fond of Ellen; and then I pretend I am; and then I feel hypocritical to myself, because I know I'm not.

"I think she'll be all right this evening," Linda said. "Probably she was just excited at seeing you, and you rushed her off her feet, Dicky."

"But what do you think I ought to do?" he asked. "I didn't want to be fresh, Linda, and if I told her I thought she wanted me to kiss her, which is the honest-to-God explanation, that would get by big, wouldn't it? I have half a mind to, at that. She deserves it."

"I wouldn't," Linda said, laughing. "I'd just wait and see what happens, and I certainly wouldn't worry."

That is what we all seem to be doing, she thought: waiting to see what will happen; all but Brad, and I wish that he were waiting too; but when Brad decides to do something you know that he'll do it well; he'll be a success and he'll stick to it, but it is rather sad to think that if he had waited he might have chosen something more interesting. Which is worse, she wondered: to stick to a thing you do not really like, or keep jumping around because you are not sure what you like best?

"I've got an idea, Linda," Dicky said suddenly. "Let's you and me beat it off somewhere and get signed up together as a vaudeville team. How about it?"

"That would be wonderful," she said, "but what would we do, Dicky?"

"We could get up a swell act. You could play the piano, and we'd both sing, imitations and parodies, you know, the way we used to fool around sometimes. We'd work it up by ourselves the rest of this summer and then we'd disappear some fine morning, and leave a note to break the news to the rest of the family. But gosh, I

91

forgot about Thornton. I suppose you'll be married by then."

·"You never can tell," she said, "and I'm certainly not going to let Thornton interfere with my plans."

What fun it would be to work up an act: with the piano, and singing, and perhaps a little dancing, an act that would really be making fun of all the usual vaudeville — the way those women sang, the tough fat ones and the little ones that thought they were so cunning, and Dicky could imitate the slick young men, so smart, so casual, that picked up the ladies' handkerchiefs when they dropped them as they walked across the stage and began foolish conversations and then started singing. You knew just how those people moved, just how they used their voices: they were funny always in a way they did not quite mean to be; and you would always be moving from town to town, and meeting all kinds of people; and why would n't that be the best way to get experience for the real stage, far better and much more fun than any dramatic school or amateur theatricals? *Just break the news to Mother*, Linda sang to herself, *and say how much I love her*. Yes, you could have a sentimental ballad in your act; perhaps that very one. She was smiling more and more; she felt like rushing home at once and looking over music, drawing sketches for costumes. Dicky was smiling, too, more than ever; his eyes were very lively and twinkling; he looked like the mixture of a young Greek shepherd and a goblin. Suddenly he laughed.

"I believe you'd do it," he said, "and you'd get away with it, too, with your looks."

Of course Dicky had not meant it; she had known that he had not meant it, but it was fun to think of. She took his arm.

"What are you going to do, Dicky?" she asked.

"Damned if I know," he said. "I can't think of a blame thing now except being out of the army."

"Was it very bad?" she asked. "Did you mind it awfully, Dicky?"

"It was a merry life," he said, "a healthy, jovial life. It's what I call good clean sport. When you had nothing else to do you could always watch the cooties running relay races over your skin: galloping dandruff, one of the boys called them. Now and then we used to catch the dear little things and freeze them up in candle grease. And that's how the army made me feel, like a cootie frozen up in grease. But if I lie around in this sun long enough and have enough swims in that water perhaps it'll melt."

"Dicky," she asked, "if you could do anything in the world you wanted — anything at all — what would you choose?"

"Ask me something easier," he said. "I don't know, Linda: I wouldn't register a kick if I could just hang around here for a year or so, and live in Robert's house during the winter and help him run the place. I'm sick of being ordered about, Linda; I'm sick to death of regulations; all I ask from now on is to be able to mind my own business. I suppose the folks will want me to go back to college this fall, though I can't picture myself getting worked up over English 37 or Economics 1A. Or it wouldn't be such hard lines to bum around the world after a bit — start out some morning with a little cash in my jeans, but not too much, and just keep going."

They had reached the highest hump of the rock. Linda looked around her: at the ocean with its soft blue edge

(not a sail anywhere, but you could imagine it covered
with a fleet of little airy boats), at the ridges of the waves
coming in so smoothly, changing to green as they curled,
and breaking in electric flashes that swept along the beach;
she looked at the green thread-like stars scattered through
the brown moss, at the road climbing into the sun over the
hill to Newport. All that was part of the world, and all
the rest of the world was spread beyond, though you could
not see it: you could start along the road to Newport and
keep on going until you had traveled through every country and across every sea. There is so much, she thought,
so much that I want to be doing, so many lives that I want
to be leading; and it seems just now as if they all were
possible. How can I keep this feeling, so light, so free?
This air, she thought, that I am breathing now is floating
around the world: nearly always the air you breathe is
just the air of a room, or a field, or at most it stops at the
horizon; but now I can feel the whole earth floating in
colored air, as if it were passing through the filmy tail
of a comet.

"Dicky," she said, "would you really run away with
me quite suddenly . . . if we could work out something
to do . . . and start around the world in search of adventure?"

"Do you mean it, Linda?" he asked, smiling at the
ground, a little embarrassed. "Sure I would. Give me
a sign when."

But she knew, really, that Dicky and she could no
more run away together than she could spread her arms
and sail off the ledge, and circle over the sea. Almost
you felt that you could do it; perhaps you could if only
you kept thinking that you could — spread your arms
and float off into the air, sweeping down at first between

the ledges, then rising and rising, until you could look back on all the islands in the bay, on the whole continent, three thousand miles across, yellow and green and brown between the two oceans; until you saw the earth as if it were a cloudy moon, floating in the depths of the sky.

V

Mark looked so content, so quietly happy, as they walked from gate to gate, that Luly could not bear to tell him. I know how Linda feels, she thought, because I know how I felt when I broke my engagement to Douglas; poor little Linda, I must speak to her again before she goes to bed: of course if she feels the slightest doubt the only thing, absolutely the only thing, is to wait. Behind Mark's head she saw the moon over the tulip tree; there were pink clouds resting along the ocean; in the half circle the trees looked very near, even the dimmest and farthest: they did not seem to be bark and leaves, but immaterial, entirely themselves.

"Mark," she said, "I was talking to Linda just after supper, and she feels a trifle uncertain. She thinks that for a time, at any rate, Thornton and she had better not be engaged."

"Not engaged!" he exclaimed abruptly, and she knew that for him the evening was ruined. "Do you mean that Linda's broken her engagement?"

"Nothing's to be said about it," she went on, "not even to the boys, but she spoke to Thornton this afternoon, and she told me a few minutes ago, right after supper."

They walked on, past the house, towards the north gate: there were lights already in the parlor and Luly could see Brad standing by the piano and taking his violin from its case; Linda was seated on the piano stool — you could see only her back; Thornton stood with Dicky and Joel by the table. Mark's feet crunched sharply on the path.

"Nothing may come of it," Luly said. "I mean she may marry him after all, Mark. It's just that she's uncertain, and she wanted him to know it, and she wanted to tell us so we would n't be making plans."

"I don't suppose there ever was a woman that knew her own mind," Mark said, "but I did think that Linda . . ."

"After all," Luly said, "Linda's only twenty-one, Mark. She's hardly grown-up. She was only nineteen when Thornton went overseas, and you remember one of the reasons we were so anxious for her not to marry him then was because we were afraid she might change her mind."

"I did n't want her to marry him then," Mark said crossly, "because I thought he might be killed; and if possible I did n't want her to be left a widow at nineteen or twenty before her life had really begun. I wish to heaven now she had married him and then she would n't be putting on this ridiculous performance to-day."

"Mark, you know you don't wish anything of the kind. This only goes to prove how right we both were."

"Of course I would n't want her to be married to a man she did n't love," Mark said, "if that's what you're driving at, but certainly she was in love with him then, and if she had married him, if he was her husband, she'd probably still be in love with him."

"I don't know why you think so," Luly said, smiling. "I have the greatest respect for marriage, and I think that nothing in life can give you greater happiness than a fam-

ily of your own, but even I don't go so far as to say that
being married to a person means that you 're necessarily
bound to keep on loving him. If you believed most mod-
ern novelists, which I don't, it apparently has just the
opposite effect."

"What I mean," Mark explained more snappishly than
ever, "is that if she were his wife she would n't be wondering whether she wanted to do this or wanted to do
that; he 'd be her husband; she 's fond of him still, presumably, or she would n't be uncertain, and she 'd be
only too happy to have him back. If you have a dress
in your wardrobe you put it on; but if you 're in a store
and see one you like, you 're not content until you 've
tried on everything in the place that will fit you and most
of the things that won't, and then in most cases you go
back to the original one."

"Are you describing me," she asked, "or women in
general? Because if there 's anything I dislike it 's trying
on dresses in shops."

"You 're not as bad as some," he said, "but I know the
feminine mind. When *I* go into a store I know what I
want and I buy it if it 's there, and I pay for it, and then
I come out."

"I don't think your figure is as appropriate," she said,
"as the ones you 're apt to use in your sermons; but if
Linda does come back to the original one, as you suggest,
which I think is not unlikely, then there 's no need for us
to be upset now, is there?"

"Oh, you don't know what she 'll do," Mark said. "I
thought she was settling down, getting more balance, but
now . . . Next thing she'll be eloping with some freak,
or doing something else utterly foolish . . . and Thornton,
what does he think? I 'll feel ashamed to see him. Poor

boy, I should think he had every reason to feel that he's been treated outrageously."

"I feel very sorry for Thornton," Luly said. "I have n't spoken to him yet, but I certainly shall to-night. I'm afraid it will be a blow if the engagement really is broken, but after all, Mark, if Linda feels she can't love him enough . . ."

They had reached the north gate and Luly stood still for a moment to look across the road to the swamp and the ledges, dim now, dissolving as in cool gray water; they reminded her through the dusk of the wild hills she imagined in *Rob Roy* or *The Fair Maid of Perth*. Yes, she thought, if Linda finds she cannot love him enough we should feel not that our evening has been disturbed but that a tragic mistake has been avoided — for Thornton just as much as for her.

Mark knew that he was deliberately feeding his irritation, letting it in as through a floodgate each time he felt it draining, letting it swish around his mind as you might indulge yourself in a forbidden drug, letting it in more and more turbulently in the hope that he would wash away his knowledge that he was doing it; but he could not quite wash it away; he could not quite transmute his disappointment into moral indignation except on the surface. It was easy for Mark to deceive himself about his feelings and attitudes, starting from the outside, but there was nearly always at the centre a stubborn clarity that would not be corrupted, that refused to be hoodwinked by his deception even if it did not always have the energy to affect his behavior. Thornton was such a charming boy; the very fact that he was not brilliant made him all the safer for Linda; he had grown up in the family; decent, sane people did n't change this way on the spur of the moment; and yet through it all he persisted in knowing that Luly was right, that if Linda felt doubtful she had much better wait; he knew it and he knew that before long he would admit it, first to himself, and then, after an interval, to Luly; but not yet — he must not think of it yet. He puffed fiercely at his cigar as he let a fresh wave of irritation gush luxuriously through his brain.

"It would serve Linda right," he said, "if she decided she wanted him after all and he 'd in the meantime fallen in love with another girl. You can't expect everybody to adjust themselves to you, you know, and the sooner she learns it the better."

"You won't be cross with her?" Luly asked, as they turned back from the gate.

"Cross with her?" he said. "Why should I be cross with her? It 's her own affair."

"I don't know that you 're acting now as if it were," she said mildly.

"You can hardly expect me to be delighted, to go in and congratulate her, can you?" he asked.

"No, but I can expect you to be gentle with her and not say anything that will make her more unhappy."

"I should have thought that Thornton was the one whose feelings had better be considered," he said.

"Thornton too, of course. But there 's no danger of your being angry with him."

They walked back slowly towards the house. She felt rather chilly, but she liked the feeling: it reminded her of autumn; it reminded her of other years when she had walked from gate to gate after supper, with the children when they were small, with Mark as a young man, with her parents. She could remember when the trees and bushes in the half circle were so thick that moonlight could hardly pierce them; she remembered the clearing in the middle among small evergreens (only one of them alive to-day and that a big tree), where she used to go to read, lying in the grass, where her father used to come and look for her when she had disappeared from the house. My life has been very happy, she thought, happier than I deserve: when I think of Father and Mother, when I think of Mark, when I think of the children . . . and this place is too beautiful; I remember Father saying that in all his travels he had never seen a place more beautiful.

"You're not really unhappy, Mark, are you?" she asked. "Even at the worst this isn't as important as so many things that might have happened. Suppose Dicky had been killed, for instance . . ."

"Oh, I can imagine worse things," Mark granted, "but I don't know that that's much of a consolation. There can always be something worse."

Luly took hold of his arm: she knew that she had weathered the climax. "And Mark," she said, "if Linda speaks to you you will be sympathetic? She respects your judgment so much, and I'm afraid she's very unsettled."

"Oh, yes," Mark said with a sigh, "I'll do my best . . . but as far as I can see, children never respect their parents' judgments. It may be just as well . . . I don't know."

"I certainly respected mine," she said, "and so did you, Mark."

"I don't know that I did. I may have. But things are different now."

"I don't agree with you," she said.

They had reached the steps to the piazza: Brad was tuning his violin; Dicky and Ellen were sitting outside

101

looking across the lawn at the water. Luly felt a pang
of anxiety as she saw them; but it would be ridiculous
for her to worry over what Dicky might do, when she had
just been urging Mark not to worry about Linda.

"You 're going to play some, are n't you, Dicky?" she
asked.

"I dunno," he said. "I dunno that my fingers will
work."

"Oh, you must try anyway," she said. "Must n't he,
Ellen?"

"Oh, he won't do anything *I* ask him to," Ellen told
her, with the laugh that always struck Luly as affected.

"You 'll play the one with my slow movement, won't
you?" Mother asked.

"I don't know," Brad said. "I doubt it very much."

"Please, Brad, I think you might . . ."

"I have n't the slightest idea which it is," he said.
"Linda, give me that A again, will you, and kindly stop
that racket until I get tuned. Of course this damn string
will stretch so I 'll have to keep tuning it up every minute.
I 'll sound like hell, if you want to know. Perhaps we
better not play at all."

"Brad, of course you must. Your last night! I 've
been counting on it all day."

He smiled grimly: so Mother had believed him, had
she? "Oh, I suppose we can gallop through something,"
he said. "Hurry up, Linda. Hand me that music.
Don't take all night, and look out there — don't tear it.
This Mozart belongs to me. Fortunately I was intelligent
enough to put my name on it before we went overseas,
or I suppose Dicky or you would be claiming it."

"You will play my Mozart, won't you?" Mother pleaded.

102

The trouble with playing for Mother was that there were always a certain few things that she wanted to hear no matter how often you had played them: you'd think she might get tired of them.

"I tell you I haven't the slightest idea which you mean," he said, "not the slightest."

He turned through the leaves looking for the one she was asking for, a good sonata, one of the best, but it would be more interesting to try one they didn't know so well. He put his fiddle to his shoulder and played the first bars of the "Meditation" from *Thaïs*. "Is that the one you mean?" he asked.

"No it's not," she said, "and it's not Mozart. It's perfectly familiar. What is it?"

"It's the slow movement of the Kreutzer," he said.

"Is it?" she asked. "It doesn't sound like it."

Through cynically drooping lashes he watched her watching him: suddenly she smiled, reproachful and delighted.

"Of course it isn't," she said. "It's from *Thaïs*."

"Oh, well," Brad said. "Beethoven or Massenet — what's the difference?"

"I think you're mean," she said. "You only played a few notes, and I wasn't half listening."

"If you're not going to listen," he said, "what's the use of my playing?"

"You play my Mozart and I promise to listen."

Linda looked up at him. "Ready?" she asked. Their eyes met for an instant: then, turning to the music, he prepared his fingers for the opening chord.

Linda thought of all the bars, all the pages, to go through before this sonata would be finished. She sighed to herself and scowled. What was the use of playing decently for Mother anyway? Mother knew music; she could criticize it very sensibly when others played; it always faintly surprised you that her criticisms were so keen; but when it was you or Dicky or Brad she enjoyed so much more the fact that it was you, her children, to whom she was listening than the actual music you made that you felt she hardly heard the music except as a kind of message from you to her: that was why she preferred to hear the violin and piano to just the piano, because it meant that two were playing. It annoyed Linda now as she thought of it: when she made music she liked it to be listened to as music and not just because she was making it. Of course that is not fair to Mother, she thought; of course I am exaggerating; but she enjoyed being unfair — partly because Mother had been so disappointed and yet so gentle when she had told her about Thornton. Mother must have told Father, and that was why he had not come into the parlor just now but gone straight to the library to smoke another cigar; Father would probably be disgruntled and irritable . . . Well, if he is, Linda thought, I will be too; certainly I won't apologize for managing my own affairs.

"Wait a minute," Brad said, as he turned the first page of the violin part. She always was expecting him to say it when he reached the bottom of the page; he always did say it; and more than ever to-night she felt like exclaiming that she knew perfectly well she had to wait. From the corner of her eye she saw Joel, smoking a cigarette, leaning back in his chair; he looked very comfortable, but probably his thoughts were not in this room at all; or else he saw that she was ill-natured and nervous and was criticizing her for it and thinking how childish she was. Thornton was behind her, on the sofa, where she could not see him: of course he was not listening to the music, but she knew he was watching her, through his eyelids so that people would not notice it too much, very sad and polite and being a perfect gentleman; she wished she could think of him as cross. Mother so seldom gets cross, she thought, that when you feel cross yourself it often annoys you that she does n't, and yet when she does you feel indignant and pounce on her and try to punish her as if she had no right to be ever, just because it happens so seldom.

Linda turned her own page, fumbled, lost her place for a moment, and went on, not caring. What if I should be a very bad actress! she thought suddenly; what if I should have no talent either for acting or for anything else? I 'm afraid I don't; I 'm afraid that whatever I choose to do I 'll want it to be something different. She could see herself going through scenes with Mother and Father, making them very unhappy, and herself too, though she would not show it, and then, after years of work, realizing that she was no good; and everyone, all her friends, would realize it too and talk about it among themselves, pitying or spiteful, depending on their mood, and be very tactful always when they talked to her; and Mother would be making excuses for her and really believing them and saying that it was only bad luck and that of course she was too good for her audiences. I just mess around, Linda thought, and I suppose that is what I 'll be doing as long as I live. She felt that she was a thin painted husk of papier-mâché, and had to struggle to keep back her tears.

It was that doubt that Brad must have felt about being a surgeon, Linda thought; but I 'm sure he did not pity himself; you cannot think of Brad just messing around. She listened to his playing; she must make herself pay attention to the music; she must be decent. But there was Thornton so near her, miserable because of her, not pitying himself either, but just miserable. . . . She thought of this afternoon on the ledges: how could she have been so gay with Dicky after she had sent Thornton off? Poor Thornton, the thing that made her saddest now was remembering how eager he was and happy to obey her orders; and then, she thought, the only thing I felt was pride that I could still order him about. She remembered a banded pigeon that once last year had alighted in the road; she had taken some corn and tried to coax it near her so that she could read the band, and suddenly a delivery truck had turned out of the north gate and run over it. The truck had not killed it at once; it had lain limply on the ground and she had to take a stone from the wall and kill it herself. She could think of Thornton now as that wounded pigeon; and I could make him so happy again, she thought, so easily with just a few words I could make him happy, and Mother too, and Father, and then I might be happy: I could n't be more wretched than I am now. She felt like a bird beating its wings faster and faster but still falling because there was no air to give them support; I must find something to stop me, she thought; I can't keep falling and turning over and over; I must be able to rest and breathe. After all, she remembered, nothing is decided: Thornton is still there. With sudden spirit she finished the first *allegro*. "Wait a second while I tune up that A," Brad said, and although she knew he was going to say it, she did not feel impatient. The *andante* is the one Mother loves, she thought, and this is the last time Brad and I will be playing it together for a long while: we must do it as well as we can.

Brad is quite a different person when he plays, Joel

thought: his music brings out something — what is it, a special kind of imagination? — that you would hardly otherwise suspect; and I get the sense of it as much from watching him, the way he draws his arm, the expression of his face, as from listening to him. I suppose there was never a person stupider about music, more bewildered by it, than I am (not that I do not sometimes love it, but that is part of the bewilderment, because I never know why: why some things appeal to me and others do not), but at least I can see that Brad understands, understands it as well as Linda does, though he probably does not think of it except when he's hearing it or making it himself, which is very sensible. I can imagine what his language would be if he could hear some of my æsthetic friends discussion Beethoven and Bach in their New York studios.

It's strange, he thought, how far away Brad and Linda seem now, as if that corner of the room, with the light shining behind Linda's head, and the white music on the black piano, and Linda's hands and Brad as he very slightly sways now and then, as if it all were a mirage put there for the time to fill the blank made by the absence of the real objects; as if that part of space inhabited by two living people were somehow immaterialized by the music, absorbed into a world as far from this one as the World of the Dead or Plato's World of Ideas. But they did not enter it at first, he thought; I'm sure they were here in this room for a time; Linda was troubled, I'm sure — uncomfortable. What is the matter? Has she quarreled with Thornton? Joel glanced at Thornton; very quiet he had been, remarkably unobjectionable; but he always is unobjectionable, Joel thought; he has a positive talent for it, and I suppose that's what I object to — he's so

thoroughly nice; it's a shame Linda does not have a lot
of aunts, because he is just the kind of a boy to be adored
by his wife's aunts; if he has a son I'll lay a bet that by
the time he's five years old Thornton will be calling him
Old Man, or possibly even Stout Fella. If he has a son,
Joel thought suddenly, it will be Linda's too: disgusting
to think of! Joel remembered how he had felt this morning on the rock and looked again at Linda; and Thornton,
he thought bitterly, still thinks that she is only a yard or
two away from him; he thinks he could get up and take
a step and put his hand on her shoulder: he could, of
course; so could I; but he would not suspect that it was
only the instant he touched her that she was there, that his
touch had called her back into space; and he would not
realize how cruel that is, cruel because it is only in the
world of space that you can suffer, and if Linda should
have to suffer, as who does not, how will Thornton understand that, how will he be able to help her? But good
Lord, he thought, let's at least be fair: I can hardly imagine anyone less capable than I of giving comfort and
relief to a person like Linda if she really needed it; I think
I am probably fonder of my friends, my few real friends,
than most people are, but if I am it may be as a reward,
or a punishment, for being so incredibly awkward in my
dealings with them.

This must be the slow part that Mrs. Waring asked for,
he thought suddenly; I can understand why: it is simpler
than the first, easier to grasp, and yet you feel that it is
simpler not because it is shallow but because it is so noble
and yet so quiet, washed so purely clean of everything
that is not itself. His eye moved to Mrs. Waring, in her
low blue chair by the table. He felt that the music somehow suggested her in its nobility and its tenderness, or it

might be that her face so perfectly reflected the music. Do her children appreciate her, he wondered; does even Linda entirely? Sometimes they do, of course; they are devoted to her; but I'm sure I didn't begin to appreciate Father or Mother until after their death. So much has been written, he thought, about the failure of parents to understand their children, that is made so important, but why is it not just as important for children to understand their parents? "I used to get up with them before breakfast and stay with each one while they practised in their dressing gowns," he could hear Mrs. Waring saying; and Linda or Brad or Dicky, slightly self-conscious, would smile good-naturedly and a trifle condescendingly at each other or at the person to whom she was talking: that moment of their mother's artless pride would then loom larger in their minds than her years of care and devotion. The very things, he thought, that reveal her submergence of herself tend to make them not entirely realize what her love must mean; and yet it plays around them, illumines them, and, reflected back, illumines her. Her tenderness, her love of all living things, is of course becoming more and more concentrated on her children, but that somehow does not take it from others: what she understands, perhaps without realizing it, is man's loneliness and hence his need for love, man's sense of inferiority and hence his need for encouragement. Ultimately, humanly, she understands people far better than I do with all my analyses; her errors, her limitations of view, her prejudices, are superficial: she speaks with disapproval of divorce; when she hears of extramarital love affairs, she exclaims, "How can people be so irresponsible!" and yet specifically, within her own experience, she rejects no one and makes an exception of each individual case; her sympathy and her conduct are not warped by the particular conventions in which she imagines she believes; and in that, he thought, she is the perfect opposite of so many of the allegedly broad-minded. Why is it, he wondered, when she looks so happy, that I can think of her face as tragic? Perhaps because I feel in her such opportunity for suffering: when anyone loves others as entirely as Mrs. Waring loves her children you feel as if she were standing on the edge of a cliff.

Brad put down his violin, frowning, trying to look as matter-of-fact as he could, and reached for a cigarette in his pocket. This is the last time I 'll be playing sonatas with Linda for God knows when, he thought; of course I won't find anyone there that will play with me the way she does; and we never went beyond the twelfth Mozart. We never played so well together, but there 's no use thinking of that: it is ended, the way everything must end. Of course we will be together off and on for a week or so; of course it is not really ended: I must play enough so that when I retire my fingers won't be all shot to hell.

"I love that sonata," Mother said, "and now won't you do one of the Beethoven?"

"I think we 'll do a Haydn," he said. "How about the fourth?" he asked Linda.

"Please do a Beethoven," Mother urged, "or at any rate one movement."

"I think I said Haydn?" he remarked, staring at Mother from beneath his lashes.

Dicky was growing more and more embarrassed at Ellen's silence. With the music it was not so bad: you could pretend to be listening; but now that it had stopped

he was beginning to feel like a fool just sitting there beside her, staring into the moonlight on the lawn.

"What's the matter?" he said at last. "Are you sore
at me, or what?"

"Matter?" she repeated. "I did n't know anything was
the matter."

"Oh, come off it," he said. "Be yourself, Ellen.
What's the point of acting up?"

"I told you this morning you thought I was acting,"
she said. "I suppose you thought I was this afternoon.
I suppose you think I let every man kiss me that wants to."

"You know I did n't mean that," he said; trust a girl
to understand you all wrong, or at least pretend to.
"I'm darn sorry if you thought I was fresh, Ellen."

"Strange as it may seem," she said, "I happen to think
of a kiss as something rather important. I don't imagine
you can understand that."

"Sure I can," he said, but what could he say next?
What was there to say? Brad was tuning up again: he
must be going to play another sonata. I wish I could
play as well as he does, Dicky thought; if I could I'd
be playing all the time. He watched the flashes of the
Sakonnet light — one white and three short reds: that
meant they had not spoken for a whole minute. Is Ellen
just a little fool? he wondered; but he could not believe it,
or if she were he did not care; this morning she had
seemed so unhappy and he had meant to cheer her up, and
apparently all he had done was to make things worse.
What he would like would be to see her laughing and
gay as she used to be: it did n't seem right for such a
pretty young girl to be so miserable.

"Of course I don't blame you for despising me," she
said suddenly.

111

You certainly never knew what Ellen would say next. She was leaning forward in her chair, her hands clasped over her knees; he could see her profile quite clearly; he could see that she was frowning, biting her lips: she looked beautiful and hopeless, as if she might be going to die or as if she had lost all her family; as if she knew she had some fatal disease. He could feel the tension of her body: such small bones she had, such soft warm flesh; you felt that anything violent was more than she could bear, that it would destroy her utterly and that perhaps at this moment she was gazing out into the moonlight at some image of her own destruction. If it were not for this afternoon he would put his arm around her, try to get her to relax, to be reasonable; but he did not dare.

"Where do you get that?" he asked. "That's absurd."

"You do despise me," she said. "Don't make it worse by lying."

"Ellen, I swear — Oh God, what's the use of talking if you don't believe me? Why on earth should I despise you?"

"You thought I wanted you to kiss me this afternoon," she said. "Didn't you?"

"No," he said uneasily, "of course I didn't, Ellen."

"Yes, you did," she said. "You must think I'm an awful fool, Dicky. You must think I can't see anything. Well, I may be a fool in some ways, but not in all. I do see things. Everyone thinks I'm a fool, but I'm not, Dicky, not the way they think. I love Linda, more than anyone, but even she thinks I'm foolish. Oh, I know. I *know*. There's no use your talking." She was staring at him intensely. "Now tell me," she said, "tell me the truth or I'll feel you're just thinking, Oh, she's a fool, you don't have to take her seriously: Did n't you think I wanted you to kiss me this afternoon?"

He was afraid she would not believe him if he lied. "I hoped you would n't mind," he said, "but what's wrong with that? Naturally I would n't have kissed you if I'd thought you'd feel insulted or anything."

"And the only reason you kissed me," she went on, "is because you thought I wanted you to."

"For God's sake, Ellen! I don't go round kissing girls for charity. Where do you get these ideas? You're all wrong."

"Listen," she said. "You were right. I did want you to kiss me. I tried to make you. You see I'm not afraid to tell the truth, if you are."

Dicky was thankful Brad was playing, because the music coming through the window gave you a sense of more time, made it somehow not quite so hard to talk; that music makes it almost the same as if you'd had a couple of drinks, he thought; later on I'll get out that pint of rye Nick gave me and see if Joel won't take a shot; I don't suppose Brad will, but he might; I wish I had some of it in me now.

"I'm not afraid to tell the truth," he said, "only you won't believe me. If you wanted me to kiss you, I'm darn glad of it. But when you say that it was the only reason I did it, you're just wrong, that's all: take it or leave it. I suppose you think I'm lying."

"No," she said, "I think you're telling part of the truth, and I suppose that's all anyone ought to expect. But you don't have to apologize. I said I did n't blame you if you despised me."

He laughed. "And you mean to tell me you were worrying all day because you thought you were a bad girl because you wanted a fellow to kiss you? You're a child, Ellen: that's the only thing that's wrong with you."

"You think so?" she said ironically. "You really think so? Listen, Dicky: you have a perfect right to despise me because I'm a bad mean person. You don't know the thoughts I have, and you don't know how just rotten I am — all through: I mean it." Her tone was once more growing desperate.

"Come, come," he said. "Why talk that way, Ellen? There's no sense to it. What kind of thoughts do you mean? About men kissing you? Because that's only natural."

"Oh, about everything," she said darkly. "Don't ask me because I wouldn't think of telling you. I wouldn't tell anybody."

Do girls have smutty thoughts, he wondered, the way boys have? I suppose they do, lots of them, even the nice ones like Ellen, and the nicer they are the more shocked they feel and the more they think there's something wrong with them.

"You couldn't think of anything half so bad as I think every day," he said. "Don't worry about what you think, Ellen. Why, gosh, I bet if you could see what the most respectable people think sometimes . . . You know when I was at high school I was sure I was some kind of degenerate, I just had no use for myself at all." He remembered playing a "psychological" game: someone read you a list of twenty words, and you were to write down the first association that came into your mind; if it was something you could not read in mixed company you were to leave a blank. Everyone had laughed when he read his list because he had left five blanks; but some of the others would have too, he thought, if they had been honest. "When I got into the army," he went on to Ellen, "I soon found out that it was just the way all boys think—at least now and then; perhaps I was worse than some and better than others: I don't know, but I should worry. And you must n't keep brooding and worrying, Ellen. It's . . . it's not right. You're too sensitive. It's morbid."

"You don't have to tell me I'm morbid," she said with a harsh little laugh. "But what am I going to do about it? Tell me that. What am I going to do about it?"

"Why, I don't know, Ellen. Just try not to . . . try to think of pleasant things and don't keep worrying about whether you're good and whether you're bad. It does n't pay."

"That sounds very easy," she said, "but suppose you can't help it. Suppose you know you're so low and bad that you can't help thinking of it. Listen, Dicky, do you think everyone has a right to live?"

"What do you mean?" he asked, puzzled.

"Just what I say." Her voice was fierce and tense. "Do you think everyone has a right to live?"

"Why, yes, I guess so. How do you mean? I still don't get you."

"Because sometimes I don't think I have," she said. "I don't think I have the right. I think it would be better for everyone if I died."

She was staring at the lawn again, with that desperate look he had noticed a few minutes ago. He put his hand on hers and noticed how tensely her fingers were clasped; she did not move, so he put his arm around her. Suddenly she pressed her head against his shoulder and burst into sobs. Thank God for that music or they would all be hearing it; not that that was of much importance when you thought of how the poor girl must be feeling.

"Ellen," he said, "don't. Don't, Ellen. . . . What can I do? What do you want me to say, Ellen?"

"You don't think I'm too awful?" she said at last through her sobs. "You don't think I'm just silly?" Then she said in a very low voice: "You don't think I'm just doing this . . . to be interesting?"

"Of course I don't," he said.

"And you won't tell anyone?"

"What do you think I am?" he asked; then, remembering how he had talked to Linda this afternoon, he felt rather cheap: I shouldn't have done it, he thought; that was pretty low; but of course then I did not know Ellen.

"I hoped you'd play that," Luly said gratefully, "but I didn't dare ask." It was the *adagio* of the tenth Beethoven, her favorite movement of all, and when Brad began the Haydn she had feared that he might not want to do anything afterward. If I could only feel always the way I feel as I listen to that *adagio,* she thought, I would never be afraid again, of anything in life or of death; if I could listen to that as I was dying, I would feel that everyone I loved, on earth and in heaven, were somehow gathered about me, to be with me always. Brad was putting away his violin; she must not be greedy, she must not ask for anything else. As a matter of fact, she did not want anything immediately after the Beethoven, and presently Dicky would be playing: she must get him started at once, now that he had returned, or he might give it up. Where was Dicky now? Still out with Ellen, she supposed. She wished he would come into the house, but she hated to go out and ask him for fear he would think she was trying to manage him, to take him away from Ellen.

"I wonder if Dicky won't be coming in soon," she said.

"Not if Ellen can prevent it," Brad said.

"You should n't talk like that," she said, not very sincerely. "Suppose she should hear you, Brad."

"What of it?" he said. "Hi, Ellen," he shouted.

"Brad!" Luly exclaimed, but she felt relieved that Brad took it all so lightly. "Joel," she said, "you 're a person I can trust. Would you mind stepping out on the porch and asking Dicky if he does n't want to play something?"

"I 'll go," Thornton said, but Joel jumped up and went out ahead of him.

"Come over here by me," she said to Thornton. "I 've hardly seen you to-day."

Poor Thornton, she thought; in my anxiety about Linda I keep forgetting him, though I suppose the last thing he wants is to be pitied. She smiled at him as he crossed the room and pulled up a chair close to hers. It made her sad to think that this must really be his home-coming because his stepmother had never shown the slightest interest in him, even before his father's death; Brad and Dicky had come back to a mother and father, but Thornton had come back to Linda, and now at the end of the journey he was not finding her.

"I 've been meaning to talk to you all day," he said, "but I seem to have been dashing around, and things have been rather mixed up."

"I know," she said. "Linda 's been talking to me. I 'm very sorry, Thornton."

"I can't blame her," he said. "She 's so young and I 've been away for so long. It was very decent of her to tell me right off; but I 'm not giving up hope."

"You must n't," she said. "This has been an exciting day for her, Thornton, and it was very hard for her when you were gone. She certainly missed you, Thornton. We talked a great deal about you. We all missed you."

"That 's very sweet of you," he said. "I certainly thought about all of you. I can't tell you how much I appreciated your letters, Mrs. Waring. Next to Linda I got more from you than anyone else, and when you had Brad and Dicky to write to . . ."

"I think of you as a kind of adopted son," she said. "I always shall."

She looked at Linda across the room, still seated at the piano, softly improvising snatches of tunes as Brad buried his violin case under the cushions to protect it from the damp; she remembered how his other violin, slightly undersize, had come unglued the first summer they brought it up here because they had taken no precautions against the fog. What a procession we used to be on the train, she thought, with our violins and our cats, and sometimes a bird cage and a turtle. As if she knew she was being watched, Linda turned her head towards Thornton and her and smiled at them gayly.

"You two look very mysterious," she said. "You 'd better be careful if it 's a secret because I 'm trying to listen."

"I don't know about your mother," Thornton said, "but you 're welcome to all my secrets."

What a night, Joel thought, as he stepped out on to the piazza. It was not so much what he could see, for the light from the long parlor windows cut across the floor in front of him and shone so brightly on the columns that the moonlight on the trees and over the lawn looked blue and dim: it was the softness of the night air which smelled of the sea and of leaves, with cooler currents flowing through it that seemed to come from the farthest spaces of the sky, from an endless and timeless region of shadow.

But it has quite definite limits, he thought; if I should travel swiftly enough either eastward or westward I would soon come to a fringe of sunset or sunrise; I would break through fiery clouds into day; there is not a moment that somewhere or other people are not fuming and chattering and going about their work: they are having meetings and discussing social problems; there are big business men and there are intellectuals and there are communists making the world over for a new humanity (and God knows it needs it). Why do I get so tired of them? Why do I get so tired of my own earnestness? Thank God we don't live forever! And now I'm being Swinburnian; perhaps Linda was right when she called me romantic the other day. What did she mean by it? She probably didn't know; she just wanted to imply that she despised me, that she thought I was absurd, which I surely was. No, she does not despise me, but since she obviously does not love me and never has, I prefer to think she despises me, to revel in morose self-castigation. But I'll be damned if I see why it's romantic to be hungry now and then for darkness, for the satisfaction of non-being; though usually darkness is just an excuse for holding hands, making love — "10,000 feet of delicious darkness," as they advertise that boat ride through the labyrinth at the Newport Beach: that's what people turn the night into, like Ellen, the foolish little bitch, no doubt at this moment trying to fascinate poor Dicky; I suppose I ought to clear my throat

119

or cough before I step around the corner. Love, he thought, it's the bunk in most cases, and marriage is ridiculous; its only excuse is to propagate the species and that's a very dubious necessity. If I had my way, I think I'd put a ban on having children for the next thirty years, and see if skipping a generation would do any good; or possibly allow only one in a hundred or a thousand to propagate and sterilize all the rest; I suppose you might be able to find one thoroughly decent sane person in a thousand, if you knew how to look for him. There is hardly anyone I know, he thought, that would come up to all the requirements, unless possibly Brad — not Dicky, he's too nervous, and certainly not me; let's have no more of me. But then, after you had selected them, and sterilized the others, they might without warning do some perfectly mad thing and show they were even crazier than the average. How can you tell what anyone will do? How can you be sure that anyone is decent or sane?

He tramped heavily as he walked to the corner of the piazza.

"Better come, you two," he said. "Your mother wants you to play something, Dicky."

"O.K.," Dicky said.

As he got up Ellen squeezed his hand suddenly; at any rate she would not be worrying quite so much, at least he hoped not. He took Joel's arm as they stood aside for her to step through the door. "Come up to my room a minute," he said, "I've got a pint of rye."

"Your mother's getting sort of anxious," Joel said. "I think she'd like you to come in and be sociable."

"I know," Dicky said. "We'll only be a minute."

He stopped at the threshold of the parlor door. "Hi,

folks," he called, "I 'll be right down, so make up your minds for some swell music. I 've got some important business with Joel first, though. It will only take a second. Thornton, are you in on this?"

"What is it?" Thornton asked.

Dicky raised his hand to his mouth and then made a face as if he were choking.

"Not for me," Thornton said. "Thanks just the same, old man."

"That 's right," Dicky said. "You 're engaged. I suppose you can't afford a breath."

"Where are they going?" Mother asked, looking a little worried.

"Oh, Dicky has some whiskey," Brad told her. "Perfectly ridiculous. Look out for him, Joel. He 's got no sense."

"Must you have it now?" Mother asked.

"Sure, if I 'm going to tackle that violin. I need some inspiration. Wait a minute and you 'll see me come reeling downstairs."

"I 'm not worrying," Mother said, but she still looked a trifle anxious.

"This is great," Joel said on the stairs. "I certainly feel the need of a drink, but we must n't stay more than a minute."

"Sure. We 'll be right down," Dicky said. Joel's right; we 've got to make it snappy, he thought. It 's a funny thing: when I was in France I 'd have gone without drinking for a month, for the rest of the war, I 'd have walked twenty miles through the mud, just to catch a glimpse of Mother through the window of a railroad train; and now, the first night I 'm back, I would just as lief spend the rest of the evening up in my room drinking with

Joel and talking things over generally; but that would be no good to-night.

He lifted his suitcase on to the bed and felt under his pyjamas for the whiskey. That bed still had the hump in the middle; it did not feel like any other bed; it was rather hard and yet wobbly because there were wooden slats instead of springs, and then a feather bed, and then a mattress; and always the first night you slept in it the sheets felt damp. How he used to love that uncomfortable feeling after his comfortable white iron bed in North Chester! And all through the night he would keep waking up and feeling sort of bruised, as if he had been dropped on to the bed from high up in the air, and he would keep turning, and drawing up his legs, and then stretching out, trying to get his body to fit into the shape of the mattress; and if he lay too near one side, by morning the whole thing would be slanting, so that once he had even rolled out in his sleep.

"Get yourself a glass from the bathroom," he said to Joel. "I'll use the cup on the washstand."

That mouldy smell, from the straw matting or the sheets or the wallpaper, he did n't know which, he would recognize it anywhere, and to-morrow morning when he woke up, he 'd be looking out the window at the magnolia leaves. That was the window Brad and he had climbed out of one rainy afternoon and run over to the Second Beach and gone in swimming after a storm; he did not remember why they had climbed out of the window unless they did n't want the family to know they had left the house, but that is what they had done: wriggled over the window sill on their stomachs, hung by their hands, and then dropped into the flower border. That is the same window, he thought suddenly; this is the same room: how

122

can it be? It seems impossible that it is that very window we climbed out of because that is all so far away and the window is here. It was like trying to figure out some problem in algebra; one moment you thought you saw it, and when you looked again there was no sense to it: to see it, to make it seem real, you would have to remember all the time between, everything you had been doing, at college, overseas, on the transport, and still carry that window, that rainy afternoon, in your mind, the way you carried figures in addition — never once let it go, until at last somehow you had brought those two times together and made them join . . . and even then would it work? But it was no use, because you could not possibly think at once of all the time between: chunks of it kept falling out as you reached for others, like books when you try to pick up too tall a stack of them in your arms. Dicky smiled to himself: I guess I must need a drink, he thought.

Joel came back with the glass. Dicky uncorked the bottle and started to pour the whiskey.

"Hey," Joel shouted. "That's enough. What are you trying to do — disgrace me with your father and mother?"

"Hell," Dicky said, "we're celebrating"; but Joel was right: it wouldn't do to get lit, not so they'd notice it, and he'd have to make a try at some sonata. He wriggled his fingers; he had almost forgotten how it felt to hold a violin.

"Well," he said, "we drink to the gathering of the heroes."

They took their drinks quickly and went downstairs. Now I could just romp through the Kreutzer, Dicky thought, if it wasn't for the trifling matter of bowing and managing your fingers.

123

"I thought you were only going to be gone a minute," Mother said as they stepped into the parlor. "If it took sixty of your minutes to make an hour, nobody could speak of the flight of time. But where's your violin?"

"Where is it?" he said. "I don't know where it is. I never thought of it."

"I know just where it is," she said. "It's in your bottom bureau drawer, Dicky, with a blue and white blanket wrapped around the case."

"I'll use Brad's," he said. "I bet you the strings on mine are all shot anyway."

"I don't know whether you'll use mine or not," Brad said. "I think it's very doubtful. Show me your finger-nails."

Dicky held out his hand and Brad felt the finger tips. "I suppose you can use it," he said, "but I fully expect it to be ruined. Whew! You smell like a saloon."

"This is going to be a real treat, fellows," Dicky said, as he took the violin from its case, "and I hope you appreciate it. If anything sounds wrong you'll have to forgive this little lady here at the piano, because she's not used to difficult music like the kind I play, but she does her best and that's all you can ask. We do our best and we aim to please. Good Lord," he said to Linda, "that one? Do you think I can play that one?"

"It's the easiest," she said. "Now let's get started. One-two-three —" she softly counted.

He drew his bow over the strings. What a noise!

"That's attractive," Brad remarked.

Dicky frowned and kept on counting carefully to himself; he would have to get through one movement anyway. He noticed Ellen sitting on the end of the sofa; she was looking at him fixedly, with serious eyes; he felt

124

as if her glance were sending forth dark trembly currents that coiled around him, binding him to her. Gosh, he thought, have I let myself in for anything? I feel sort of responsible for her now; I feel as if she sort of depended on me already . . . What did I say out there, anyway? He winked at her but she would not smile. Now he had lost his place.

"I can't do this," he said. "I told you I could n't."

"That was beautiful," Brad said. "Perfectly beautiful, but now you better give me my violin before you drop it."

"Wait a second," Dicky said. "Wait a second and I 'll give you some real music."

Pack up your troubles in your old kit bag, he played,
And smile, smile, smile.

As Linda took up the tune, he lowered his violin for a moment. "Now then," he called. "Everybody join in. Show some spirit, you there, in the back row! Why are n't you singing? Yes, I mean you. We don't want any grouches around here. A grouch never did anybody any good, did it, fellows? I guess he 's figuring out how he can scare the Boche." Dicky laughed sanctimoniously. "Now then. Put a smile on that face. Just imagine you 're looking at your best girl. She 's waiting for you, remember that. And will she be glad to see you when you step up to the old front porch in your uniform!"

What 's the use of worrying? he sang,
It never was worth while,
So — o — o —
Pack up your troubles in your old kit bag
And smile, smile, smile.

125

Linda played the tune gayly; she could imagine herself in the ladies' orchestra at a restaurant; she ought to be chewing gum; and afterward some attractive young man from one of the tables would step up to her and ask her if she would have supper with him somewhere. Anything may happen, she thought; I have n't decided; who knows what I may do?

She looked over her shoulder to see if Thornton were amused; he was smiling but still sad: one thing I must do at any rate, she thought, is speak to Thornton and be really nice to him; I cannot let him go to bed with that patient kind expression on his face. It is strange, she thought, that ever since I told him we could not be engaged he began to seem more and more natural, perhaps because I stopped being afraid of him. I wonder if that was partly why I felt so gay with Dicky: not just because I was free of Thornton but because it was only after I spoke that I began to feel that he really had come back. That would be queer, would n't it? It seems as if you never knew exactly why you feel a certain way, but if you 're going to do anything about it you have to pretend to yourself you know the reason; even then you are not quite sure, you cannot really entirely pretend, but you act as if you could and if you guessed right, then it turns out later that you acted wisely, but if you guessed wrong, then you wonder how you ever could have done such a thing: yes, I imagine in most cases it is really guessing and whether you happen to be lucky. If I could tell Thornton I would marry him after all, she wondered, then would I be afraid of him, would he suddenly become strange again? Would it be very exciting? She swung around on her stool as Dicky finished, and tried to flash Thornton a private signal that he must not be unhappy.

126

"Are n't you going to play anything more?" Mother asked.

"Not to-night," Dicky said. "I can't let you hear too much at once or you won't appreciate what a rare treat it is."

"You must get Linda to go over that sonata with you," Mother said. "If you tried it over once or twice and practised some of those scale passages, it would go very well."

"What do you mean it *would* go well?" Dicky exclaimed.

Mother smiled. "I mean it would go even better," she said. "I was enjoying it, but apparently you were n't, because you stopped."

"Oh, we were all enjoying it," Brad said. "I was hoping Dicky would play through the whole eighteen of them."

As Linda got up from the piano stool Ellen crossed the room to meet her. "I must be running along," she said, "but I want you to come out for a second first. There's something I want to tell you."

It was her rather tense voice. What is this going to be? Linda thought; am I going to hear her version of this afternoon? I wonder why it is that Ellen is constantly confiding in me the kind of things that I would be most curious about if it were anyone else, but just because it's she I cannot feel any interest in hearing them; and yet Ellen is one of my best friends; I'm fond of her, and I certainly want her to be happy.

In the hall Ellen grasped her hand and held it tight: whenever Ellen took hold of your hand she clung to it as if she were a small drowning child, so that you felt rather brutal when at last you took yours away, as if you were leaving her alone to be swept down the stream like Ophelia.

"What is it?" Linda asked in the sympathetic voice you felt you almost had to use with Ellen when she was at all intense: a voice that she could not make herself feel was ever quite sincere no matter how genuine her sympathy was; but I do not mind using that voice, she thought, when I'm alone with Ellen; it is only when there are other people around that I feel guilty. It is as if I could keep saying to myself: You are sincere, you really do mean it, and could count on believing myself, but as if I were afraid other people would not believe me.

"I just wanted to tell you," Ellen said, after a long pause, while her fingers clutched more and more tightly, "that you won't have to worry about me, Linda."

Linda laughed. "But I wasn't thinking of worrying about you," she said. "Why should I?"

"I mean about Dicky and me," Ellen said. "No, don't interrupt me. I know how your family feel, how close you are to each other. It's very beautiful and I admire it, and I love you all. You believe that, don't you?"

"Of course I do," Linda said, thankful that no one was listening.

"And I know Dicky's young and I'm young . . . and I thought you might be wondering or your mother might . . . I wanted to tell you that we're not engaged or anything like that . . . and that I wouldn't think of being engaged to him if you didn't want me to, because you come first. You know that, don't you?"

"But Ellen," Linda said, "I don't know why you thought anyone would imagine . . ."

"Sh — sh," Ellen said. "Here they come, but I *know*. Not you, perhaps, but the others . . . and I wanted to

128

tell you . . ." She stopped, as Dicky and Joel came out of the parlor. "Well, good night then," she said, in a voice that told clearly she had just been confiding secrets, and lifted her face for Linda to kiss.

"I'm going home," Joel said, "so I'll walk around by your house."

"I wouldn't dream of it, Joel," Ellen said. "I'm not afraid. Really I'm not."

Joel took hold of her arm and led her to the door. "Come on! Come on!" he said. "Don't be foolish. Good night, Dicky. Good night, Linda."

Linda caught his eye: he looked ironic and accusing, and she smiled apologetically. As she turned away from the front door, she glanced into the library. Father was sitting in the green rocking-chair, scowling over a book.

"What is it, Father?" she asked. "A detective story?"

"It's my chess book," he said. "I don't know why I study it, because the more I study the worse I play."

Father's voice did not sound annoyed, as she had feared it would; he seemed only, like Thornton, rather meek and woebegone.

"Aren't you glad they are back?" she asked.

"Oh, yes, I'm very glad," he said. "I have a lot to be thankful for. I'm quite aware of it."

"You don't sound as if you had," she told him. "I'm afraid you don't deserve it."

"I'm afraid I don't deserve much of anything," he said.

"Go on with your chess," she said gayly. "You won't get any compliments out of me."

Brad joined Dicky by the front door. "In about ten minutes," he said, "I'm going up across the fields to

Joel's, after he's had time to dump Ellen, and we're going for a walk along the Second Beach. Want to come?"

"I'd like to," Dicky said, "but, gosh, I'm beginning to feel sleepy as hell, Brad. I think I'll be toddling along as soon as I've killed one more cigarette."

"I guess we'll take a swim," Brad said. "You better come."

"I would, but I feel sort of queer, sort of washed out now that my drink's died on me. I went to sleep at about two last night and woke up at about four. Just at present I don't know exactly where I'm at. This freedom business, and being out of the army and having decent food and being back here again, sort of throws a guy off his base. I'll have to sleep on it before I can believe it."

They walked across the piazza and down the steps and stood together on the path.

"This place is beautiful on a night like this," Brad said. "I hate to be leaving it to-morrow."

"Yes, what's the idea?" Dicky said. "Can't you work it so you can stay on a week or two?"

"I don't like to ask Mr. Norton. He's been so darn nice about the whole thing."

"Yes, old Norton's a good scout," Dicky said. "I don't know that I wouldn't rather be going in with him than going back to college, and I suppose that's what the folks will want me to do."

"Sure," Brad said. "You might as well finish college when you've got the chance."

As he stared through the shadows of the trees in the half circle, he thought of the last time he had met Dicky, their one meeting in France: he had walked past the hotel on the square in Châlons, glanced in the dining-

room window and seen a red-haired chap, an American
private, who looked sort of familiar; he had walked on
for a few yards, and then just on the impulse walked back
and looked in, and there sat Dicky with a bottle of wine
and a cigarette. How they had talked and talked: about
the Grove and the family, and where they had been and
where they thought they were going, and when they
thought the war might end; they had written a letter home
signed with both their names, and Brad had got even
rather tight: that day and the night of the armistice, he
thought, and you could n't have told it from looking at
me.

"Remember Châlons?" he asked.

"Do I? It was the twentieth of October, not a year
ago, can you imagine that? We 'll have to make it an
anniversary."

"Sure we will," Brad said. Standing now with Dicky
on the path, he felt rather homesick for that afternoon in
Châlons, for the blue uniforms at the other tables, the
sound of French words, the old yellow-gray square outside the window, and Dicky's face, gay, familiar, and
young, part of home, part of your life before the war.
Over there, that life seemed far away but very complete
and bright, like a lamplit room you had left and could
sometime return to, some dark night open the door and
find yourself there again as if you had never left; now
that the war was ended and you were at home again,
now that you were going to work, it seemed as if that
other life were sort of crumbling away, as if the room
when you tried to enter it were not a room at all, but just
a reflection of a room in a dark windowpane, and when
you turned quickly around to see the room that was
reflected, there was nothing there.

131

Dicky threw away his cigarette. "Well," he said, "I guess I'll be turning in. Good night."

"Good night."

Brad walked down the path towards the south gate. Joel and Dicky and I went walking around Sachuest the night before I left for camp, he thought; I bet we all wondered if we would all be here again, and here we are. Going in with Mr. Norton is not so bad as going overseas; you know you can get out of it if you really want to . . . you can always get out. Perhaps if you can't do what you most want to do you can do something else so very well and make such a success that afterwards you are glad you could not follow your first choice. I guess you can be interested in almost anything if you know enough about it: look at Tom Bucklin spending hours and hours studying the differences in half a dozen two-cent stamps. I might get out my stamps sometime, he thought, and have a look at them; I must have a few pretty good ones. He stopped at the gate and glanced up and down the road; then, lifting his head, he stared at the sky: you could not see many stars when the moon was as bright as this; they seemed to be hidden, floating behind a milky veil. The smell of the seaweed, the stars, the soft branches of the trees, were suddenly more than he could bear. His eyes filled with tears. I'll be remembering this, he thought; it will always be here. I'll be remembering it. I'll be coming back.

Linda felt very light as she walked down the path to the garden with Thornton, so light, so easily blown away that she did not seem real: I might be the ghost of myself, she thought, or just the vague idea of a person floating through somebody's mind. Does Thornton feel

132

that way too? she wondered. Thornton moves lightly always; I love to watch him; lightly and easily and yet rather slowly; he moves with a faint drawl, just the way he talks; I dance with Thornton better than with anyone else — even Brad or Dicky; perhaps that is because he taught me to dance. If you listened hard enough, she thought, it seems as if you could hear music now, as if you could dance to it, dance in the air and just touch the tops of the grass. That music would not be made from the sounds you can hear, the crickets and the faint brushing of the pines, and the bell buoy over there by Sakonnet (how hard the bell is to find through the other noises, but when you do find it how clear it sounds, in spite of the miles of cold black water between); that music would come out of the greenish, pinkish light around the moon: it looks at first very dry and empty but suddenly you know it is full of a tense fluttering and dancing like the notes from delicate plucked instruments, like the notes from the big quiet lutes held slantwise across the knees of the angels in old Hindu frescoes. You listen for it, she thought, and you cannot hear it at all; you cannot imagine hearing it and you think you must have invented it or dreamed it, and then you hear it again for part of a second, and you feel that perhaps the whole night, these shadows over the grass, and the smell of the water, and these dark trees rising from behind each other, rounded by the south-west wind into beautiful wavelike curves — you feel that none of it is really there, that you are not there, that everything is just a mirage built out of that music, and that if the rhythm changed then everything would change with it into something you cannot imagine, or perhaps turn into nothing. It makes you feel gay, she thought, and yet at the same time it scares you, as if you might step

out of the world, out of life, and never find your way
back. She slipped her hand through Thornton's arm.

"I'm glad you're here, Thornton," she said.

He pressed her hand against his side with his arm, but
did not say anything for a moment.

"I was hoping you'd want to come out with me," he
said at last, "but I was afraid you would n't."

"Why were you afraid?" she asked.

"Well, I don't know. I thought perhaps after what
you said . . ."

Yes, he really has come back, she thought; but the
question is now, where am I? Perhaps I am beginning to
turn very quietly and smoothly into nothing, so stealthily
that I won't be noticing it until it is too late, and then
when I cry out to be rescued I'll be so far away that my
voice will not reach him; he will turn to look at me and
find that I have gone and think that it was all a dream.
Perhaps when I saw him to-day and he seemed strange
it was really I that was strange, that could see only part
of him, part of everything around me: but of course most
of the time you see only small parts of people, even the
people you know best, and even when you know the other
parts it does you no good if you cannot at that moment
see them and feel them, because it is not those parts that
are hidden, but the thing in you that can see or feel
them that has gone mysteriously away, and you have no
clue where to look for it. All that I love in Thornton
could not have gone in the moment I saw him on the
rock. This is Thornton whom I have always known,
Thornton, my lover, who kissed me and held me in his
arms before he went away and made me so happy I
could hardly bear it; and now the strange me to-day who
cannot find so much that is really myself is sending him

134

off as soon as he returns, sending him off so that perhaps when I return he will be gone; and if I found him gone I would never be as brave and kind and decent as he has been.

He stopped at the entrance to the garden for her to pass in front of him between the boxwood that nearly filled the path; but she did not withdraw her arm and they brushed through the boxwood together. He reached for her fingers with his other hand. The smell of the boxwood is comforting, she thought: it fights against the nothingness you feel in the moonlight; it makes the garden real so that you can believe in the flowers and the stems, and the roots in the damp ground, and moles moving through earthy tunnels, and caterpillars eating leaves, and moths softly flying. Or is it just the touch of Thornton's hand? I like him to be holding my hand, to feel his fingers tightening, slowly, very slowly, because he is afraid I will pull my fingers away.

"This is beautiful," he said, "is n't it? But when I see something like this I guess the cue for me is to keep my mouth shut because I can't describe things. I never could."

"I 'm glad you can't describe things," she said. "I hate people that go around describing things, because I don't think things can really be described . . . and certainly you can't describe a person; at least, if you do, you won't get the person but only a description."

"I guess you 're right," he said, "but sometimes you can get a pretty fair idea of people, can't you, from books or even from someone else talking about them?"

"Oh yes, an *idea* of people," she said. "What 's an idea?"

"You 've got me," he said, and laughed softly. He

was squeezing her hand now very hard; his voice was happy. She felt excited, but for the first time to-day she was at the centre of her excitement; she could not judge it, she could hardly even be afraid of it, because it left nothing of her to judge, to be afraid, nothing that was not part of itself. If she drew away from him now, it would be like pulling up by the roots something that was growing inside her, pushing out leaves and buds, pressing, twining like a wild soft creeper about her veins and her nerves.

They walked over the grass more and more slowly. Suddenly he released her hand, put both his arms around her, and held her tightly against him. He is kissing me, she thought; he is my lover, he has come back, and now he is kissing me — now I am awake . . . or asleep? I hardly know.

VI

"What do you think?" Luly said, as she stepped into their bedroom. "Linda is going to marry Thornton, after all."

"No!" Mark exclaimed. "Not really?"

"She told me when I went to her room to kiss her good-night. She thought I could n't have told you she was doubtful, because you did n't seem cross with her. I refrained from mentioning that she might not have found you so mild if she had seen you a little earlier."

"I would have been glad to see her earlier," Mark said. "I was n't cross."

"Perhaps not," she said, smiling, "but it would have taken considerable clairvoyance to see that you were n't."

"I was disappointed naturally," he said. "I think Thornton will make her a good husband. But after all it was her own business. She 's the one that 's marrying him. I 'm not and neither are you."

"Quite," Luly said. "You can't get me to quarrel with that." He won't admit how delighted he is now, she thought, because that would be admitting how much he cared when I told him earlier, and not till his dying day will he confess that at first he was thoroughly upset and irritated. "They want the wedding to be fairly soon," she said, "but I should think it would be well to wait until after Christmas or even until spring."

"Why wait?" Mark asked. "I never could see the point of long engagements except in cases of financial necessity. She's an adult. She knows what she wants. For God's sake, let's not start managing our children's lives for them if we can help it."

Luly knew that she ought to be amused by his inconsistency and yet she could not help feeling hurt by his fierceness. "I don't think I try to manage my children," she said.

"Oh, I'm not blaming you," Mark said, and her hurt feeling faded at once as she recognized that he was apologizing. "I'm afraid it's a universal feminine trait."

"It's not a bad idea," she said gently, "occasionally to look for the beam in one's own eye."

"I have many faults," Mark said, "but trying to manage people is not one of them."

"No," she said. "I don't think it is. Not generally."

Luly took off her blue woolly kimono, put out the lamp, and opened the window by the bed. A wave of cool wind broke softly through the room, lapping into all its corners. There were speckled clouds across the moon, but its light still gleamed on the water; she could make out a few boats at anchor in the Third Beach cove, though it was hard to see them, such small dark spots against the brightness: they kept changing their sizes and shapes like tiny black stars dancing in a sky of cold fire. She must not stay here any longer or she would get chilled, but she hated to leave it, because it was so beautiful.

"All in all, it's been a very satisfactory day," Mark said drowsily.

"Very," she agreed, and got into bed beside him.

Yes, she thought, it has been a happy day in spite of worries; I suppose it is impossible to keep from worrying

138

about your children if you are fond of them, worrying about what may happen to them, though it does seem foolish and even rather ungrateful. I can hardly blame Mark for being inconsistent when I was first worried because Linda would not marry Thornton, and then I could not help being just a little worried because she decided that she would (poor Mark, he never used to be so touchy; no one realizes how he felt the boys' absence); and there's Dicky, I worry about his flirting with Ellen, and Brad — I keep feeling that it's cruel for him not to be a surgeon, in spite of what he says; but at least, she thought, I do not have to worry about what they are inside; that would be the awful thing, to have a child that you knew was false inside and hard and not to be trusted: that would be almost as bad as having a child that was an idiot.

She listened to the wind. To-morrow there might be rain; if the wind kept on rising like this there might be a storm. She could imagine it passing through the rigging of those small black boats in the harbor, whirling the fine sand in clouds along the beaches, tearing through the trees around the house: it pushed the day far, far down into a dark place where it brightly floated with other days, floated, changing its shape when you tried to fix it, no nearer, no farther, than all the rest. The three children were born in this room, she thought. I remember how windy it was the night Brad was born. That was the year the grapery was taken down after most of the glass had been smashed by hail. I remember Father pruning the huge bunches of black and golden-green grapes, and always he would let me have a bunch, of whatever color I chose; I remember the earthy smell of the greenhouse like some lovely still garden in the

139

tropics (and all these big trees that are moving now in the wind, he planted them, when he was only twenty, younger than Brad); I remember the tornado that came up the coast from the West Indies when Dicky was a baby, and blew down nine trees in a few hours, and the grass was covered with leaves the next morning as if it were autumn. I love the wind, she thought; I used to love it when the children were overseas, except that it would make me wonder if they were too cold; but when I was listening to the wind somehow it made them seem not so far away, perhaps because I could imagine it blowing from them to me — or perhaps because it made everything seem so far away that the longest distances in the world amounted to nothing.

PART III

December 1928

December 1928

I

LINDA got out of her car, walked up on to the piazza, and stood looking around her, trying to catch some scent of the warmth and the dampness that usually drifted between these columns; she took a few steps and noticed that even the sound of her feet on the boards was different from in the summer: sharper, with a short dry echo. Why have n't I done this before? she wondered. I have n't been here in winter since I was a child; for two or three years I 've thought of it, but for me to think of something, to think how nice it would be, is an almost certain guarantee that I 'll never do it. The wonder is that I 'm here now.

She went back to the door, tried it, found it locked, and rang the bell. No one came. She would go across to the cottage and get the key from Robert.

But another car was turning in the north gate: no Lincoln this time, but a Ford; they had planned to meet at about three and both had arrived almost exactly on schedule. Dicky waved and called to her, but drove past the end of the house to put his car directly into the garage. Linda ran along the path to join him.

"Hi there," he called as he jumped out of the Ford,

his face wrinkled all over by his smile. "This is pretty slick. Christ, what a day!"

"Isn't it?" she said. "I thought we might go walking before it gets dark. Would you like to?"

"Sure thing," he said. "That would be swell."

As he kissed her it seemed to her that his face felt very cold and rough. "You wouldn't rather get warm first?" she asked. "I could make some tea."

"No — no — " he said. "We can have that later, when we get back. I want to stretch my legs. But wait a sec."

He went to the car, opened the rumble, and came back with a quart of whiskey. "How about a shot of this," he said, "to give us a little pep for starting? Want me to get a glass so you can have some water with it?"

"No," she said. "I only want a drop."

She took a sip from his bottle. "Terrible!" she exclaimed. "Dicky, how can you drink it? It's disgusting."

"I can drink anything," he said, "that's not poison."

"It's ridiculous for you to take stuff like that. I've a great mind to smash the bottle." She raised her hand as if she were going to throw the whiskey against the side of the garage.

"Don't do that," he shouted. "I'd kill you if you did that."

"As a matter of fact," she said, "I won't, because the glass might scatter and we might pick up a piece in our tires."

He took the bottle from her. "If you don't like this," he said, "why didn't you bring something yourself — a quart of Scotch or a bottle of Benedictine? I don't suppose you did?"

144

"No," she said. "I certainly did not."

"Saving it for your horsy friends, I suppose."

She watched him as he raised the bottle to his lips; he looked better than she had feared he would look and she wondered if her worry about him were all for nothing. Suddenly, she thought, you see a person as doomed; you feel that you must act at once, that things cannot be allowed to continue; and then you see the person again, as I am seeing Dicky now, and instead of someone ravaged and distraught you see a healthy and reasonably happy individual who simply will not fit into the dark tense story you have been imagining; and it's just the same, of course, with your own life: at moments it seems all waste, all tragedy, and then, the next day, you feel that you are happier than most people, that what made your life seem tragic was not your life itself but only some special part of you that might have led a quite different life, that might have given you its own color and made you a different person, that part peering out at you for a moment and regretting that the other person whose soul it would have been was never allowed to be born.

"How is Ellen?" she asked.

Dicky put the cork in the bottle and the bottle back in the car. "Not so good," he said. "But they don't know. The doctors don't know. I don't think one of them knows a damn thing about it, if you ask me."

"When will she be able to come home?" Linda asked.

"You've got me," he said. "Personally I think she could come home right now. I think she'd like to, poor kid . . . but I dunno. She changes so much. Still, it's her father's funeral. I'm not paying for it. Four hundred bucks a month, can you imagine? Pretty nearly twice as much as my total salary. No wonder they like to keep them when they once get hold of them. Brad made a big mistake when he decided not to be a doctor."

"Brad seems to be getting along pretty well as it is," Linda said.

"Oh, I guess he's making out all right," Dicky said. "He's doing pretty well for an honest man."

"Why Dicky," she exclaimed, "how cynical!"

"Oh sure," he said smiling, looking about him at the sun on the white side of the house, at the network of shadows over the dry fawn-colored grass, "I'm one of those smart guys that nobody can fool."

They had been walking towards the south gate. The path was hard beneath their feet, unyielding except for a soft film of dirt strewn with gravel and bits of broken shells; by the time we are back, she thought, that too will have frozen.

Across the gray beach drifted streamers of white sand, smokelike, moving with the faintest scratching noise from the brown marsh grass to the water. It's the way it used to be, Dicky thought; what a relief not to find people; I'm getting pretty darn sick of people. The sand bar by the mouth of the creek was covered with a flock of sea gulls; big fellows they were; you never saw so many here in summer; the crowds must scare them off — sensible birds. As Linda and he came near, they rose slowly, quietly, flapped out over the bay and alighted on the water: they looked like big gray and white ducks except they were too long and slim; if you squinted your eyes you could see them as a fleet of toy boats. One old fellow still remained on the sand bar; showing off, was he, or just too lazy to move? Dicky picked up a bleached quahaug shell and shied it along the sand in his direction; the gull ran a few steps, spread its wings, and flew to join the others.

"That's calling his bluff," Dicky said.

"I think you're mean!" Linda exclaimed. "He looked so proud."

"It's good for him," Dicky said. "Next thing he'll be getting into trouble."

What do they think about? he wondered. They're stupid-looking critters, but comfortable; I think I'd take a chance of changing places with one of them: spend your life flying about the rocks and beaches, swimming, diving for fish, nothing to worry you . . . but if they're like most people they don't know when they are well off. It's funny to realize that this beach is here all the time: you go away and you don't give it a thought, or if you do you're thinking of it as it was the last time you saw it; and then when you come back you find it again, waiting for you. If this were one of those countries where they have volcanoes and earthquakes you might come back some day and find it gone: that would be strange too; but now that we are here, Linda and I, with this wonderful air, and the water and the sun, and the sand so fine and gray, and the mops of dry seaweed, and the boats dragged up on the stones for the winter, and no one snooping round to bother you — gosh, it's hard to believe that there is anything else: this is the real stuff and all the rest doesn't amount to shucks. And yet, he thought, our apartment is there, now, this very minute, if I were there to see it. He could see it in his mind, but somewhere on the other side of the world, on some other planet: smaller than usual, the way it looked when you first came back to it in winter, even if you had turned off all the radiators; he could smell the sweetish violet soap in the bathroom, rather sickening to him always, like tasting a sweet creamy dessert that had been kept for several days; and that sanatorium's there, he thought, and Ellen in that big gray room. If I had to stay in that place for a month, it would be enough to knock me off my bean even if I was perfectly O.K. when I went in; but they seemed to think it would pull her round: well, if it straightens her out, I guess it's worth the four hundred; I guess it's worth all you could give. He could see Ellen as she stood by the door of the living room, very pale in her blue kimono; he could hear her choking voice: "I've swallowed two bichloride tablets, Dicky." "You've what?" "I've swallowed two bichloride of mercury tablets." He had n't believed her; he had laughed in disgust; this was carrying things a step too far. "What's the idea?" he had asked. "You said I was driving you crazy —" She had gulped, choked; for a moment he thought she was going to be sick all over the carpet. "And I would n't want to do that, you know." Then he had jumped up, and she had run to the bathroom, and locked herself in: through the door he could hear her vomiting; and then the joke of it: when the doctor came at last and they had broken down the door and she had been examined, there was not a trace of poison; he had been right — but then how the deuce could she make herself sick like that? And she swore up and down that she had taken them; you could not get her to change. Just out of curiosity, he thought, I'd like to know whether she really believed she had taken them or not; just out of pure and simple curiosity I'd like to know, but I don't suppose I ever will. But why bring that up?

He looked across to Sakonnet: a strip of land like a pennant between the blue bright water and the blue hard sky. He scuffed his foot into a tangle of seaweed, brittle on top but underneath wet, rotten, falling slimily to pieces; a fishy smell filled his throat and nostrils.

"This was a clever idea of yours," he said to Linda. "How did you happen to think of it?"

"Oh, I have clever ideas now and then," she said, "but usually they remain ideas."

The thought came to him that this might all be charity on her part, that she had guessed he wanted a change, that he was in a bad way; but hell, he thought, I must n't be so sensitive; suppose she did; she 's my sister; what have I got to be proud and dignified about? They were walking now over large bluish stones; a Portuguese fisher- man, in the last shack on the beach, was pulling up a boat on a roller; there was a little dirt yard around his house, with lobster pots piled as high as the roof, and a few hens scratching; a tarred fish net was hung along the posts of the fence. Dicky looked at her as she walked between him and the water: you would never believe she was thirty-one. Her face was rosy now — her cheeks, her ears, her nostrils — but very clear and smooth; she wore a leather jacket, a brown fur cap, and a little brown animal about her neck.

"You know you 're a damn good-looking woman," he said. "Too bad you 're not on the stage."

"At least I 'll never know that I 'd have been a failure," she said.

Thornton 's all right, he thought; he 's a good fellow; he does n't put on side, not to speak of; but I should think he might be rather dull as a steady diet; if I were a girl I don't think I 'd get much of a kick out of sleeping with him. Perhaps Linda feels about him the way Ellen seems to feel about me: good God, let's hope not!

They climbed over the rocks into the field that sloped eastward towards the lighthouse: it was all short brown grass with a couple of haystacks, but along the edge, beside their path, grew a tangle of dead goldenrod and briars, and asters, they must be, with a little fuzz still left on them that shone pearly-white in the sun. Of course she has Pat, Dicky thought; he's about the most attractive child I know; that is something; but thank heaven I don't have any children. That's one of the things Ellen was dead right about, though I did think I'd like to have a son; the chances are if it had been anything it would have been twin girls: that's the way things seem to be run in this gay life of ours. But just imagine a child with Ellen and me; between the two of us we would drive the poor kid crazy. It's a hell of a responsibility to bring anyone into this world; the chances are every time it's kinder not to; and yet when you have a day like this, when you can be in a place like this . . .

Offshore surf broke very white on the rocky islands. Now that they had rounded the point the only houses you could see anywhere were beyond that water where they could not bother you; you could feel the sun raking across those waves, shining down through their glassy blue sides; you could feel how warm it would be in front of those little houses across the channel. But soon it would grow cold: the sun would be setting and all the windows would be flashing like the headlights of automobiles.

"How about going up on that rock where the path

turns," he asked, "and laying off a bit for a cigarette? You 've got me winded."

They stepped down on to the flat gray-blue rocks, picking their way between pools, and climbed to the top of the mound at which Dicky had pointed. Below them the waves would break on a reef a few yards off-shore and plunge, all foam, to break again at the foot of the rock where they were sitting: you would see a flash of green, with seaweed waving through it, and then there would be nothing but a swirl of the softest white lather. They have been coming in like that for a good many years, he thought: when this point was an island, as it shows on the old maps; when there was no one here but Indians, and before there were any men at all, most likely; it 's sort of peaceful to think of — I don't know why. When you saw that flash of green with the seaweed waving through it, it was like having a glimpse of another world.

"It would n't be such a bad idea," he said, "just to slip off this rock into one of those waves, like that fisherman last November that was drowned. That would be a fine way to die, do you know it? Only I would n't want my body to be found, with a funeral and flowers and all the rest of it. I can't see that for dust."

"I 'm afraid it might be a little cold," Linda said; but the waves as she watched them did not look especially cold; or rather they looked as if you might find them cold but if you did it would be your own fault — because you were too weak and tender, spoiled by your warm houses and your clothes. If you were strong and free like a seal you ought to be able to plunge into that frothy water down there among the rocks and swim out as far as you wanted, out to the horizon or beyond, and then swim back, and shake off the water as you pulled yourself up on the wet rocks, and put on your clothes and go quietly home without anyone's suspecting your journey. Perhaps that was all Dicky meant; the foam looked so inviting with its soft sparkle and its flashing blue shadows; you felt so quiet and cool and far away out here that you hated to think of ever going back; or was there something more, something despairing and bitter in his voice or just beneath his voice, something that he just would not show you? It is hard to come near Dicky, she thought; it is for me, and I think it is for everyone; perhaps it is because you feel that most of the time he cannot quite reach himself; you can imagine him chasing himself around corners, reaching one just in time to see himself vanishing around the next; and the Dicky you see is the one that is pursuing, slightly cynical and discouraged with the capture he cannot make, never, or almost never, the pursued. It is hard to come near Thornton, she thought, but that is very different. With Dicky it is something positive you are trying to catch; you know it is there — something tender and naked and bright — and you feel sad because you 're afraid you never, that no one ever, can run it down, least of all Dicky himself; but with Thornton I 'm afraid it is only an absence you are chasing — that is, when you take the trouble. Knowing Thornton is like wading out and out on a very shallow beach; the water is pleasant and not cold; there is a smooth sandy bottom, and at first you think that soon it will get deeper; but it never does; you keep on and on and still it is only up to your knees, until you feel that you might wade beyond the horizon without wetting your bathing suit. Linda could picture Thornton talking confidentially to

her, to her or to strangers, it made no difference, in his
rather drawly voice, with bright caressing glances, with
half smiles, with movements of his hands, — not exaggerated, just a few, just the right movements, — with
a cigarette between his fingers: likable, even charming,
but you felt that beneath this play of movement, this
pleasant arrangement of voice and glance and gesture,
he was attempting to cover, perhaps without realizing
it himself, a lack of endurance, of weight, or of passion,
just as you might conceal the shallowness of water by
continually rippling its surface. I'm afraid, she thought,
that when I succeed in making Thornton at all interesting or exciting it's by imagining how he would appear
to someone else, or to myself if I were someone else, the
way I used to make meals seem interesting by thinking of
olives and sardines as the kind of food that the ancient
Greeks ate, or trying to think of my oatmeal as the
porridge to be eaten by a hungry traveler at an inn in a
Scottish novel. But it may be my fault entirely with
Dicky and Thornton both, just because I myself am
lazy and changing.

Dicky tossed his cigarette down into the foam among
the rocks.

"I suppose we ought to be jogging," he said, "or we'll
find Joel waiting for us."

"Joel?" she exclaimed.

"Sure. Didn't I write you? No, I guess I must have
seen him after I wrote my letter. I asked him down
and he's coming. You don't object?"

"Of course I don't," she said. So Joel was to be here.
How it changed everything! A minute ago, peacefully,
if rather sadly, she could have sat on this rock looking
out to sea until the sun went down and you were driven

on by the cold; now she wanted to be moving at once —
why? In order to be sure to be at the Grove to meet
Joel, or simply because when everything had started shifting and tumbling in your mind it was hard to keep your
body still?

"I figured this would be a good chance to see him,"
Dicky said, "before he goes away."

"Is he going away?" she asked.

"Sure. Did n't he write you? He 's going to Persia
or some ungodly place like that to dig up things. That
friend of his, Pete Merwin, is taking him along on his
expedition."

"Joel never writes me," she said. "At least he has n't
this year." What is more, she thought, he would have
gone away without letting me know and then sent me
a long letter from Persia or Mesopotamia. How like
Joel! But of course it is my fault that he has not written: I acted like a fool, but I don't know what I should
have done; I don't know what I would do if it happened
again. But it will not. Joel is far too proud.

They climbed back over the rocks to the path along
the top of the bank, leading now straight westward.
There is nowhere that gives you such a sense of being
at sea, she thought, especially now, in the late afternoon; and how short the afternoons are in December:
while Dicky and I sat there, not more than half an hour
surely, the day turned almost to evening. She squinted
at the orange sun, hanging over the fields straight ahead.
I 'm glad Joel is going, she thought; yes, I really am glad;
poor Joel, he has got at last the kind of thing he wants;
of course he is delighted. This will be Joel's third, or
is it his fourth job in the last five or six years, and Dicky
has had three; I wish Dicky would be sent on some ex-

pedition, some far voyage; I should think what Ellen
and he both need more than anything is to get away
from each other for a year at least. Perhaps when Ellen
is through with the hospital I should ask her to visit me
for several months. Could I bear to? Perhaps I could,
because then I could feel at least that I was of some use
to somebody: that would be strange, would n't it?

"Did you and Joel have a row or anything?" Dicky
asked.

"Of course not," she said. "Why?"

"Because I had a heck of a time getting him to come.
He was afraid you would n't want him."

"Oh, that was Joel," she said. "Of course he always
thinks he 'll be in the way, and he 's about the one person
I know that never is."

"That 's a fact," Dicky said. "He never is, is he?"

How terribly I 'd feel, she thought, if he had not
come, if he had decided to go off to Persia without seeing
me; I think I would have had to go to see him; but
you cannot blame him for not wanting to see me — or
is he still in love? Perhaps he feels simply disgust. They
had been standing on the piazza; it was a dark cool night;
she had been so amazed when he kissed her, so completely
taken off her guard, that all she could do was laugh
(such a silly cheap laugh), and then they had both walked
into the house, and he had hardly spoken the rest of the
evening; and she had been noisy and foolish, partly because she was embarrassed and partly because she was
very glad and proud that Joel loved her, because she
always had felt that he disapproved of her. I wonder
when it began, she thought, as she had thought many
times during the winter; I wonder why I never fell in
love with Joel instead of Thornton: how can they be

compared for a moment? What is there in Thornton that begins to be as fine, as interesting, as genuine, as everything in Joel? Perhaps, she thought, it was thinking about Joel and wondering how I would feel if I saw him again, and worrying about what he must think of me, that made me restless enough really to come here after I had planned it so often.

"How's that for a view?" Dicky asked.

They had reached the end of the western point. The sun had set hardly a minute ago, and now the water was a pale green-blue, unbelievably clear and shining; the sky was pure orange; and between them the line of the cliffs was very black, with a concentrated darkness that you felt would spread and spread until it covered the whole sky and the ocean. The air had grown so cold that you could not imagine sitting still on a rock: you must keep walking fast, walking along the shore beside those low bright waves rolling in to break on the Second Beach, walking while the night came on, a cold night, very still, with no moon, but a sky crowded with stars; walking not back to the place you had started from, but on and on with that sunny pale afternoon between you and everything else, until you came to a dark night country where you would find a lamplit room with a fire, and no one in the world but you and Dicky and Joel; and outside frozen grass, and twigs scraping against the roof, and Jupiter and Sirius and Orion.

LINDA glanced from Dicky to Joel, each leaning back in his armchair with the shelves of brown old books rising behind him. She thought she knew how Dicky felt: his lips, his eyelids, slightly swollen and stiff so that he would not move them unless he had to. Joel looked exactly as he had looked when he arrived, as he had looked while they were getting supper in the kitchen: self-contained and distantly ironic; his face with its large nice features, its heavy eyebrows, its friendly-looking moustache, made her think of some pleasant region from which she had been exiled; he has the nicest face of anyone I know, she thought, the gentlest, the strongest, the most trustworthy, and only now, when it is too late, do I begin to appreciate it. She took another taste of her drink.

"I 'm very angry with you, Joel," she said, trying to smile so brightly that it would attract his attention, smiling all the more desperately as she realized how flip and pert her voice must sound.

He stared into his glass. "That 's good," he said. "I like to be regarded with violence. It 's such a rare sensation that it makes very little difference what kind."

"Are n't you curious to know why?" she asked.

"Curious?" he repeated, as if she were a child using a

long word incorrectly. "Oh yes, I'm always curious."

"I don't think I'll tell you," she said, "because I can see you're not even faintly interested."

"Oh, you mysterious women!" Dicky said. "Now go ahead and coax her, Joel. That's your next move. I know them all."

"Shut up, Dicky," she said, but she did not mind him really: if there was bitterness in his tone it was not meant for her.

Joel looked as if he were trying to decide just how far he should humor her. "Go ahead, tell me," he said. "I'd like to know. The only danger is that if you tell me I may apologize and then perhaps you won't be angry any more . . . and there are so few people that bother to be angry with me."

"It's because you did n't write me that you were going to Persia," she said. "Joel, are n't you ashamed?"

"I've got so much to be ashamed of," he said, "that I can't be bothered with details like that, even if I granted there was a reason."

"Of course there was a reason," she said. "Did n't you think I'd be interested?"

"Oh, naturally," he said. "Everybody would be interested."

"If you're going to talk that way," Linda said, "we might as well give up. I've never known anyone more deliberately disagreeable and spiteful." She clung to her smile as if it were the one thing that would save her from toppling into a gulf of crossness and tears, but her voice was sharp; she wanted him to feel that she was not joking.

"I'm sorry," he said, but he would not meet her eyes.

"Have a heart, Linda," Dicky said. "Don't ride the

poor lad. Who the hell cares whether they get letters? Good God, if your feelings are going to be hurt every time someone does n't write to you, you 're in for a hard life. Finish your drink, that 's what you need. The thing I can't understand is why everybody seems to get all heated up about everything, no matter where you go. Seems to me it gets worse every year. People getting excited and indignant, and getting their feelings hurt! Christ, I can't see it!"

Dicky's voice had now the same slight stiffness, the heaviness, of his lips and eyelids; she felt that he was going farther and farther away, that a bungling self-righteous person was creeping into the empty body he had left.

"Nobody 's getting excited, unless you are, Dicky," she said, "and nobody's feelings are hurt."

Dicky smiled slowly, with an effort. Linda felt that he was trying to look sly but could not quite remember how. "You don't say," he said. "Well, I 'm glad to hear it."

"Dicky," she said, "I hate you when you talk like that. You 're disgusting."

He raised his hand part way to his forehead in a salute. "All right, officer," he said, "I 'm sorry. It won't happen again."

The lamp and the books and Joel's face blurred: walking back with Dicky, she thought, through the cold night, with the stars coming out in that clear green-blue sky, I probably was happier than I had been for months, perhaps for years; and I don't think I was ever more glad to see anyone than I was to see Joel when we heard his car crunching over the gravel and ran out to meet him on the piazza.

159

"Are you really interested, Linda?" Joel asked. "You're not just talking? I'm so sick of people just talking . . . and that's what most people do most of the time — at least in New York."

His voice was kind — a little shy; it was Joel's voice at last. He sees how miserable I feel, she thought; he is taking pity on me now, but it's rather late for that.

"Of course I'm interested," she said fiercely, "and you know it perfectly well . . . and of course it's not just that you didn't write me, Joel; but you have been so offish ever since you got here that I think I have a perfect right to be angry, and I'm going to be angry."

"Let's all be angry," Dicky said. "Let's have a contest."

"I'm sorry," Joel said. "Probably I have seemed rather skunkish. It's just that I've been leading such a completely fatuous life for so long that I'm afraid I've exhausted my patience and ruined my nature. I get up in the morning, go to the office, leave it, and go to bed at night; no writing, no decent reading even, to speak of; no thought for the world, or people, or for anything else."

"But it won't be that way now, will it?" Linda asked. "I should think you'd be so excited, Joel, and so pleased! I'm sure I would."

"Yes, it ought to be different," Joel said. "At least I should think it's bound to be different, and pretty nearly any difference is bound to be an improvement."

"But what is it, Joel? What are you going to do exactly? I didn't know you knew anything about Persia or Egypt or any of those old civilizations. But you know so many things, Joel, so many out-of-the-way things

160

that nobody would suspect. I imagine that you are the wisest person I know. I really do."

"Wise enough to stay single," Dicky said.

"That's not wisdom," Joel said. "It's luck, and as for my wisdom in general," he said to Linda, "I know just as much about Persia and ancient civilizations as I do about anything else — which is nothing."

"Now Joel," she said reproachfully, "why do you say that? Are you going to be mean again? I thought you were beginning to be natural, the way I think of you."

"I'm not being mean," he said, so earnestly that Linda felt that the evening she had imagined, or another evening not too different, might slowly fill the room as they talked. "Honestly, Linda, I don't know a blame thing about it: that's the joke. It's perfectly absurd. Pete Merwin blew into the office about three weeks ago — I thought he was in California — and asked if I'd like to join an expedition to dig up some old city or other in Persia. It was just like having Santa Claus come into the room. I don't think I could have stood New York a month longer. I told him I didn't know any more about such things than the man in the street, but I could handle a shovel or cook or haul water or dig latrines or do any dirty work there might be. He went down to Philadelphia that afternoon and all I've done since by way of preparation is get out a couple of books from the Public Library."

"I think it's wonderful," Linda said: the thought of it made her feel gay all through, the thought that someone might appear and carry you off to Persia; it made you feel that anything could happen, that anything could change, that the most incalculable things might cross your path as they did in fairy tales. Of course

161

as a rule they did not; probably nothing of the sort would ever happen to you, but that made no difference: it was the thought that after all they might; and I'm so glad Joel's the one, she thought; there is nobody else I can think of who deserves it so much. She beamed at him now; she wanted to show him her face, her eyes, her voice, to let him know surely and completely, inside himself, how very glad she was. "I did n't know such things could really happen," she said.

"They can't," Dicky said. "There's a catch in it somewhere. The blessed Saviour will trick you off to Persia and then He'll give you leprosy, just for the fun of the thing. You wait."

"I've no doubt there's a trick to it," Joel said, "but I would n't hold it too much against Him even if He did give me leprosy; I'd consider on the whole that I'd had a fairly decent break. After all, it would n't be such a bad way to end — as a leper in Persia, crouching in the sun by the gate of a mud village, begging and shooing the flies away from your sores. On the whole that seems a shade better than mouldering year after year in a New York office building, helping our splendid bourgeoisie run down the steep place. As a matter of fact, I suppose you'd be put in some mission hospital, over there somewhere, and there'd be a couple of doctors who would be decent fellows or they would n't be there. . . . No, the more I think of it, the more it appeals to me."

"Joel," Linda exclaimed, "you don't think you'll really get leprosy! You don't think there's really a risk!"

Joel smiled at her. "Not much of one, I'm afraid," he said.

If he caught leprosy, she thought suddenly, I'd go over and take charge of him; I'd be a nurse in the hospital.

162

That would be something worth doing; that would be really coming to life. But how foolish, she thought, how romantic! I used to make plans like that when I was very young, things that I could do for Thornton. But it's not foolish now, she told herself passionately, as if she were trying to convince some skeptical observer, as if her whole life depended on her ability to bring conviction; it's not just sentimental, because then I was young and ignorant, it was nothing but a gesture; but now I *know*, I know that I could if I wanted to and I *think* I would want to: what makes you sentimental and dramatic is not what you plan to do, not the thing itself, but the fact that you're just playing with it to be excited and pleased and would not really do it; it would have been sentimental, she thought, if Christ had thought how noble it would be to be crucified and then had led a comfortable life and taken care not to be and still thought how noble He was even to think of it; but I'm not doing that, she pleaded; I don't think I'm noble, I think I'm absurd, I'm ashamed of myself; I would not have anyone guess my thoughts for the world, least of all Joel. But I would, I could do it. I would never be able to do such a thing out of sheer goodness, like Father Damien or any really great person, but I could for someone like Joel, I could for Joel; and then perhaps the goodness might gradually come. Leaving Pat would be the worst, she thought; that would be the thing I could hardly bear; but I could come back when he was grown-up and he could come and see me perhaps; I'd leave him with Mother. Mother would be the only person, she thought, who would understand me if I did a thing like that; at first she would disapprove, she would do all she could to prevent me, but later I'm sure she would understand.

"You know," Joel said, "of course it may be just because it's a new thing and because it's come so suddenly and because it's so different, but I can't think of anything more exciting than to go digging for the signs of an old civilization — actually digging it up out of the earth — even if you did n't find anything but a broken dish or a piece of a skull. I don't know why it should be so exciting. Perhaps it is n't really; perhaps it won't remain so; but it's the thought that all that life is there, and everything you'd turn up would help you to imagine it: that it was all there and not just for a short time, but for years or centuries or sometimes thousands of years . . . one city built above another like the various cities on the site of Troy; that it was there and that now it's gone: that's what is exciting, the fact that it's gone. But you can't think of it as gone if you can't think of it as there, if you see what I mean. It's like adding up a huge sum of figures, very slowly, so you can keep it all in your mind, and then putting a minus sign in front of it. Think of the Ægean civilization, for instance; two or three thousand years of life getting more and more elaborate and finished and self-conscious, a whole world, that must have appeared to them as *the* world, the centre of the world in space and time both; and then think of its being forgotten so that for a couple of thousand years or more nobody knew there had been such a world, until about fifty years ago they began to discover it. I should think that would have been far more exciting than discovering America, because after all America was *there*, it was just starting as far as Columbus was concerned; and this was over, done . . . it was discovering a tremendous absence. Does this make sense?" he asked. "I guess not. I'm sorry."

"I think I see what you mean," Linda said. "I *think* I see."

She frowned as she looked at Joel. She saw him at any rate, his face beautiful as he talked, kind and glowing and eager; it made her think of Pat's face as he told what he had been doing through the day. You could think that Joel had melted the air around him, the air that usually kept you separate, that kept everyone separate from others, or turned it magically into something that flowed between you, that drew you together; as if for the time you did not stop being *you* at the outer edges of your skin, as if the whole room were part of you as you listened and part of him as he talked. But behind him and around him she could see, too, little by little, what he had been saying. You could think of all the people that had lived, all the cities, all the nations that had come and gone, and having come and gone would never and could never be nothing, but were always *there*, absent; the hard thing to imagine was that for them *there* had been *here*, that each one of them, each generation, each individual, had lived each one of its moments on the rim of the future just as you were living now this actual moment, as you thought of them. When you try to see the past, she thought, you can't help thinking of it as protected by what came afterwards; when you think of the Egyptians or the Greeks or the Elizabethans or anything that is gone, you can't help seeing what was their future, what for them was unknown time that might be filled with anything, you can't help seeing it as already there, over them, around them, like soft invisible down or layers of warm semitransparent water keeping everything just as it is, so it cannot change, burying them deeper and deeper, finished lives that can only be looked at from a distance as you would look at the moon or a star through a telescope, that cannot be looked at at all when the water grows too deep, just as there must be quantities of stars that cannot be seen by even the strongest telescope, many, many more, probably, than the ones you can see. Yes, it's almost impossible, she thought, to think that each one of those people was outlined always against the future, like a figure seen against the sky, like Dicky as I watched him this afternoon on the rock; you look down at them always; you see them living and moving, but always with time about them, with layers and layers of slowly drifting time hiding them and protecting them and preserving them. It would be as hard, she thought, to think of a Babylonian girl or a Greek slave or an Egyptian queen, no matter how much you knew about them (that would make no difference), to think of them living for even one instant exposed, one whole side of them, to the future, the real future of things that have not happened, as it would be to create them magically, here in this room. Perhaps if you could think of them that way, entirely not in our past but in their present, perhaps then you could bring them here for that instant; perhaps that is the secret of magic.

"They may be digging us up sometime," Dicky said. "That's a droll thought. I wonder what they'll find digging around this part of the woods a couple of thousand years from now. They're welcome to my bones. I'd make a neat little skeleton for a museum. They could mount me in a case with a couple of broken whiskey bottles. Prehistoric glassware found near the corpse."

Linda smiled. Yes, she thought, that quiet golden water is beginning to cover us too; it has covered part of us already, but so thinly we hardly notice it: like the clear golden varnish on that portrait of Grandfather there above the desk, like the dust that you find on the tops of these old books when you pull them out of the shelf; quietly, gently, it is creeping into this room, through the cracks around the windows; it will bury us entirely before long, as dust, little by little, gently, steadily falling, buries ruined cities. Most of Mother's and Father's lives are already under the surface, under that warm transparent glaze (and death is simply the moment of complete submergence: the moment when the past which had almost covered you covers you entirely): and before very long this whole room will be filled, the trees and the house will be covered. She could see herself a girl buried under a thousand years; she could see herself and Joel and Dicky in this lighted room, with the trees and the stars outside, with the lamp reflected in the window-pane and the books rising to the ceiling, and it was all a thousand years ago; no one remembered it. She turned her head to feel herself moving, looked at her arms and her hands: that is the way someone moved, she thought, someone felt herself moving a thousand years ago; but nobody suspects; nobody can guess how she looked or how she felt; nobody can disturb the warm clear cover of the settling years. Even if there should be a sudden volcanic eruption out of the ground, she thought, and we should be preserved in lava or hot ashes, sitting here, just as we are, like some of the people in Pompeii, even then they could only guess and imagine — only look at us from a distance, peer down at us from miles above. I wonder how we would be found, she thought, in what positions, and who they would think we were. They might guess that Dicky was my brother, because we look something alike, because we are small-boned and thin;

perhaps they would think Joel was my husband, that this was our house.

Dicky got up, poured himself some whiskey: he did not move unsteadily but just a little slower than was natural, like a figure in a slow-motion film.

"Dicky!" Linda said reproachfully.

He looked at her with the bottle still in his hand. "I know," he said, half quizzical, half in irritation, "I know all about it. You think I'm taking too much. You're darn polite, but you think I'm getting drunk. Why do people always think you're drunk? That's another thing I can't see. They think you're drunk or getting drunk or have been drunk or going to get drunk. It's ridiculous. And what if you did get drunk for a change? If you understood psychology you'd know it was a damn good thing to get drunk now and then and give your subconscious a chance. Haven't you guys any pity on your poor subconscious? Suppose you stop crabbing and let me put a little more of this into that soft drink of yours. I told you you needed it."

Why not, Linda thought, as she held out her glass; why should I feel sharp and superior because Dicky's voice is not quite natural, because his thoughts are slower and less reasonable than they would be if he had not been drinking? If I had lived six years with Ellen I might be a dope fiend by now, or else in another sanatorium. They got drunk at Agathon's feast, she thought, twenty-five hundred years ago in Athens, all but Socrates, and that was only because no wine could affect him. If it doesn't disgust me to think of Agathon drinking, and Phædrus and the young Alcibiades, it surely is not fair to be superior and horrid to poor Dicky.

"Well," she said, "here's to Joel's trip."

"Sure," Dicky said. "Many happy returns, Joel."

"You know, Joel," Linda said, "the more I think about it the more I feel that I simply must go too. Don't you think you could get your friend to take me along to do the washing or the cooking or something of that sort? Don't you really?"

"I wonder if you would like it," Joel said. "I wonder if I will, for that matter. Perhaps I'll get so bored I can't stand it, or perhaps I'll get into some row or other and come slinking back with my tail between my legs."

"Of course you won't," Linda said. "I know you don't think you will really. You're just saying that."

"Of course I am," he said. "Of course I think I'm going to have a wonderful time. You're the one that's just talking, I'm afraid, because you think I need encouragement, which I don't. This is really one of the times I don't."

"I'm not just talking," she said. "I would *love* to go. Don't you believe me?"

Joel smiled at her. "There wouldn't be many comforts," he said. "Persia sounds very pretty. It makes you think of Omar Khayyam and carpets and roses and silky cats, but as far as I can gather it's mostly dust and dysentery. No, I think it's just as well you're not coming."

Linda bent forward and put her glass on the floor beside her chair. The glow went out of the room; the past, the future, in which these minutes had been floating, were swept bleakly away like the flowers in Klingsor's garden. So Joel would not even let her pretend that she might go with him; he thought of his new work as so different from her, from the world she lived in, that it annoyed him to hear her suggest any chance of connection between them. I know just what he thinks of me, she thought, just what I am, no doubt; one of those "charming" well-dressed women with "intelligent" interests that most of her friends, her respectable conservative acquaintances, slightly mistrust as having a tendency to be queer or arty or highbrow; that really living people, free creative people like Joel, regard with faint pity or contempt as someone who might perhaps have been one of them if she had not let herself be swamped by her surroundings, by her money. But I'm not such a person, she thought fiercely, or if I am what has he done to help me? What right has he to fling it in my face? I don't call it very kind. I don't call it very decent. He is partly teasing, of course, but that is what he means.

"So you think I need to be comfortable, do you?" she asked. "Well, perhaps you're right. It doesn't make much difference, does it, since there's no question of my going?" She got up from her chair. "Good night," she said. "I'm sleepy."

"Linda," Joel said. "You're not going up yet? Linda, did I sound nasty? I swear I didn't mean to."

His voice was kind once more, affectionate, really unhappy. She would like to look back and smile; she would like even to stay a little longer, but she did not dare to turn because the kindness in his voice had made her eyes fill with tears.

"Stay a little longer," he asked. "Won't you, Linda?"

But she could only shake her head in the doorway, without turning.

"Hell," Dicky said, "don't let that worry you, Joel. She'll be all right in the morning. She's got more sense than most of them, if she is my sister, but you can't expect them to be rational."

"Damn fool!" Joel said. "I certainly am a damn fool."

"What's the matter with you?" Dicky asked. "You didn't do anything."

"I did just what I'm always doing," he said. "Just said the worst possible thing at the worst possible time."

"Come on," Dicky said. "You're dreaming. You didn't say anything. What did you say?"

"Let's not talk about it," Joel said, "if you don't mind."

"O.K. by me," Dicky said. "Hand me your glass."

Why did I do it? Joel wondered. What devil made me bring in that dig about comforts? Not so mysterious, I guess: jealousy of Thornton, simple meanness, wanting to rub it into her that she has married a rich man whom she is too intelligent not to find dull: or perhaps she doesn't; perhaps he isn't; I'm hardly in a position to judge Thornton objectively. But it doesn't make so much difference, I suppose, what I said just now; it's only the last of a series of mistakes. The first one was coming here at all, or rather the first one was kissing her last summer: charming performance that! What a repulsive passionate object I must have seemed, eyes squinting, doubtless, and features bloated — thank God, at least it was dark! I don't feel so sorry about that, though, because after all I could not help it; just then as she stood beside me I could not help it or I wouldn't have done it. It came over me then that in all the years I had loved her I had never done anything but stare at her like one of the more stupid animals and now and then make unpleasant remarks (witness the one I made just now); it came over me that I had been a fool; and as she stood there beside me looking through the columns, I felt that she was not only the Linda of that moment but the Linda of all the different moments, the different days and years, when I had not spoken and might have, when I had not touched her, when my shyness or my caution, or various complications of pride and voluptuous self-denial and ideas of fairness (themselves three-quarters pride), had made me turn away while she married Thornton (and I knowing all the while that he was not worthy to touch her, and knowing that I really was, not through my own merit but through my love for her, my appreciation of her). Yes, that moment by some damnable power of its own managed to gather into itself all the moments of my denials, my repressions, my waverings, and the Linda that I suddenly kissed (like a movie gangster kissing his woman) was the Linda of a thousand different moments, and my kiss the fulfillment, the release (brutal, absurd, no doubt, as it seemed to her), of a thousand desires. No, that could not be helped; it was foolish, outrageous, but I'm not even sure that I regret it; in fact — why not be frank? — I'm sure that I do not regret it. It has put a link between her and me of a sort that was not there; at worst it cannot make much difference to her and to me it is tremendously important, so why pretend to be more quixotic than I am? But this coming here to-day: I could have prevented that; I knew that I should not come, yet here I am; but again, he thought, to be quite honest, do I really regret coming? I'm afraid not. As I looked at her just now, not daring to watch her too closely for fear that she would stop watching me, I knew that her face as it was then would stay with me for my torment and delight. I knew that if there had been a chance of my having a peaceful trip it was gone, but I was fool enough to be glad. Though how can you measure gladness? How can you set up peace of mind, detachment, the pleasure of work well done, with the joy of a caught look, a lifted hand? How can you say when you are the happier, the more miserable? Surely a little while ago, as she listened to my talk of the past, I was very happy; I hardly remember ever being more happy: it seemed then that it was my interest in what I was saying, in the ideas I was trying to explore; but really of course it was her interest, the feeling that she was with me; for she was with me then, more, I think, than she had ever been. When you love, he thought, very often your thoughts are not of her you love; you may forget that she exists, or almost forget, as you go about your business; and yet your interest in everything else, no matter how remote, is given a special color by your beloved; the joy that you may feel in what takes you from her is a joy that is borrowed from her presence. I hardly was aware of her face as I talked, yet now I know that I saw it every moment; I felt that for once I was holding her spirit in my hands, not daring to look, not daring to move, lest I should startle it like a bird that I had coaxed to alight on my finger; and then suddenly I dashed it to the ground. Why? Pure wantonness? Sadism? Was it not the longing to feel the power which I thought I had won, to use it to the full before it should be withdrawn of itself? All my life as she has looked at me with that calm, that gracious disinterest, I have tried to pierce her with irony, with criticism, because I could not otherwise touch her, and always I have failed; always Linda has not really been touched, though she may have pretended to wince, out of pity; but to-night, just now, he thought, I touched her at last; to-night my arrow drew blood, and I find that I do not regret: I triumph. The back of her head, the line of her cheek half-seen, as she did not quite turn, not daring to, the tears that I guessed were in her eyes, made me feel like lying down on sharp stones for her to trample upon, grinding her heels into my face; and yet I triumph. It was not jealousy of Thornton that made me speak. When I felt Linda's eyes upon me, when I felt at last that I had pierced an entrance into her spirit, I never thought of Thornton; no one was concerned in those moments but Linda and me.

"What's the matter?" Dicky asked. "Still brooding? For God's sake, don't you begin to brood or the evening's killed. That's the best thing I do, just sit and brood, and liquor does n't seem to help."

"I'm not brooding," he said. "Where do you get that idea?" An interesting comment, he thought, upon my usual expression that when I sit here growing more insanely happy each minute I should be thought to brood.

"No?" Dicky said. "Well, that's fine. Neither am I. To hell with it." He emptied his glass and mixed another. There was not more than half a pint left in the bottle, which might save future inconvenience.

Dicky was taking his drinks faster now. The whiskey and ginger ale no longer seemed to have much taste; it slipped over his tongue without penetrating; it hardly seemed to touch his throat. The cold, that was about all you felt: it might be so much water you were pouring into a radiator, with a taste of alcohol now and then, not so much when you swallowed as afterwards; alcohol, he thought, to prevent freezing. He smiled. But, God, he thought, no danger of freezing in here; it must be about eighty. His smile did not last. You might know that Linda would get sore at nothing and go to bed, he thought; you might know that Joel would just sit there and brood. Jolly companions! A merry evening! He looked at the shelves behind Joel's head: suppose you had to read all those books; suppose you could not leave this room until you had read every one. Between the top of each row and the shelf above there was a line of shadow; that would be so much gained; you would read all the bottom row and then you could skip that crack; how many rows all together? He raised his eyes, slowly counting, from shelf to shelf; it was hard work staring upward; the lamp hurt your eyes. Why bother to count? That's one thing I don't have to do, read those books, he thought; that's one thing I don't have to worry about.

"I've got an idea," Joel said. "Why don't you come with me, Dicky? You're the one that ought to go."

"Sure," Dicky said. "That would be fine."

"I mean it," Joel said. "It would be fine if it could be arranged."

"All right," Dicky said. "You arrange it."

"Why wouldn't it be fine?" Joel asked. "Wouldn't you like it?"

"Oh sure, I like anything."

"But seriously, Dicky, have you ever thought of going away?"

"I've thought of lots of things," Dicky said, "and some of them won't bear repeating. So don't ask."

Go away? he thought. Go to Persia? Go anywhere? That would be fine, but how about Ellen? *But living alone,* he sang, *in a home of our own, is heaven enough for me.*

"I could write to Pete," Joel said. "If he'd take me

175

he might take on one more. The two of us together
would make a fine detail."

Go away? Dicky thought: it was funny to think
you could go away, that there were really places to go
to; you could not see them, could not imagine them;
they were not really places, they were maps, descriptions
of places; in those books, that's where they were. There
was a dark green book about South America with lots
of pictures that he used to look at sometimes on rainy
days, and one day he tore one and put the book back
quickly, and never told and never took that volume
down again; there were books about Africa, and one
about Norway and Sweden; it told how you harnessed
reindeer and how you kept your feet warm in the snow
by packing dry moss in your shoes.

Go away? he thought: that's what they would all like;
they all want to get me away. Her father would, I
know, and so would that slick doctor, damn him, like
the photographs of famous Viennese specialists who
recommend yeast. Get me away so they could have
her entirely in their power and turn her against me.
Damn that doctor's impudence: some of the questions
he asked her about herself and me! I wouldn't have
answered them but I think she liked it; I think she kind
of fell for that doctor; but she was damn sweet the
last day, she didn't want me to go. "I love you, Dicky,"
she said. "You know that, don't you? I told that
doctor I didn't, but I do. I'm afraid of that man.
He gives me the shivers." But that was probably because she knew I was jealous. "And why do you keep
talking about a child?" I remember she said once.
"Aren't I enough of a child to keep you busy?" Good
God, I shouldn't have left her there, when she gave

176

me that look like a dog you 're leaving to be chloroformed. I ought to have jumped out of the car and yanked her away from that bird and driven off as fast as I could; yes; and then have everybody say I had killed her or driven her crazy; and perhaps I am killing her; perhaps it 's my fault — Oh, Christ! He felt as if a hand had quietly wrapped around his heart, had begun to squeeze it gently, gently, until in sudden agony it would burst. If they could get me to some stinking Persian town, he thought, with a phony water supply . . . boy, would n't that be grand!

He gave Joel a long sly look. "So they 've been after you, have they?" he asked. "No, thanks. I pass."

"They?" Joel exclaimed. "Who? What?"

"Laugh," Dicky said. "Damn you, that was a joke. All right, don't. I apologize."

I suppose one of my reasons for being here, Joel thought, at least it certainly should be one of my reasons, is to keep Dicky company, to help cheer him up if such a thing is possible; but ever since I arrived I have hardly thought of him: in this room it has been only Linda's and my presence that I have felt, not Dicky's even as an intruder. It was as if Linda and I (yes, I 'm sure that Linda too) had been drawn into a vortex — our thoughts whirling about each other, combining into colored rings, the color partly from hers, partly from mine, a new color different from either's yet requiring both, a fiery pin-wheel kindling into sparks (softly glowing, fading and rekindling), every most trivial thought on the outer-most edges of our minds, making them whirl around the central flame (that flame almost invisible at the centre except for the trembling of the air), but plunging everything else, Dicky and any thought of him, any thought of his thoughts, into blackness. Dicky's thoughts: they too must be turning, slowly, painfully, I fear, on their own axis; they bore into him, no doubt, into all that is tender and soft, like a dentist's drill; let us hope that habit, and just now his drink, is able to dull, to blur, what must be their incessant grinding. If you could see people's minds, he thought, nakedly burning in the unimaginable space where minds exist, it would be like looking at the stars through a telescope able to contract not only space but time: you would see them whirling about each other in pairs, pulled outward perhaps by the tug of other minds but unable to escape, or passing comet-like and alone, powerless to stay in fixed relation for a moment with any other; you would see them drawing together, drifting apart, jerked this way and that, all of them waxing and waning, growing hotter or colder, dimmer or brighter, moving in and out, each one doubt-less having some imponderable bearing on all the rest; a dance like fireflies on a lawn with no apparent rhythm, although perhaps if you were far enough away, if you could find the proper vantage, you might make out some rhythmic sequence that kept returning, like a phrase of music or even some unchanging total form of which the continual shifting of every part, of each distinct atom that glowed, faded, whirled, attracting others, itself at-tracting, was only a process like the pulsing of blood through flesh, the breathing of air.

"You're a cheerful duck," Dicky said. "Just sit there with your mouth shut! What the heck! This isn't a funeral. It isn't even church."

"Can't you sit still and be cheerful?" Joel asked.

"No, I'll be damned if I can. Why should I?"

178

It's strange, Joel thought: you see someone rushing on to what you know is certain doom, and yet you cannot stop him any more than you can change the course of a star; often he could not stop himself even if he saw the doom; often no doubt he does see it. It seems that some way of rescue should be devised, some way by which the maddest, the most suicidal of our actions could be controlled. So far, I'm afraid, there is nothing, except in the more extreme and obvious cases a locked cell and a strait-jacket. You could see from the first, from the moment of his return, poor Dicky being captured; I could see it, his mother saw it, Linda and Brad both saw it; Dicky saw it himself and tried to back away, but it was too late: Ellen had made him love her (through pity, through desire, a sense, that was partly fear, of responsibility: who can tell?) and now I imagine he cannot stop loving her, and the joke of it is that I don't think Ellen herself really wanted it. She wanted something; she's always wanting things, she doesn't know what; and Dicky was there; she saw that with care, with persistence, she could take him; no doubt she feared that if she did not she might some day regret that she hadn't, she might find that what she might have taken someone else had taken. Yes, he thought, the whole thing was clear from the first, and clearly wrong for everyone concerned, and yet the least effort to prevent it would only have made it the more inevitable. I could no more have turned aside Dicky than Dicky, if he knew my thoughts of Linda, could turn them aside; and yet such thoughts, for me, can be only disturbing, a torment and a waste, because they can lead to nothing. Still, knowing this, I cling to them, I rejoice in them. Dicky could not affect them, nor anyone in the world, because this evening

Linda and I are set apart, divided from all that is not ourselves (Linda? How do I know? Perhaps I'm crazy) by light years of empty space.

Linda lay quite still, hoping to catch a sound from out of doors; but there was no wind; no twig scraped against the roof: was that the ocean that she heard or just the hum of the silence? The air was pleasant on her face and arms but it remained the air of this room, not the air that flowed among the gray stiff branches, that trembled with the flicker of the stars over the fields, that lapped the sides of the waves; she could not reach that air; she could not push through the cold quilt of the silence; even the barking of a dog, she thought, a step on the gravel, could not reach me; they would make soft dents on the outer surface of these black downy folds, dents that would fill up as soon as the pressure was removed: they could not reach me. Nothing can reach me.

She felt as if her mind were dissolved, a liquid in which sediment was floating like the lees of wine when an old bottle is shaken: the sediment was drifting down, beginning to settle into a pattern which meant endless wakefulness; she must keep restlessly thinking, stirring it up, until somehow it would settle into another pattern.

She tried to think of the rock where Dicky and she had sat in the sun this afternoon: it was like turning the pages of an album in search of a special picture; you knew it was there, it must be there, perhaps you had passed it. "It was warm and sunny on the rock. The surf was beautiful." She formed the words with her lips, but they had no meaning. Trifles swarmed around the edges of her mind, floated sprawling through it like bacteria across the field of a microscope: unwritten letters, unpaid calls, small delays and forgettings. That note of Mrs. Brown's, she thought, that should be answered. I must do that as soon as I get back; I must remember; I suppose we'll accept; and I never called up Henrietta about the rehearsal; I meant to bring the script to begin looking over my part; and Mother, I must write to Mother; it is nearly a month and she has not been well; it's horrid of me not to write. Mother's apt to be wakeful; sometimes in the middle of the night she knits for hours: is it like this, I wonder? What does she think of? Probably of us — of Brad and Dicky and me. She must worry constantly about Dicky (I don't think they have come up to bed; I hope he doesn't get too drunk). What will happen to Dicky? If only Ellen could die! Perhaps the next best thing would be for Dicky to die, but that seems too terrible (and I'm sure I left the key in the Lincoln and the garage is not locked, but never mind). Death, she thought, sometimes Mother must think of death because she told me once that she lay awake planning which of the things she would give to each of us; and she worries about that pain in her side. My tongue is a little sore at the very back; I must not smoke so much; people get cancer of the tongue or the throat from too much smoking; perhaps this soreness in my throat will slowly turn malignant; perhaps I will die of cancer of the throat. Everyone must die in some special way, of a disease or an accident: they drown, they are run over by automobiles, they get softening of the brain, like Oswald; it is always *something* and it's often horrible. If I should die of cancer of the throat, it would be to-night, it would be this very moment that I first recognized the thing that was to kill me; this moment as I lay here on my back, with my arms too cool and my body a little too warm, would divide my life in half. "When did you first notice anything?" the doctor would ask, and I would answer: "I noticed that my tongue felt sore one night when I was lying in bed, but I thought it was just my imagination." When I was a little girl I used to be afraid I had leprosy; I used to dream of lepers; someone would touch me on the street and it was a leper. If you went to Persia I should think you would be afraid that you would meet lepers, that they would touch you in the street: how could you tell? But I don't think I would be afraid with Joel; I cannot imagine him afraid: and Joel is going away; to-morrow and the next day I will be seeing him and then perhaps not for years.

Where am I going? she thought. What is happening to me? It seems that I am going nowhere, and yet I must be moving because nothing stands still. It's like a long train: you go on and on but the country does not change. Will it be this way for Pat? Poor little Pat, I wish he were here beside me. How can I bear to leave him, not to have him always with me, because so soon he will be changing? Why is it that when people grow up they cannot talk together? If I could talk to Mother the way Pat talks to me, it would make her happier than anything I know; and I love her just as much, — yes, when I really think of her, I do, — just as much as when I was a little girl; but I cannot talk to her, not the way I could; I'm sure Dicky can't; I don't think Dicky has talked to anyone for years; poor Dicky cannot even talk to himself. I don't think Brad talks, but with him perhaps it does not make so much difference, because you can tell that he is there, awake, near you, by just looking at his face. Of course I talk and talk to everyone, but not really: that is no more I that am talking than when I am saying my lines in a play. Or is it just living with Thornton? Thornton talks nicely but you never can remember what he says: you only remember that it is just what you would expect, just what he always says: he talks to me as he does to his dogs and horses; he strokes my shoulder; he is proud of me; he thinks he has drawn a prize, a blue ribbon. If I'm skittish he merely walks away — very sensibly. How horrid I am about Thornton! How mean I am! How empty! Do people get emptier and emptier as they grow older? Many do, I'm afraid; certainly I do. Have they always been the same: Pat, then I, then Mother and Father? If you only knew, if you only could see, you could go back without a break to the beginning of man, — in what forests, I wonder? — back to the beginning of life. It's strange to think of. You can't think of it. I must not try; I must go to sleep.

But still that scattered dust kept drifting down through the spaces of her mind, like sand falling through miles and miles of black water, to settle on the bottom of the ocean.

III

"It's the stairs," Joel said. "Do you think you can make them, Dicky?"

Dicky, lurching away from him, nearly falling, did not answer. Thank God he's been sick already, Joel thought; let's hope he won't be again. "Put your hand on the banisters," he said. "Can you put your hand on the banisters?"

Joel placed Dicky's hand on the newel post; the fingers gripped it. That was good. Not daring to leave him alone, Joel walked behind Dicky, took his arm firmly, near the armpit. "Now," he said. "Let's go."

They climbed the first three steps, but Joel had almost to lift Dicky by his shoulder. Dicky's fingers dropped from the railing; he pitched forward; Joel just caught him in time. I could carry him, he thought, if he would let me; but he wouldn't; I'm afraid he would strike out at me. Joel went behind him, put both his arms under Dicky's armpits, clasping his hands tightly across his chest; Dicky's head rolled forward; he retched: for a moment Joel thought he was going to be sick again. "Now," he said, "just try to lift your feet, Dicky. We're going upstairs to bed. You're tired. You want to go to bed."

Pressing his knees into the back of Dicky's, he forced

184

him to move his legs. The first step was hard, but then for three steps Dicky went up quite easily. This is fine, Joel thought; now if I can get him to his room before he passes out . . . But Dicky suddenly, standing up straight, threw himself backward. Oh God, Joel thought, now I've done it! He reached for the banister, caught it in time to prevent their falling on their heads but not to check a backward stampede down the stairs, with Dicky a dead weight upon his chest, a stagger across the rug at the bottom, and a crash against the opposite wall. Dicky slid to the floor and lay there. He can't be hurt, Joel thought, because I got the brunt of it. Well, at least now I can carry him. Thank God he does n't weigh much.

"Joel, what is it?"

He looked up quickly. Linda stood at the top of the stairs. She wore a pink dressing gown or kimono that looked as if it were made of soft light flannel, like a child's kimono, and she looked like a child, a girl of fourteen or fifteen, with her oval face, her eyes wide open and anxious, her hair drawn tightly back from her forehead. It might be in a braid between her shoulders; he remembered when she always used to wear it in braids. How slim she looked! How pathetic in her anxiety and wonder! He could feel rather than see the clearness, the softness of her cheeks, her lips, the fineness of her hair; all that was a part of her, inseparable from the sound of her voice, the shape of her thoughts — those thoughts that had always slipped by him, that he could never capture. She made his lips smile and his eyes fill with tears, as when you see a great dancer do something so beautiful it cannot be believed: you watch her body move, you hear a phrase of the music, and then for an instant you are hearing no music, your eyes forget that they are seeing; and your mind is pierced with the delight that only then, for that instant, you can remember; all the beauty that you have known and forgotten is suddenly restored; all that separates you from beauty, that divides you from yourself, is burned through.

"Joel, what is it?" she asked again. "Why don't you answer? Are you hurt? Is Dicky hurt? Joel, you *are* hurt."

"Nobody's hurt," he said. "I've just been clumsy as usual. It's a shame I waked you up."

"I wasn't asleep," she said, and came down a few steps towards him. "Is Dicky very bad?"

"He'll be all right. I didn't think he was bad at all until a moment ago. He was sitting perfectly still on the sofa. I noticed he hadn't been saying anything for a minute or so, and suggested going to bed. He didn't answer and when I tried to help him up I found he could hardly walk. But we made it safely until we reached the stairs."

Joel stooped and started to lift Dicky again by the shoulders.

"Wait a moment," Linda said. "I'll help."

She hurried down. He had no idea of letting her help him with Dicky, but he would not say so until she was downstairs, for fear that she would go back to bed. She stood on the bottom step, her hand resting on the newel post where he had put Dicky's hand a minute ago. "Now," she said, "tell me just what to do. It ought not to be hard for the two of us."

"Nothing for a moment," he said. He put his arm under Dicky's shoulders, the other under his legs, and lifted: it was harder than he had thought, because Dicky

186

was so limp, but not at all impossible. Dicky could not weigh more than a hundred and twenty-five, perhaps not so much.

"You 're not going to carry him up that way?" Linda asked.

"Yes I am," Joel said. "I 'm going to take him right up and get him to bed in five minutes. He 's been sick already, so he ought to have a decent night. When he wakes up to-morrow he 'll feel rotten of course, but he ought not to be so bad by noon."

"Then what can *I* do?" she asked in a desolate voice.

"There 's one thing I wish you would do," he said. "It would be great."

"What is it?"

"Will you do it?" he asked. "Will you promise?"

"Of course I won't promise, but what is it?"

"Will you go out to the kitchen and make us some coffee?"

"But you can't give Dicky coffee. How could you get him to take it?"

"I mean for you and me," he said. "Will you, Linda?"

"I 'd love to," she said. "Yes, I 'd love some hot coffee. Poor little Dicky. You would n't rather have me undress him?"

"I should say not. Now, if you 'll let me by . . ."

She stepped down on to the rug at the foot of the stairs, and Joel climbed them with Dicky in his arms. The stairs were narrow so that he had to take care not to bump Dicky's head against the wall or get his feet caught in the banisters.

He took him to his room, laid him on the bed, and undressed him; then he looked for his pyjamas, first in the suitcase, then in the bureau drawers, in the closet: Dicky

187

must have forgotten to bring any. Well, he would be warm enough with plenty of covers. Joel lifted him again — how thin he looked! You could see his ribs, his sharp thigh bones, and yet there was a grace that was almost boyish in the spare taut symmetry of his body. Joel pulled back the covers, laid him on the sheet, and pulled them up again, tucking them about his neck. His face looked now quite pale; he was breathing heavily.

Joel stared down at him for a moment before he put out the light: what's in your mind? he wondered. Is it quite asleep, withdrawn into itself, beyond the reach of pain and worry; is it peaceful and dark, sightless, unhearing, like the minds of the dead? Or are you dreaming, Dicky? I hope not, because the chances are that your dreams will not be pleasant. You are one of the few people that I call my friends. I suppose I love you, if by that is meant that if you were to die I would really miss you, that at moments you would seem nearer to me, more a part of me, than most living people. You are damnably unhappy: I can feel your unhappiness inside you like something fibrous and hard that you cannot absorb, cannot understand; I can even feel it somewhere inside myself; it is part of my sense, my confused and fumbling sense of life; it does not pass me by, you must not think that; but just now your unhappiness — and all the misery, all the unreason in the world — cannot really touch me, cannot touch my happiness as I think of her, think of my loving her.

The kitchen was warm. On the stairs her ankles had felt a little chilly, she had wanted to hug her kimono tightly about her; but now the heat from the coal stove was delicious, and she was glad that her ankles were bare.

She lit the kerosene lamp on the table; one of the nice things about having the electricity turned off was that you could use oil lamps and candles. Of course you could use them anyway, but you never took the trouble if you could reach out and turn on a switch; and even if you did, since you knew the electricity was there, that it could be turned on at any moment, it was not quite the same thing: it seemed artificial, slightly absurd, like reviving old folk dances and native customs. There are not too many lights here, she thought, but the lights at home are almost indecent; they make it seem a little like a wealthy house in a movie, or a very expensive, very homelike hotel: all kinds of reading lights everywhere, and special lights on every porch, big lights and small lights, so that you can arrange any number of effects, like a stage setting; and lights out of doors between the house and the stables, and the stables and the cow barn, and on the way to the garden; and yet if I turn one on and it does not work I get impatient and feel that it must be fixed at once; and Thornton feels so too. I am apt to be rather sharp about it; Thornton is very quiet and reassuring, but we both agree in our minds (one of the few things that we probably feel about in just the same way) that it is very important for that light to be fixed at once.

She smiled to herself. This kitchen with its old iron stove set into the wall and the dark red-painted bricks behind it, the copper boiler between the stove and the sink, the faint tap now and then of a coal dropping through the grate, the smell of raw coffee — how could it be possible that now she was here, when just a minute ago she had been upstairs in the dark, struggling to find her way out of a cold, endless labyrinth between sleep and waking? She opened the draft of the stove, took off one

189

of the round lids, prodded and stirred the coal with the poker until she could see a volcanic network through the blackness. It would take some time for the water to boil in the coffeepot; she hoped not too long, because she would like everything to be ready for Joel when he came down; she would like him to be amazed that she had been so quick. She put the coffee into the pot, and three cups of water; if she left the smaller lid off the stove, the bottom of the pot could sit directly above the flames. Now for the table: she would put on the red checkered tablecloth she had seen in the drawer this afternoon and had not bothered to take out for supper, and use the dark blue English china; she would cut some thin slices of bread, and butter them, and get out a jar of the Dundee marmalade that Joel especially liked — at least he said he did; it might be just talk. She wished there were some flowers or berries that she could put in the centre, so that it would be quite different from what Joel would expect, much prettier and more festive. As she moved about the kitchen she would look at the coffeepot every other minute to see if there were signs of boiling.

And this too, she thought suddenly, this might be covered by a thousand years, by two thousand years; our sitting in the library after supper, Joel, and Dicky and I, my thinking that it would sometime be existing only in the past: that time has come so soon; it is the past already; already it is thinly, ever so thinly covered. You can see most of it quite clearly, but not the tiniest peak pricks through the surface; and now if there should be a sudden earthquake or eruption it would not be the three of us that would be found in one room together, but I would be here alone. You could imagine, she thought, that something might happen in this room only, some strange convulsion of time, so that suddenly, in one instant, it would be covered by two thousand years; so that it, so that I, would be existing only two thousand years ago, and all the rest would be *now*, quite naked to the unlived future. Then Joel, digging, might discover my bones, the skeleton of a young woman, that is all that he would know; and this twisted chain that I forgot to take off when I went to bed would be around my neck, the gold perhaps crusted and greenish, or perhaps it would be bright as ever; but he would not know what I looked like, what my hair was like; he would not know the color of my eyes, how my voice sounded, or anything that I had thought; and I, as I lay there, as Joel uncovered me and looked at me curiously, delighted that he had found something at last, his face eager, his body warm from digging, I would not know that it was he; I would not be there, because I would be two thousand years away.

She looked once more into the coffeepot. Around the edges there were foamy bubbles; now in a few minutes . . . Turning away from the stove, she saw Joel; he stood watching her, just inside the door. He smiled, and she smiled too, with a rush of gladness; it was as if he had come to her, so quietly, with her not knowing when he came, from across two thousand years.

He went to the table. "This is great," he said.

"But it is n't finished. I hoped it would be. The coffee 's not quite done, and if you 're hungry we may need more bread."

"I 'm very hungry," he said. "Where 's the bread knife?"

She watched him cut the first slice. It started very thick and dwindled to nothing before the bottom of the loaf. "Here," she said. "Give it to me. I 'm not fussy, but I draw the line at slices like that. You might watch the coffee to see that it does n't boil over."

"It 's boiling now," he said. "It smells as if it was done. Shall I take it off?"

"No," she said. "Leave it a minute or two to get some strength."

"I don't know whether I can wait," he said.

"Well, you 've got to," she said, "whether you can or not."

"If you photographed me now, Linda, hanging over the coffeepot and sniffing the steam, with an expression of impatience and delight, perhaps we could sell it as a coffee advertisement. It would do for any brand, you know."

She smiled but did not answer. "There," she said, "I 've cut eight slices, Joel, but they 're very thin. You must eat six and I 'll take two."

"Why not four apiece?" he asked.

"I'm not hungry. All I want is coffee. I 'm only taking the two to be polite, so you won't feel embarrassed."

"That would n't embarrass me," he said. "*You* could n't embarrass me, Linda."

"Why Joel, I think you 're very easily embarrassed. So am I, for that matter, but I 've learned not to show it. You have n't, and I don't think you ever will."

"You could n't embarrass me to-night," he said.

"Now I suppose you can take off the coffee, Joel. I was going to pour it into another pot. I was going to have everything beautiful, but you came back too soon. Is Dicky all right?"

"Perfectly," he said. "You sit down. I 'll pour it."

She sat down at the table and watched him pour the coffee into the cups, very slowly so that the grounds would not come with it. Then he sat down opposite her, his

192

back to the stove. It is true, she thought, Joel does seem different to-night: he seemed different just now, when I saw him suddenly there by the kitchen door, from what he has ever been, different even from what he was in the library; though perhaps then he was beginning to change, change into this new Joel. Generally I feel quite powerful with him, as if I could tease him as much as I wanted, but now I feel that I could not, that it would have no effect. He seems different, she thought, and yet he does not surprise me; it seems quite natural that he should be this way, as if this were what I had always been looking for, what he had always kept just out of sight: and now suddenly I find it waiting for me. What is it, I wonder? Is it his voice? Is it the way he smiles? It is exciting and yet very peaceful, very comforting, with the kind of peaceful happiness things have when you remember them long afterwards. When I saw him just now in the doorway, standing so silently as he watched me, he might have been Apollo or Hermes, or a half-divine hero, entering the house of someone who had always prayed to him, lovingly and yet with doubt at heart, come at last to reassure her, to take her with him to the Islands of the Blest.

"Joel," she said suddenly, "why is it that I 've never seen you before? Why are you this way to-night?"

"I 've always seen you, Linda," he said, "always: but perhaps I never dared to look at you except when you were not looking."

"And now you 're going away."

"Not for a little while," he said.

As she finished her coffee she felt her cup trembling slightly in her hand.

"Don't you want some more?" she asked.

He shook his head.

193

They cleared the table without speaking. She rinsed the cups and plates, passing them to him to dry.

"You go on," he said. "I'll turn out the lamps."

She walked through the pantry, the dining room; she had reached the top of the stairs before she heard him below in the hall. She knew he was standing there, watching her as he had done when she first saw him in the kitchen — but now he was not smiling: she knew that he was not smiling. It is within my power not to look back, she thought; if I do not turn my head he will not come, even now he will not come. But no, she thought, no, I could not bear it. She looked over her shoulder: he stood there just as she had known he would be standing, gazing out of the shadow, not smiling. She met his eye — turned away; but still it was his glance that she saw as she heard his feet on the stairs.

PART IV

July 1929

July 1929

I

LULY looked down at Pat, seated on the turf beside her chair, with his arms clasped about his knees, and wondered if he had noticed how she stumbled over the words. She hated to catch herself stumbling, to hear her tongue form meaningless sounds as if she were sick or crazy; it made her feel ashamed, even before dear little Pat. Pat smiled up at her, more with his eyes than with his lips: deep blue eyes, very bright when they were wide open, very intelligent; their brightness, their intelligence, were apt to surprise her because his eyelids were heavy, because as a rule he kept them partly lowered and you did not have much impression of his eyes. She would admit now, which she would not at the time, that he had been an ugly baby; but she had said from the first: "Mark my words; he 'll be a handsome man," and everyone had laughed at her. Well, she knew babies, she knew little boys. It is so irritating, she thought, to have people think you make a remark just because you happen to be a mother or a grandmother, as if that made you feeble-minded; just as it 's irritating beyond words to have people think you feel in a certain way because you happen to be a minister's wife.

She smiled back at Pat now a little tremulously, because she could see that his smile was meant to encourage her, to show her that he had noticed nothing strange in her voice, and she found that very touching, like a simple tender phrase of music (another thing that distressed her lately was the way tears would come to her eyes on any occasion: it seemed so weak; it was so unpleasant for others); and Pat moved his lips as if to send her a kiss, but so gently that she need not take it for one unless she wanted to, and then looked down and prodded the turf with a twig as if he were hunting for insects or cater-pillars.

"Do you think you will like *Quentin Durward?*" she asked.

"*I'll* say!" he exclaimed, still encouraging her.

"I think I'll stop now," she said, "because I'm a little tired."

"Oh, that's all right," he said. "When a book has long words like that I don't like to hear too much at first because you have to listen so hard. You have to keep listening to the words and then you get mixed up with the people."

Perhaps he was too young for the Waverleys. She had looked forward for years to the time when she could read them to him; she had been excited this morning as Mark and Brad and Dicky had started across the fields to church: it was like getting on a boat for a long delightful journey, just she and Pat.

"We'll do some more to-morrow," she promised, but she knew really that she could not. "Or we might get Grandpapa or Mother to read it to you and me both."

"That would be swell," he said. "And sometime, Grandmama, will you read me that big book with the scary pictures? That's the one I've *always* wanted to read. The picture of the ape, the great huge monkey carrying off the lady — that 's the scariest. It makes my heart quiver to look at it."

She smiled at him more gayly. "Do you like to feel scared?" she asked.

He looked thoughtful. "Not really scared," he explained. "Not too scared; but I love to see Angel when he 's scared. When he sees a dog his eyes get so big and shiny! And do you know what he ate last summer? You know those big ladder spiders?"

"He did n't eat a spider!" she exclaimed. The thought made her rather sick.

"No, he did n't, but you know those big grasshoppers they catch in their nets? He ate one of those!"

Pat was trying to entertain her, trying to cheer her up, but she must not keep him. "You don't have to stay here," she said. "If I want anything I can ring for your mother."

Pat got up. "I 'll go to my room and get my sketch-book and then I 'll be right back," he promised.

She watched him cross the lawn towards the house. The columns looked very white this morning, with the green shadowy trees on either side of them; and in the open window of her bedroom she could see the jar of pink and white peonies that Pat had brought her yesterday. Now that he had gone, everything seemed quite still, though the leaves were moving: the air, like invisible water, shook them in its current; the sky seemed very far above them, very empty; she felt warm here in the sun, but there was something cold in the thick fresh foliage of the trees with their white sparkles, their almost black shadows. This is where I wanted to be, she thought, here at the Grove; this is where I was afraid I would never be able to come after my accident; but now that I am here

199

it is not the same; it still seems far away; even the children are not the same, except at moments; even Mark is not quite the same; and I am becoming more and more of a burden, which I hoped and prayed I would never be. If I could get back my strength, she thought, either that or die! But I would like to see Pat grow up; I would like to see Dicky happy once more; I would like to travel with Mark, to visit some of those cathedral towns again, so quiet, so lovely; it would n't be very expensive.

She looked anxiously towards the house. Being alone now made her restless, impatient, half frightened (how could you not be frightened when everything seemed so empty, so far away?) ; she knew it was foolish when Mark and the boys would be back from church before long, when Linda would come out to sit with her until it was time to meet Joel (his train was not due until after twelve and by that time Mark would be here). I used to like to be alone, she thought, when there was so much that I could do; I never understood people who always needed company: it seemed so weak, so superficial. It is weak, I know; it 's because there is nothing I can do. She felt tears gathering in her eyes: this was like a disease; she hoped at least now that no one would come until she could dry them; but there was Pat hurrying across the lawn, such a good little boy — of course he would come back. She closed her eyes and leaned her head against the pillow as if she were asleep.

As Linda crossed the lawn, she saw Pat raise his head from his drawing and put his fingers to his lips: Mother was asleep, her head resting sidewise against the pillow, her mouth slightly open. When she was asleep she seemed more like herself; her face looked tired but calm. When she was awake now her expression often would keep changing: sometimes the corners of her mouth would be drawn down; sometimes there would be a strained half-startled look about her eyes as if she were suffering; sometimes her lips would grow more and more puckered as if she were tasting something unpleasant; and yet when you spoke to her she answered as a rule in a listless voice as if the looks that crossed her face had nothing to do with her thoughts and feelings. When you were with her it was this strange surface life of her muscles and skin that took hold of you, that prevented you from seeing her, feeling her own presence; and after a time you became exhausted struggling with this life that was not hers, and you would even grow annoyed and lay the blame on Mother herself. Always when she was there the whole family had been apt to lay the blame for anything on her because she was always ready to take it; even when she protested at first you could bully her into believing she was guilty, because someone must be guilty and it was so much easier for her to believe that it was herself than one of her children. Now as Linda watched her sleeping profile, she remembered several times in the last few months when it had appeared to her during the night: it was then the profile of Mother as a girl, young and intense and beautiful (perhaps the image of some old photograph she had forgotten, because each time it was exactly the same), and she would look at it lovingly, eager to show her love, but that young profile of Mother would not speak, would not look at her, for always it remained a profile; once, even, she had started to get out of bed to go into Mother's room, but then as she grew wide awake she had decided not to, for fear of disturbing her. This morning, she thought, I cannot think of Mother; I can think of nothing but Joel's return;

201

and yet now that in so short a time I'll be seeing him I cannot even think of Joel; the nearer he comes the less I can think of him: all he does is prevent my thinking for more than the briefest snatches of any other person.

She looked over Pat's shoulder. He was drawing a leopard standing upright, in complete armor except for his head; his pose was heroic, a shield was flung across his shoulder; his spotted face looked calm and noble and gentle. Pat glanced up at her. "He's the knight that won the battle I was drawing yesterday," he explained. "See the scarf on his arm? That's the one the young lady leopard gave him. You'll recognize it when I color it." He had drawn a whole series of animal knights, suggested by the stories of King Arthur she had been reading him: leopards and panthers, and sometimes rabbits, just as heroic, just as noble, with ears laid smoothly back; they stood like this victorious leopard, modest and virtuous after their conquests; they fought each other on horseback, with shattered lances flying, with cloaks waving in cloudlike sweeping folds; they kneeled gently before their ladies, who, in low-necked dresses, with scarves across their shoulders, extended their paws graciously and serenely; and all were so spirited and courteous, all of them went in such a quiet dignified way about their business, even when it was the most desperate fighting, that they suggested nothing so much as Pat himself. Linda looked away. She felt tremendously guilty towards Pat; she ran her fingers through his hair, backwards over his large intelligent head, down through the pale silky hairs on his neck, rather a thin little neck for such a massive head. What she would like more than anything, she felt at that instant, was to fly far away somewhere with Pat, to a place where they would not know anyone except each other. If only

I could keep from remembering Joel, she thought, if I could get away from Thornton so he would not irritate me, I could be quite content just to live with Pat. He squirmed now as her fingers tickled the back of his neck, and turned his head so that he would see her face. There was always something gracious in his manner and a little shy, as if he realized that he was a child, only nine years old, that he was not going to pretend to feel or act any older because that would be foolish, but that he knew there were limits, from the point of view of any grown-up person, to what a nine-year-old could understand, limits that you would overlook because you loved him, but that he could not expect strangers, or even grown-up friends, to overlook except from politeness; and it was this quite natural and objective sense of his own youth that made him such good company, that made you feel that without his being precocious in the least he could not be thought of as being either old or young. Nothing can be settled, she thought; it is worse than foolish to plan, to consider, to worry, until I have talked to Joel — and even then I see no solution; I can see no solution to anything.

She heard Mother move and, turning, saw that her eyes were open.

"Did you have a nap?" she asked.

"I guess so," Mother said. "Perhaps a little one, sort of halfway. I rarely go to sleep during the daytime. I guess I took just little whiffs and then I woke up and then just little whiffs again."

Linda smiled. At times this summer Mother would use phrases that were strangely childlike: Linda could imagine Pat describing a light sleep in just those words; and whenever this new childlike Mother appeared, her face would be her own once more, a sweet, very kind, but rather helpless face, not sad itself but apt to make you sad because it was so helpless, so confiding. Linda bent over and kissed her: her cheek was flushed and felt very warm from the sun that had been shining on it.

"Don't you want me to take off one of your blankets, Mother?" she asked.

"No, I don't think so," Mother said. "If my feet get too warm I can hang them out and get them cool again."

"Why, Mother," Linda exclaimed tenderly, "that sounds like hanging out clothes."

Mother caught her smile and smiled with her; Pat smiled too. "That's just what I was thinking," he said. "Isn't it funny? I was just thinking of that that very moment."

"That's what Grandma used to say," Mother explained, "and Mother did too. When her feet were too hot she would hang them out of bed to cool off."

Pat got up. "I feel hot now," he said. "I think I'll go to the beach. I don't have to wait for Uncle Brad and Dicky, do I, Mother?"

"No," Linda said, "not if you're careful."

"You used to think I didn't go out far enough," he said, "and now you think I go out too far. That's always the way."

"When your Uncle Brad was about your age," Luly said, "one day I wanted him to put his head under and he wouldn't do it, so I waded right in and ducked him. I waded right into the water with my shoes and stockings on."

Pat stared at Linda, raised his head suddenly like a terrier, and laughed heartily. "Gosh," he said, "I bet he was scared when he saw you coming. I'd have been awfully scared if Mother had tried to duck me last summer. Did he cry, Grandmama?"

"I don't remember," she said, "but he was a surprised boy. I think he had the surprise of his life."

Pat looked at the ground, wrinkled his forehead, pulled down the corners of his mouth as if he were about to confess a secret crime. "Can I have a blueberry muffin before I go?" he asked. Linda loved that hesitating voice: he might be saying: "I don't suppose I can; I won't be hurt or surprised if you refuse; but if you knew how much I wanted one, I'm sure you would let me have one."

"Do you think he better before swimming?" Mother asked anxiously.

"I guess he can have one," Linda said.

"Oh, thanks," Pat exclaimed. "Thanks awfully," and walked away towards the house with measured swift steps, a compromise, Linda knew, between his eagerness to get the muffin and his feeling that too swift a departure might seem greedy and impolite.

"I don't think it will hurt him," Linda explained to Mother. "Doctors don't seem to think that eating a little before bathing is as bad as they used to."

"I know things change," Mother said, "and I don't believe it makes much difference what you eat. I'd be thankful if your father could be persuaded not to make me take that awful oily stuff that's supposed to be so wonderful. Nothing will convince me that anything that tastes so bad will do me a particle of good and I don't believe that anything I want will hurt me. Years ago in Savannah there was a little darky girl on the place. She was so ill that the doctor told her mother she could give her anything she wanted. Well, she craved crabs and blackberries, and her mother gave them to her and she got well." Mother smiled more and more happily; she chuckled to herself. "Speaking of the way things change," she went on, "I was thinking of the time your Great-Aunt Eliza . . . she was a tartar if there ever was one, but a most charming and intelligent old lady . . . You know there used to be an idea that lobster and milk could n't be eaten together, that it was deadly poison . . . and she decided to try it. So she hired a trained nurse to sit by her bed in case she should be ill, and she happened to wake up in the night and the nurse was asleep and snoring. Aunt Eliza was perfectly furious. I can see her face now, the way she used to tell it. 'I might have died,' she said, 'and that woman would n't have known a thing about it.' " Mother chuckled again. "I would n't have been in that woman's shoes for a good deal," she said.

Linda laughed too, and as she laughed she saw that the smile was fading from Mother's lips, the expression retreating from her face. Then in a moment the eyes once more grew lively and eager, the dullness withdrew so quickly that you hardly believed it had been there, just as you may almost doubt afterwards the sudden twinge of a tooth. Linda turned to follow her look and saw Brad and Dicky walking towards them through the trees from the south gate.

"Are n't you coming over to speak to Mother?" Brad asked. "You better."

"Sure," Dicky said. "Sure I 'll come," and he turned from the path to cut across the lawn with Brad. Ellen, he supposed, was still in her room, probably not out of bed, but he would not feel easy until he had seen her, found out for certain where she was and what she was doing. He scowled, crossing the lawn, felt that he would flush once more with anger and shame if he could n't make himself stop thinking of her; but he could not, he knew it, not at

206

least until he had seen her. He tried to make his face clear as he came up to Mother and Linda. Cheerful and considerate, he thought, that's me: smoothing his forehead, twisting up the corners of his lips, and then, as Mother smiled at him, really smiling not because he felt happier but because he felt so sorry for Mother, because in a way since her accident all he could do was smile at her and hope that his smile might manage to give something of what he ought to be giving her and knew was there somewhere inside him for her, but so hard to get at, so tangled with other things, that probably he could never lay his hand on it again.

"Well, how's everything?" he asked heartily. "How've they been treating you in my absence?"

"Very well, thank you," she replied. "First Pat was entertaining me and then Linda."

"That's fine," he said. "If there are any complaints you know who to come to."

"It's just as well there haven't been any complaints," Mother said, "if I had to count on hunting you up to see about getting things fixed."

"That was a mean one!" Dicky exclaimed; but it's quite true, he thought, I should be seeing more of Mother; here we have been here almost a week and I have not really talked to her; but what can you say? That's the trouble. He looked this way and that: first to the strip of ocean — perhaps he could persuade Ellen to go sailing this afternoon — then at the house.

"What did you think of Mr. Fairlamb?" Mother asked. "Did he preach a good sermon?"

"Rotten," Brad said. "He's one of those very earnest young Christers, sort of a socialist, too, as far as I could make out. Believes in production for use and not for

207

profit and all that. Well, that might go down big if your
state was unselfish, but if people were unselfish capitalism
would be fine too — so there you are."

"That's putting it simply," Linda said.

Brad looked at her with exaggerated contempt. "I've
been suspecting it," he said. "You're turning radical.
I suppose it's Joel's influence. You say you have been
corresponding with him, which strikes me, by the way, as
hardly decent since you're a married woman."

Dicky bent down, picked a blade of grass, and began
chewing it. He was beginning to wonder how he could
get away; during this last week, whenever he was with
Mother, he would begin to fidget, begin almost at once
to make plans for escape. He spit out his blade of grass,
hitched up his belt.

"It's just as well you did n't try to come to church,
Mother," he said. "I had to hoist one old dame off the
floor this morning. She tried to sneak out before com-
munion and took a flop in the aisle, and I went up to her
and took her under the arms and gave her a hup and she
went on." He looked at her kindly, grinning as hard as
he could, in the hope that just for a moment he could make
himself feel the way he would have felt telling this same
thing to Mother a year ago, and almost believing that he
had succeeded. He bent down and kissed her forehead.

"I guess I'll breeze into the house," he said, "and see
what mischief Ellen's been getting into."

"Tell her from me," Brad said, "if she does n't get up
by ten o'clock to-morrow, I'll go into her room and yank
her out of bed by the foot."

"She'd like that," Dicky said.

Brad looked down sorrowfully at Mother. She has
more color, he thought, than she had when she came here,

but I 'm afraid that 's only sunburn; I 'm afraid she is not any stronger. He raised his head as a car turned in the gate: it was the Lees bringing home the Old Man.

"Who is it?" Mother asked nervously. "Is it callers? I can't be seen this way. Run into the house, will you, Brad, and tell Myra that I 'm not at home."

"Apart from the fact that you can be seen plainly from the driveway, that would be great," Brad said, "but luckily for you it 's just the Lees bringing home the Parson, so you don't have to worry about how you look."

"Well, I hope they don't get out," Mother said querulously. "I 'm disappointed in the Lees. I thought they were going to be such nice young people."

"I understand you disapprove of them because they serve cocktails," Brad said. "I can't believe it. I thought to myself as I looked at the decanter on the sideboard and the family wineglasses underneath — I thought: Oh, the inconsistency of it all!"

"I did n't buy them," Mother said proudly. "I inherited them."

"That makes it all the worse," Brad answered. "The Lees are n't so bad," he went on, looking down at her with one eyebrow raised. "When I go there what they give me is a glass of milk, because I insist on it."

"I was thinking of Dicky," Mother explained.

"Don't you worry about him," Brad said. "He 's all right. He 's on the water wagon now. He 's showing more self-control than anyone." But how long he will stay on, Brad thought, now that Ellen is back, is another question; it must be hard lines on her to come here and find there 's a *real* invalid in the family. "Hullo, Parson," he said, as Mark joined them. "Luly 's just been staging a scene because she was afraid the Lees would come over to

209

see her and she does n't like them because they give cock-
tail parties."

"I have not been staging a scene," Mother protested,
half grieved, half smiling. "I simply said I was disappointed in them. Did n't I, Linda?"

"I like the Lees very much," Mark said testily. "For
heaven's sake, Luly, do live and let live."

"Now don't *you* get on your ear," Brad said. "Mother 's
all right now. I 've succeeded in calming her down."

He watched the Lees' car turn out of the north gate.
If he had thought he might have asked them to join the
party at the beach this evening, though perhaps it would
be more fun with no outsiders: we 'll go on the roller
coaster, he thought, and the merry-go-round, and every
fool thing there is; it will be a party to welcome Joel.

"Apparently that Mr. Fairlamb was n't very exciting,"
Mother said to Father.

"Oh, he 's a good young man," Father said, "but dull
beyond words. People get such impossible ideas under the
guise of love for their fellows and all they generally do is
make them uncomfortable. You 're not a nihilist, Linda,
are you, or an anarchist, or anything like that? I hope
not."

"I think she 's one of those absurd parlor radicals,"
Brad said. "And by the way, Parson, if you 're going to
insist on those Cremos I see I 'll have to provide you with
some decent cigars, at least while I 'm here. I could n't
afford to go around La Salle Street with a five-cent stink
in my clothes. No one would do business with me — not
the kind of people I do business with."

"I always accept small favors humbly and gratefully,"
Father said, "but I expect to end my days in self-support-

210

ing poverty. In fact when your mother passes on I'm going to an old man's home. That's just what I'd like — a nice peaceful old man's home."

"You would n't think it was so peaceful," Mother said, "if you'd ever been at the board meetings of an old man's home."

"I could always go to my own room," Father said. "Now if you would only pine gently away and let me put you in the cemetery . . ."

"Don't be too sure of yourself," Mother said, smiling, liking to be teased. "Perhaps I'll live longer than you."

"But you've said you wanted to die before I did, have n't you?"

"Yes, I have," Mother said. "Often. And I meant it."

"Well, then," he asked, "what are you kicking about?"

"I'm not kicking," she said. "I'm simply making an observation."

Everything is O.K. now, Brad thought comfortably; everything is happy and peaceful. I'll be running along.

"Going to the rock?" he asked Linda.

"I'm meeting Joel presently," she said.

"That's so," he said. "I think this interest in Joel is highly questionable myself, but that's up to your own conscience."

"And Brad," Linda said, "Pat went down to the beach. He was rather hoping that you'd come there."

"He was, was he?" Brad exclaimed. "He's got nerve!" But he smiled to himself as he thought of Pat running over the sand in his blue bathing trunks, thin, brown, laughing, and teasing like a gently lively little dog. If I could be sure of having a son like Pat, he thought, I might run the risk of getting married.

Dicky opened the door of Ellen's room softly; he'd be hanged if he'd knock. It was bad enough her insisting on a separate room: it made you feel so nice and proud when your wife refused to sleep with you and took every occasion to let people know it.

The room seemed dark after the bright lawn; it did not seem now the room he had always known, with the top shelf in the closet that was such a good hiding place; though the furniture was just the same: the four-poster in the middle with its stiff white curtains, the glassy pictures of the Seven Ages of Man around the walls. Ellen made every bedroom her own as soon as she took possession. Perhaps it was more than anything the perfume that you always noticed, a perfume that sometimes annoyed, sometimes attracted him, that he could never take for granted.

Ellen just now was sitting up in bed, reading; she was wearing her pink satin kimono; her hair was loose.

"Well?" she said. "Did you have a nice time at church?"

"Oh sure," he said. "I had a swell time."

She looked prettier than ever now that she was back from the sanatorium; she looked delicate and wistful and quite irresponsible. It's funny, he thought: my family, Brad and Linda and Father, I can't think of as being any special age; I can't compare them with anyone else; they just are, that's all; it was the same with Mother until her accident, and that is why she seems so different now: she never used to be any age and now suddenly she is old; but Ellen always seems young; you cannot blame her; you cannot treat her as you would an ordinary person.

"I'd have gone with you if you had asked me," she said.

"Humph!" he said. He had asked her last night at

212

supper and she had said she did n't want to be disturbed, but why bring that up?

"Are you cross?" she asked, gently reproachful.

"Cross? No," he said. "What gives you that quaint idea?"

"You are," she said. "I don't know what I can do about it."

Her face looked as if she had expected great things of life and then little by little had learned not to expect them. He remembered how night before last she had come to his room after he was in bed, leaned over him and kissed him, her hair falling about his face and neck; "I know I 'm very trying, Dicky," she had said, "but remember I 'm just back from a sanatorium. It takes a little time to get used to things. And I 'm not well — remember that — I 'm really not well," and he had felt that he loved her more than ever, that if she was not well, it might be his fault, because he had not known how to make her happy: that 's what that damn doctor had implied, and who knows, he might be right after all. That was the trouble: if she really were sick, you could think of the Ellen you loved, the young appealing Ellen who was gentle and kind and sorrowful, as the only real one, and all the rest as just her sickness; and then when you lost your temper you were blaming her for her sickness and making her worse; but then again, he thought, as he looked at her now and felt how he would like to go to her, put his arms around her, and rub his face in her hair, that may all be the bunk: it 's a pretty safe bet, as far as I can discover, that anything is at least seventy-five per cent bunk. But what if it is? What does that do for me? Suppose I left her and then she killed herself or did something crazy just out of spite, how would I feel then? Pretty fine? Yes?

213

"Brad's slinging a beach party to-night," he said. "Want to come?"

"Of course I want to come," she said. "Supper, Dicky?"

"He thought we'd better wait until after supper," Dicky said, "on account of Mother. She sort of hates to have us go off too early."

"I could stay with her," Ellen suggested. "I'd love to if she'd like to have me; but I don't suppose she would. She hates me."

Dicky smiled at her shrewdly: just try to keep Ellen at home, just take her at her word, and see what would happen.

"You better come," he said; "I did n't know whether you'd feel up to it."

"Now you're being sarcastic," she remarked. "It's not becoming to you, Dicky. As a matter of fact my main reason for wanting to go to-night would be to watch Linda and Joel."

"Linda and Joel?"

"Why do you pretend to be so innocent?" she asked. "What's the point, Dicky? You blame me for pretending, and what about you?"

"I don't get you," he said. "I don't get you at all."

"You amuse me," she said, with a taut smile, "you really do. You and Brad both. You pretend to know so much; you talk as if I did n't know anything, and then you don't notice the most obvious things in the world. Do you mean to tell me you have n't guessed that Linda and Joel are in love?"

"Don't be ridiculous," he said.

"Will you answer me a simple question?" she asked. "Just why is n't Thornton here this summer?"

214

"Because he's cruising with Jim Ballou. You know it as well as I do."

"And you think he'd be gone all summer if there wasn't some reason, do you? As a matter of fact I suspected something might be wrong as soon as I heard he was going."

"You would," Dicky said.

"I would and I did," she said, "and when we saw Joel in New York, and I saw the self-conscious roundabout way he was asking for Linda, I guessed then and there what was up, and the way Linda's answered things I've asked her about Joel and Thornton has made it perfectly clear."

"Don't be ridiculous," he repeated irritably. If Ellen were going to spread concoctions of this sort she would be making trouble.

"You noticed last night at supper the neat way Linda arranged to be the one to meet him?" she asked.

"I thought Linda was your friend," he said contemptuously.

"She is. She's my best friend, and I don't blame her in the least. I never did like Thornton and I think Joel's *most* attractive. I never realized how attractive he was until I saw him the other day in New York. Talk about sex appeal!" She laughed. "If Linda wasn't my dearest friend," she went on, "and I wasn't pretty sure she was in love with Joel, I think it's quite possible that I'd have an affair with him myself."

Dicky laughed roughly; so she was coming back again to the subject of "affairs." Good Lord!

"You try it," he said, "and see what happens."

"You wouldn't know anything about it," she said, "so don't flatter yourself."

"Look here," he exclaimed, "what's the point in talking

215

about men this way, Ellen? You 've talked about nothing but affairs and how handsome this man is and what fun it would be to pick up a good-looking sailor, and stuff like that, ever since I called for you at Dr. Winkleman's. It 's all very well if you want to tease me, and make me uncomfortable, — which it does n't do, by the way, except that I hate to see you make an ass of yourself, — but there 's such a thing as running a joke into the ground. It begins to get tiresome."

As he watched her eyes harden and grow dark, her face become set (how many times, he thought, how many dozen times, have I seen her face change in just that way?), he knew that it was foolish, useless, for him to have lost his temper, but good Lord, there was a limit to what anyone could stand. "So you think I 'm joking, do you?" she said fiercely and yet softly, as if she were keeping her voice small so that her words would thrust themselves more deeply into the tenderest pockets of his mind. "You think I don't mean it. You think I 'm cold, do you: just because I was always cold to you, and no wonder? Well, I 've learned some things in the last few months: I 've learned what 's the matter with me and what 's the matter with you."

Dicky bit his lips, sucked in his cheeks; she 's crazy, he kept muttering to himself; don't pay any attention; it will pass; she 'll be sorry.

"And you learned all this at the sanatorium," he asked, "from your precious Dr. Winkleman? It must be some place."

"Never mind where I learned it," she said, "and never mind who I learned it from. Sometime I may tell you and you won't thank me. I could tell you a lot, but you can take my word for it you would n't thank me."

"Do you know what you remind me of?" he asked. He hardly knew what he was going to say, what words to choose; but as he looked at her pale sharp face, thrust a little towards him, the eyes staring so venomously into his, he knew all at once that she hoped he would call her names: that the more insulting, the coarser they were, the more she would enjoy it. He began to tremble all through as if he had stayed in swimming too long, and hated himself because he could not stop. Then he turned his back on her and went out of the room, taking care to close the door quietly because he knew that she would like him to slam it.

Through the branches of the tulip tree Linda saw Dicky come out the back door and start walking down the path to the garden.

"Oh Dicky," she called, "Brad did n't go to the rock. He went to the beach."

"O.K.," Dicky called back. "I guess I 'll keep on to the rock."

So Ellen had been making another scene. As she watched Dicky's white shirt move through the dark acid-looking shadows under the trees Linda thought of her own scene with Ellen night before last: Ellen had come to her room and asked her why she was so cold to her, and Linda, thinking of Dicky's misery, had talked to her for the first time in their acquaintance with complete frankness. "You say people don't like you," she had told Ellen. "You say they don't take you seriously. How can you expect anyone to like you when you act like such a selfish little fool? If you don't behave yourself and act like a sane person, I 'm through with you, Ellen. I mean it." Ellen had flung her arms about her and admitted everything. "You don't know how much good you've done me," she had sobbed. "It shows real friendship, Linda. If only other people would be frank with me like that and not try to deceive me! And promise me one thing, that's all I ask. Promise me that you will scold me again when you think I need it. . . . Because I will. I know I will . . . and if I can count on you . . ." What can you do after that? Linda thought: what's the point of going through that identical scene regularly once a week, or once a month even: because that is what it would be.

"I never like it when one of the boys goes off the rock alone," Mother said. "Your grandfather was a splendid swimmer. He went swimming once in the North Sea where the water's so very cold; but he always said when you went in swimming off the rock it was just as well to have somebody with you."

"If you're going to be meeting Joel," Father said, and she knew he was virtuously controlling an impulse to speak sharply to Mother, "I advise you to be on your way. It's five minutes of twelve."

"Yes, I know," she said, and knew that she had known it for the last ten minutes, ever since Dicky had gone into the house; had known it and yet had kept putting off the instant of starting. Why? Because there was so much that was confused and uncertain about meeting Joel, so many questions that might have so many different answers. Was he really well again, cured of his jaundice? Poor Joel, it was like his entering the army in quest of heroic adventure and being put in charge of venereals in Iowa. We joked about leprosy, she thought, but certainly it never occurred to us that he would come back before the work had more than started because the food disagreed with him; I think he would have preferred leprosy. And why

218

did he stay in New York instead of coming here at once? And what happened there? But she knew that the real question was whether Joel when she saw him now would be the same Joel she had loved, or would this be like Thornton's return, and those few days with Joel prove merely a foolish sordid mistake? Everything I have done so far seems to have been a mistake, she thought, everything I have done and everything I have not done; so I suppose this will be too: when people are always making mistakes it must be themselves that are wrong; you like to blame the things outside, but you know really that it is you. Of course when I think of Joel and me, and how we feel toward each other, I don't think of Pat or Mother or Thornton or anyone else; and everyone always has to be thought of somehow: sooner or later you must think of them, but the trouble is they won't stay still for you to see them, for you to be able to feel what they must be feeling, for you to know which is the more important, your feeling or theirs, for you to be able to guess just how far and in what way your own changing will make changes for them.

"If you're going into the house," Father said, "I wish you'd tell Myra to bring out your mother's medicine. And Linda," he called, as she started towards the piazza, "tell her to bring out *Barchester Towers* when she comes. It's on your mother's work table."

That was nice at any rate, that Father would be reading to Mother, that you could think of them for hours every day going through Trollope. On the bank Linda turned to wave at them; and as she looked back over the lawn, with Mother in her wheeled chair, a blue and white homespun blanket across her knees, and Father beside her, rocking slowly back and forth, Father with his cheeks, the top of his head, so burned, so very pink in contrast to the black clerical clothes that he would not wear, if he could help it, except on Sundays — as she turned and waved to them, a small cloud passed over the sun and every color changed: the lawn and the trees became dark and bluish and yet intensely green; beyond the hedge and the fields, all pink grass tops and daisies, the ocean, still in sunlight, seemed thrust far away into a sunny airy world that had nothing to do with this shadow; and for a minute everything in life seemed no longer complicated, surrounding, distracting you on every side, but thin and clear, spread out like a series of brittle glazed pictures: Mother and Father here on a lawn by a tulip tree; Brad playing with Pat on a beach with neat waves, and figures crowding the sand all around them; Dicky poised on a rock about to dive; Joel on a train with spirals of smoke blown across the fields and over the bay to Conanicut. They were all there, Mother and Father and the rest (even Thornton was somewhere, a thousand miles beyond the horizon on a yacht in the midst of a blue tropical ocean), all existing at the same time, *now,* this very minute, in different places, each one part of a picture (and every one of them you could see, all the pictures in the world, now, this instant, if you could only be there), and all of them were bright and clear but very thin, so thin that you would push your finger through them if you were not careful — push your finger through and find what? You never knew, you never could know, because you did not have time; because before you could touch them, touch any of them, they were changed by magic, they were not quite the same pictures: just as the lawn now was changing as the sun burned through the white rim of the cloud, restored the sparkles to the trees, brought the ocean near again, and made her suddenly realize that time was passing. If she

did not get on her way at once she would be missing
Joel.

Mark watched Luly disapprovingly as she kept screwing
up her face after the medicine. "Ugh!" she exclaimed.
"Ugh, that's perfectly disgusting. I think I'll ask Dr.
Dwight to give me something that does n't taste so
horrid."

Mark beat a tattoo on the book with his fingers but did
not speak.

"That woman likes to pet me," Luly said after a
moment.

"Myra's very fond of you," Mark said curtly.

"Well then, I wish she was n't, because I only like to be
petted by people I'm fond of."

"Oh, do try to accept things as they come!" he snapped.
It was no use, the devil was in him: he had made a resolu-
tion not to lose his temper, not to be even ruffled, all day
long, no matter what happened.

"I won't always accept things I don't like," Luly said,
"any more than you will. She drives me almost distracted
talking about fixing me so or fixing me so, as if I were a
baby. I asked her once how she thought I got along
before she was here to fix me."

Mark kept himself this time from replying. He turned
the pages of the book in search of his place. He knew just
how he looked at this moment: hunched together, with his
lower lip thrust out, and small reptilian eyes. A fat ill-
natured lizard, he thought; that is what I look like; that
is what I feel like: but I hate people to complain; I cannot
help feeling annoyed when people make a fuss. He was so
used to thinking of Luly as strong and active, someone to
depend on, someone to advise him, to manage him, to make

221

things run smoothly, that he simply could not force himself now to see her differently. She is old, he thought; when that man's car knocked her down it aged her ten years; and the old are always difficult: the trouble is that I'm beginning to grow old too; I used to be sweet-natured and long-suffering, but I'm not any more; I think God should begin to give people a discount on their behavior when they reach sixty or possibly sixty-five, and then increase it by a rapidly sliding scale so that when you're seventy, say, you can do anything you want, and make yourself just as disagreeable as you care to, without its doing much to lower your average.

"I wish Dicky wouldn't go off the rock alone," Luly said, "and I wish Ellen would try to be a little more considerate."

"He'll be all right," Mark said, gentle at last, but he hardly saw how anything could be all right for Dicky unless he could shake off Ellen. Divorce, even? The Episcopal Church was strict about divorce: people loved to manage other people's business, tell them what they could do and what they could not; and the Church was just as bad really — at least it could be made just as bad when it spoke through the mouths of pious young fools like this Fairlamb.

"I think perhaps the best thing would be to have your children die young," he said, "and then you'd always have happy memories of them: when they grow up they do nothing but get into trouble and cause their parents worry."

"I think that's rather an exaggeration," Luly said.

"Of course it is," he said. "An exaggeration? Yes — but not so much as you'd think . . ." Mark had found his place; he ran his eyes over the first paragraph: he felt

222

as if he were standing on the threshold of a room full of delightful or amusing people, with a view from the window of gray cathedral towers. Those were more interesting days than the days in which we are living, he thought; I should have lived in England in the middle of the last century; I think I would have appreciated it more than a lot of the Victorians.

"We 're going to see some more of Mr. Slope," he told Luly. "He rather reminds me of myself: the same earnestness and zeal."

He began reading, and as he read he remembered other times, in other years, many other years, when he had read aloud to Luly; and this reading to-day seemed to attach itself to the rest, to become part of all that other reading: not just an end tacked on to something that had gone before, but mixed through all of it, even from the very start, like spring water spreading through a deep quiet pool. From the time they were engaged Luly had liked nothing so much as his reading aloud to her; and now his voice grew more lively, suggesting the different characters: he was not thinking any longer that Luly was old and sick, and that he was growing old, too, and soft and fat, and getting less and less patience with everything every day.

At the end of the chapter he stopped to glance at Luly. She was asleep. It was just as well; probably she was happiest now when she was sleeping. If she could sleep enough, if she would eat enough, she might grow stronger, though he doubted it very much: she had worked too hard all her life. I have never known a woman like Luly, he thought — never; it 's too bad she has to go through this, she must hate it so; I can 't see God's idea — no, I really can't; unless it is to make death acceptable . . . to her and to all of us.

223

Luly's head stirred, her lips trembled as if through her sleep she had noticed the stopping of his voice. "Mother?" she said at last, plaintively, anxiously, like a child. "Mother?"

II

LINDA walked down the platform, away from the little station. It was warmer here than at the Grove, though there was still a faint breeze: it brought to her a smell of cinders, of tepid smoke, a stale fishy smell from the harbor; it stirred the dust on the street, sifting it into the vacant lot behind her car, and making even grayer the trampled grass (trampled by boys playing ball; but now the lot was empty: everyone must be at the beach or swimming off the wharves). Joel will be arriving, she thought; in a few minutes Joel will be arriving *here*. So much may happen in railway stations, such exciting meetings and departures! The trains going out of them, connecting with every other place, seem to set them apart, to give them a different quality from the rest of the town, the ordinary business streets and the houses where people live. This station itself is so insignificant, with its little waiting room always too hot, and its news stand, and the carved initials, the penciled names on its walls, it is so ordinary, so like thousands of other stations (only the smell from the wharves and the whistles from the boats are different), that you hardly can believe it exists except when the trains come in or puff slowly out, except for those few moments that may be so important and exciting; you can imagine that at all other times, if you happen to

225

pass by, to think to yourself, "That is the station," it only puts up the barest show of existence, just enough for you to take it for granted and not be surprised that it is n't there.

There *was* the sound of a train: a curl of white smoke cast a shadow across the roofs: the station, the platform, the dust on the street, even those empty cars on the other track, became more and more charged with life, as if the vibration of the approaching train, — the train bringing Joel, who must now be standing up, putting on his coat if he had one, feeling for his bag, wondering if she were going to meet him, — as if that vibration sent through everything, through metal and wood and living nerves, an electric current so intense you could hardly bear it.

The engine appeared in the cut: a minute now! She walked quickly down the platform toward the station, so that she would be beside the cars when the train stopped. It was passing her; she looked into the windows as they moved slowly by, searching for Joel, but she could not find him. Where was he? How could she have missed him? Then between her and the station Joel, with a huge bag, an old felt hat (it was the hat that told her it was he), swung off the front end of the first car just before it stopped, turned, waved his arm, and came to meet her, one shoulder pulled down by the weight of his bag. A moment ago, she thought, while she hurried down the platform to meet him, smiling, staring at him hard in her effort to see him, but still not quite able to manage it (like suddenly changing the focus of your gaze from something dim on the horizon to something intricate and sharp that you were holding in your hand), a moment ago he was somewhere else, in a time and place that belonged

not to here and now but to his months away, to the far
other places where he has been traveling: he was a remembered Joel who changed as I kept changing, a possible
future Joel who was simply a reflection of the one I
remembered, like a cloud that you look at upside down in
a lake; and now the Joel I am meeting, this thin, rather
yellow Joel steadily returning my gaze, has just by his
appearance at the instant he stepped off the train become
the only real one, and that remembered changing one,
who might be anywhere in the world since he was not with
me, has vanished as quietly as the smoke that a minute
ago was casting its shadow on those housetops.

"Joel," she said. "How are you?"

"I'm fine," he said. "This is great, Linda. I hoped
you might meet me."

"Of course I was going to meet you," she said, pretending to be hurt by his doubt, to be teasing him, simply
because at such a moment you had to pretend something or
you could not find words. "What do you think I am?"

He put down his bag; they shook hands; like people
on a railroad poster, she thought, except that there is no
porter to smile in the background; then for a moment
they stood, not speaking, simply staring at each other, forgetting even to stop smiling, though their smiles were the
smiles of a moment before and had nothing to do with
this moment.

She turned away with a deep comfortable feeling that
his being there did not depend on her looking at him.
"I left the car across the street," she said.

"I know," he said. "That's where you always leave
it, don't you? I saw it while the train was pulling in,
before I saw you."

It is not like Thornton's return, she thought; I need not

227

have been afraid; perhaps I was never genuinely afraid; perhaps all the time I was deliberately torturing myself as an insurance against possible disappointment, or a peace offering to the gods, the way Greek mariners threw bits of their cargoes into the sea. If we had met by ourselves he would have put his arms around me, we would have kissed each other instead of shaking hands; but it makes no difference: the most formal nod, the most passionate embrace, neither one could have had anything to do with that moment of getting used to seeing him, of knowing that he is here.

As Linda drove through Newport, Joel looked eagerly at the houses and streets, at the glossy sunlight on the leaves: he would have liked to dip his hands and arms in it as if it were spray. The air was so smooth, so sweet, so filled with the suggestion of clouds and gardens and boats, that he wanted to take it not only into his lungs but into his veins, to shed his skin like a snake so that it would touch him more closely; but all this, the light and softness of it, was part of Linda: it existed only for her, through her; even his feeling of other years, other summers, that, for him, buried this town, this whole region, as deeply as the lost city of Ys under the Breton sea, in a crystal fluid shot through, when it was faintly stirred, with the softest of prismatic lights, even this had become to-day only a reflection of Linda. Always it was Linda's presence that he was feeling: the presence of this Linda whom he had seen on the platform, who now was so near him that he could touch her with his hand if he did not feel a strange physical shyness, as if they both were children; but this Linda was herself only a sign, a promise, of the elusive, the unchanging Linda who kept, and would always keep, just beyond the

228

glance of his eyes, the touch of his hands, and would come only now and then, for the shortest of stays, to the room that was ready day or night to receive her, in the deepest centre of his mind.

"How cool it is up here," he said. "What beautiful weather!"

"Was it hot in New York?" she asked.

"It was like hot glue," he said. "It smelled like a swamp full of alligators and snapping turtles. You know the way alligators smell."

"No, I don't," she said, "and I'm sure that you don't either; but if it was so unpleasant, Joel, why did you stay so long — almost a week, wasn't it? I think I have a right to be very angry with you."

"Oh, I'll tell you," he said gayly. "I'll confess everything, and what a tale it is! You wouldn't believe it, Linda, but until I arrived here, just a few minutes ago, I was pretty desperate. That was one of the reasons I didn't come sooner, by the way. My mind was like a moist collapsed lung, or some kind of slimy luke-warm jelly, the kind of jelly that might be spawned by a fish, full of eggs that didn't hatch and were getting staler and staler every day."

"But are you well, Joel?" she asked. "You look very thin. You're sure you've recovered?"

"Oh, I'm splendid," he said. "It was nothing more than a long bilious attack, that's all; some kind of germ, I guess, that they finally got rid of. The hospital wasn't so bad, though it was hot as Hades most of the time and it was apt to stink. What made me sore was thinking what I might have been doing if I didn't have to be there."

They were driving now down the hill to the First Beach: its shoddy pink plaster, the white skeleton of the roller coaster behind it, looked gay and neat this morning against the blue.

"I've noticed you're not telling me anything," Linda said. "I'm beginning to get very suspicious, Joel. I didn't know what had happened. I could imagine anything after your letter day before yesterday."

"Not really?" he asked. "Was I as bad as that? It was nothing, as a matter of fact. I mean, you can see the whole thing as perfectly ludicrous, as a farcical joke, but the joke's on me. That's the trouble. My letter didn't seriously worry you, did it, Linda?"

"Well," she said, "I made a certain allowance for your literary style, Joel, and you did volunteer that you hadn't done anything yourself, though of course I wasn't sure whether I ought to believe you."

He laughed. "I knew I'd be seeing you so soon," he explained, "and at the time it seemed so absurd and so wretched that I couldn't bear to write it out. But look, Linda, if you really want me to tell you, though now it seems completely unimportant, at least as far as it concerns me, why don't we park the car somewhere before we get to the Grove, and talk for a few minutes. Will you? Let's do that. In the dunes behind the Second Beach. That's just the place."

"It must be after half past twelve," she said. "We don't have lunch till half past one, but the family will be expecting us. What could we tell them?"

"Oh, tell them we had errands," he suggested, "or that we ran out of gas or knocked down a child or two and had to take them to the hospital."

It was such high tide that there were no cars on the beach, and the waves broke only a few yards from the

230

foot of the dunes.   As they sat down beside each other on
the sandy crest, Linda turned her head to look backward
over the marshes, and there, two miles away, beyond the
Third Beach and the pale bright fields, was the Grove,
shining between the trees like the miniature white façade
of a temple.   "If Brad happened to be training his telescope in our direction," she said, "he could easily recognize us."

"Well," he said, "we've certainly been most respectable
so far, Linda."

She met his gaze for the first time since their shaking
hands at the station, and as she saw his brown deep-set
eyes staring at her so fixedly, his mouth slightly strained
into a smile, as she caught the feel of his thickness, his
gentleness (he might be a prince, she thought, just turned
back into human form from some kind shaggy animal),
she remembered him suddenly as he had looked when he
first stepped into her bedroom that evening last December.
But his arms now were around her body; he was kissing
her and it seemed impossible that for months he had not
been kissing her.   Then, as abruptly as he had taken her,
he let her go.

"Joel," she said, slightly laughing, out of breath, "is
that what you call respectable?"

"I call it damn respectable," he said, "under the circumstances," and as he spoke he settled himself a few feet
below her on the side of the dune.

"And now, Joel," she said after a minute.   "Tell me.
Tell me everything."

"Oh, all right," he said, "but it seems now so utterly
ridiculous, so beside the point.   I'm afraid you'll think
I've been very mysterious over a little thing, but at the
time it did seem pretty damnable, I admit.   I wrote you

231

that Dicky and Ellen met my boat, did n't I? I guess she 'd only been out of the sanatorium for a few days. They asked me to dine in their apartment, and Dicky had to go out afterwards to interview a man to see if he could sell him something, whatever he 's trying to sell; and that damn little minx, believe it or not, began to make love to me. You know she 's mad, Linda. I honestly believe it and it turned my stomach, literally. It was as if a sly evil animal had crept in and was staring out at you or rather evading your eyes even while she stared. It made me think of *Lady into Fox* . . . and the worst is I could n't feel sorry for her, though I suppose I ought to. I just felt disgusted, and presently I got up and left, and I will hand it to myself that I don't think she even guessed that I caught on."

"It does n't surprise me," Linda said, "not in the least, but I don't think it means anything, do you?"

"I don't know what it means," he said, "but I know I could n't stand it."

"I 'm sure it 's just one of her ways, Joel. Poor thing, she 's always contriving new ones and they are always so much alike. But as far as you 're concerned, I don't see how you can blame her. It's your own fault for being so beautiful, so perfectly charming."

"That 's right," he said. "Laugh at me. I deserve it."

"I 'm not laughing at you," she said, "but you have n't told me yet why you did n't come sooner. You did n't have other affairs, did you, Joel? I see I shall have to be fearfully jealous."

"Oh, it 's nothing interesting," he said. "I was look-ing for a job, that 's all — something decent to do; so I would n't be coming up here and urging you to get a divorce and marry me with my complete financial status about ninety dollars in the bank."

"Did you get one?" she asked.

"No," he said. "Of course I did n't." *

"I 'm glad, Joel."

"Why are you glad?" he asked reproachfully.

"Because it will give me more time to decide what I must do."

"There can be only one possible decision as far as that goes," he said, "but I suppose, apart from the way I feel, that there is no hurry. You see, I could have got something, I 'm sure, something pretty good, in the tea business, with either of the companies I 've worked for. I know quite a lot about tea, from the business end; it 's the one thing I do know anything about, strangely enough; but I just could n't bear to, if I could avoid it — going back into business."

"What kind of a job are you looking for?" she asked.

"Oh, nothing revolutionary," he said, "at least not just yet. Perhaps I 'll come to that one of these days. What I 'd like now would be some kind of a job in a museum, in connection with American Indians, or possibly field work in the West. But I can't think of jobs this morning. Tell me about Thornton, Linda. How has he taken all this? You say I did n't write details; well, you certainly did n't either. I suppose I ought to feel guilty toward Thornton, but I don't in the least. I never did for a moment, perhaps because I 've always been so jealous of him."

"Have you, Joel? I 'm glad you have, but there was no reason for it since I 've really grown up. If I did n't write you it was because I did n't know what to write: I would n't know now, Joel. He was certainly shocked when I told him, and hurt and very much surprised; I told him as soon as I got home; I did write you that; but I think it was more at the idea that his wife should have a lover — a 'nice girl' like me, from a respectable home — than any sharp personal feeling. He was very quiet and reasonable when I talked to him, with the air of being willing to understand my point of view, to make allowances, that you only see in people who you know never could really understand. It may be mean of me, Joel, but I couldn't feel grateful to him, because I kept feeling that his quietness was not in the least for me but all for himself: so that he could think, 'How quiet, how considerate I'm being, how thoroughly decent, how infinitely superior to her!' His main idea from the first was to keep up appearances — for my sake, he said, which of course is nonsense — even if we stopped living together as husband and wife."

It's strange, she thought, that never since we were married have I been quite able to imagine what he was feeling at any given moment: now and then perhaps I have come pretty near it, when he has grown white and angry at seeing some animal mistreated (the only times I've seen him very angry); once or twice when he has been playing with Pat or talking about Pat, though then I'm not so sure; but never in connection with me. You can think of him as not feeling anything quite genuinely; you can think of his modest genial manner as a cloak for a persistent conventionality, a subtle egotism (it's so much easier to think of him that way now that I must guard against it); or you can think of him as simple and easygoing, truly modest and kind, but certainly there are no deep darks and no very high lights; certainly for years I at least have been able to find nothing that could stir my curiosity in more than the faintest way, although I realized my ignorance.

"But he would give you a divorce?" Joel asked after a moment. "Do you think he would, Linda?"

"Yes," she said, "I'm sure he would if I insisted, though it's the last thing he wants. But it's not Thornton I'm thinking of, it's Pat. If we should be divorced he would insist on having Pat for at least half the year, and it's only right that he should, and that's what I can't bear to think of, Joel. That's what I put off thinking of as much as I could until I should see you."

"Yes, of course there *is* Pat," Joel said; and he wondered how he could have forgotten him. "Pat wrote me about the nicest letter I've ever received," he said, "to thank me for the stamps I sent him. I hoped he'd write me another, but I don't blame him for not writing because my answer was so childish, such a little-boy kind of thing. I realized that as soon as it was in the mail." What a joy it would be, he thought, to have Pat with me, what a privilege for any grown-up person! Pat and Linda, what a combination! And then Linda and I might have another child, though I don't see how he could approach Pat; one might even start a school, he thought, a kind of advanced school to make children see life as it is, and how so much that passes for life is dead, and that beauty may be achieved but only through courage. . . . Why haven't I thought of such a school, he wondered, as a possible solution for me? Only a few children at first: you would have to feel your way; the simplest kind of a room . . . Good God, he thought suddenly, here I am again planning vague happy things as if I and not Thornton were Pat's father; but of course as things actually are the existence of Pat (dear little boy; how ludicrous that life should contrive a situation where he should loom up as an enemy, an obstacle to happiness) means that possibly all my thoughts of Linda, of our life together, are just as far-fetched, as impractical, as most of my other ideas.

He scowled at the sea: at the small waves spreading their overlapping fringes to smooth and darken, to scatter with bubbles, more and more of the sand; at the straw-colored water of the shallows (still the sand that you were seeing through the water, and if you were bathing now you might see pink transparent-looking crabs scuttling over the ridges of the bottom); at the flashes of white flame, more brilliant even than the swords of the marsh grass, far more brilliant than the foam, sun reflections, themselves reflected in the green curl of the waves; and then beyond, as the water deepened, at the deepening color — emerald, peacock-blue azure: you could not tell where it changed, you could not tell at any given spot just what color it was; and in spite of its brilliance it was somehow airy, im-material, a filmy background for those stabbing, blinking sparks. When you look at a sight like this, he thought, when you feel the sun and smell that far-away air (the same air that is pushing that faint blue ship over the horizon), there seems no excuse why everything should not be simple and natural and beautiful. It was always in some such place that I imagined Linda; I kept thinking that I had only to see her again for everything to straighten out, to become beautiful like this; that all that was neces-sary was somehow to escape from that hellishness; but how could I have thought for a moment that she would give up Pat? I worked out no schemes; I did not think of him at all in connection with our plans, just as I never stop to think at the time I should.

He turned from the sea to look at Linda so close beside

him. She too was looking at the water, or the horizon, her shoulders slightly drooping, her neck bending forwards, her chin raised so that the sun shone directly on her face; her eyelids were half closed to keep out the brightness; her lips were curved downward sadly, but not enough to disturb her air of being withdrawn by herself into some far country, perhaps under the sea or behind that dense soft sky, and leaving this wistful face, this smooth delicate body poised on the rim of the dune like a sea bird resting for a moment on the edge of a wave, simply to reassure him, because she was kind-hearted and gracious, that sooner or later she would return. She might be Andromeda, he thought, or Ariadne, or any beautiful young woman, in any time or place, in Crete or Egypt, in Brittany or Ireland, sitting alone, withdrawn and gazing over the sea; and yet of all those possible ones I know that it will be Linda who will come back; and I feel that if I have to leave her, if I cannot be on hand to greet her after her plumy secret flights, there can be no more joy for me in living.

"Well," he asked, "now that you have seen me, Linda, what's the verdict?"

Linda looked at Joel, almost startled, his voice sounded so gruff, his face was so grim.

"But how can I tell?" she asked. "You mustn't be angry with me, Joel. How can I tell? The thing is, you see, the moment I saw you I knew that I loved you as much as I thought I did. If I were courageous, I suppose, I might admit to myself that I've found that I can't give you up, and it's that that makes me realize, now for the first time, what it would mean to me to give up Pat, to have to share him with Thornton."

If only, she thought, you could see both things at once,

237

equally near or equally far away; but I cannot: I see first one and then the other, and the one I am not seeing I am simply remembering, and I cannot compare the two. It is like the time I was visiting the Chases in the country — I must have been about Pat's age — and Mother telephoned to see whether I would like to stay longer or whether they should drive out to get me; and I could not make up my mind; I remember I cried into the telephone; and at last I told them to come and then I was more and more sorry, because there were baby puppies, and Helen had planned for us to take our lunch to the brook field the next day, and I kept seeing the brook field and could not bear not to be going; and then when Mother and Father arrived I got up my courage to tell them I wanted to stay after all, and they were very kind, not cross or amused, and had tea on the piazza; but then as I watched the carriage driving down the lane without me, taking them home, I suddenly felt that I would die if I could not go with them. I 've been that way, she thought, about so many things; and it 's not so much deciding between the happiness that each will bring you if you choose that one as the regret, the sadness, you will feel if you do not choose it.

Suddenly she remembered Pat, years ago, standing beside her in the animal tent of a circus, among the crowd; they were looking at the hippopotamus and people were rather laughing at it, and she exclaimed to Pat, "How ugly he is!" and Pat beside her frowned and said in a gruff voice: "I like him. It 's not the looks that count, it 's the goodness." She had told it several times as an amusing remark; but she never would forget Pat's little scowling face, the reproving fierceness with which he defended that huge torpid beast. She turned again to look behind her

238

across the marsh and the blue harbor to the Grove, so white and neat among its trees: Pat was there under those trees or in that house, not suspecting or dreaming of what was in her mind, counting on her absolutely, without question; Mother and Father were there, and Dicky and Brad; perhaps even now they were looking across at the dunes and the sea beyond.

"Linda," Joel said so abruptly that it startled her, "I don't know why I asked you just now what you were going to do, because I know there's only one possible thing. I let you get away from me years ago when you married Thornton, and I've cursed myself ever since. It's not going to happen again."

He scrambled to his feet and sat down very close beside her.

"No," she said, "Joel, no — it's late — we must be getting back," but she knew that her words would not stop him, and knew, as for the second time this morning she felt his kisses, that she had not been so happy since those winter nights which afterwards, when Joel was away, had hardly seemed real, because you could not believe in such happiness.

Then all at once, to her surprise, she found that she was sobbing.

WITH a look of pious resignation Mark put down one more game for Brad in his book. "Do you know what that makes?" he asked. "Two hundred and twenty-nine for you against one hundred and forty for me. It does n't seem respectful, Brad. It does n't seem decent. I should think you 'd be afraid she-bears would come out of the swamp and devour you, the way they did the children who shouted 'Go up, thou bald head,' to Elisha. I 'd a good deal rather have you address me in those terms than run off with nearly every game the way you do."

"Yes?" said Brad. "Why don't you do something about it, then? Why don't you show a little intelligence?"

"I do show intelligence," Mark said. "That 's just the trouble. I show intelligence but no instinct. Now you have the instinct, Brad, and while I would n't go so far as to say you have no intelligence . . ."

"No, I would n't," Brad said, "if I were you."

"I 've always wanted to preach on the text, *Go up, thou bald head*," Mark said, "but I could never think of a sermon to go with it."

"By the way, Parson," Brad said, "when you preach at the chapel these next two Sundays, for God's sake stop in time. You 're getting an awful habit of running on after you 've finished."

240

"No, am I, Brad? Not like that young Fairlamb this morning, I hope. That would be too terrible. But I have the excuse of age, Brad. One of the tragedies of age is that the more senile you get and the less people want to hear you, the more garrulous you grow. I realize it. I shall have to limit myself rigidly to twenty minutes, with a possible emergency allowance of two or three more."

"Fifteen would be better," Brad said.

"Oh no, Brad, you must n't be too brutal. We 'll say twenty, because it 's not as if I were a dull preacher; you must take that into consideration. I do have an instinct for preaching, even if I don't for chess."

"Humph," Brad exclaimed, "I should say your average is about one in three either way."

"One in three! But that 's an enormously high batting average for sermons."

Mark put away the score book in the top drawer of his desk.

"What 's the matter?" Brad asked. "Afraid to play another?"

"I promised Pat I 'd do stamps with him presently," Mark said. "The last time I promised you lured me into a game against my conscience — so I think I ought to keep my word to-day."

"Clever alibi!" Brad exclaimed. "Well, I don't know as I blame you." He yawned and pulled out his watch. "It 's ten minutes of three," he said. "I 'll give Pat till three and then if he 's not here we 'll play. My time 's valuable, but I hate to stop with two twenty-nine. I 'd rather make it a round number."

Mark caught himself sinfully wishing that Pat would not arrive until after three; not that he did n't enjoy putting in stamps with him but because the temptation was so keen to be able, perhaps, to mark down a game to his own credit to balance this one for Brad. It's Satan's usual mode of approach, he thought; I can feel him working in my mind with the identical tactics he employs when he's urging on gamblers to lose their fortunes and turn their helpless offspring into the street, or brokers to speculate on margin with the funds of widows and orphans; but after all, in regard to its possible results, it is comparatively harmless, and perhaps if I didn't allow the devil these mild triumphs he would seek his revenge by some major onslaught that I might be too weak to resist (though that argument, I'm afraid, is so Jesuitical that God would reject it at once as insincere, unless perhaps from the very highest churchmen). My real excuse, he thought, is that I do need something now and then, something interesting and impersonal, to take my mind off domestic affairs, if I hope to keep any remnant of my better nature and not become a hopeless victim of senile irritability and nerves. This will be a trying summer, he thought, trying in every way, with poor Luly so helpless, with Dicky on the hair trigger most of the time, with that impossible Ellen.

"I think it would be nice if you'd have a little music to-night, before you leave for the beach," he suggested. "I think your mother would appreciate it. She was saying the other night that you hadn't played since you got here."

"Sure," Brad said. "We could have a sonata or two, I suppose, if you think Mother would like it."

"How do you think she's been these last few days?" Mark asked.

"Well," Brad said, "I don't think she seems much weaker

than she did when I was in North Chester, and that was nearly two months ago."

"The doctor says there's nothing organically wrong with her," Mark said, "but I can't believe it. She is failing, Brad, if not from day to day, from week to week. She has less and less energy, and less and less interest . . . and of course she's growing fussy. If she could have her way, she'd have you sitting in the room for her to look at indefinitely. She's like the omphalopsychites who spent hours looking at each other's navels. She'd like to have all her family seated about her. I'm beginning to get a line on men like Charles M. Baxter who haunt the bedsides of senile old women and get millions out of them for their pet charities. Anyone could get anything out of your mother he wanted to."

"Not if *she* did n't want him too," Brad said.

"You could make her want to," Mark said.

"I doubt it," Brad said. "Mother's very weak, of course, but she knows more of what's going on than you give her credit for."

"Well, perhaps she does," Mark admitted, "but I hate to think so because the more she realizes things the harder it must be for her. I say she's fussy; well, of course I am too . . . and she has every excuse for being and I don't; but of course your mother's a saint, and one of the disadvantages of sainthood is that no one makes allowances for you. I seem to be in pretty robust health, but if I die one of you would have to look out for her, and I think you would be the logical one, Brad, because then there would be no question of her being a parasitic in-law, which is an impossible thing under the best of circumstances. Of course Ellen would be out of the question; Thornton would be very decent, I'm sure, but I should hate to complicate his household; and I think perhaps you 're her favorite, Brad; she talks about you a good deal. I have no favorite; I don't like any of you."

"I think she may get her strength back this summer," Brad said. "I really do, Parson. I 've had sort of an idea of your retiring and my lugging you both abroad in the fall if I could manage the time."

"Well," Mark said, "I don't know . . . but I 'll be very much surprised if she gets on her feet . . . ever."

It is doubtful charity, he thought, to wish for recovery for the aged, unless you are pretty sure they can get back their normal strength and energy — and that almost never happens; they sink and recover a little and sink again, and the stronger they were, the more they did with their lives, the more pitiable it is. Suppose I were to have a stroke, he thought, or some lingering disease so that I could not read or walk about or play chess: I might resent at times being a Christian and hence forbidden to put myself out of the way. Of course such a condition might offer me a chance to achieve sainthood, but I 'm afraid that 's beyond me; I can hardly aspire to it. Saints, I feel sure, are born and not made; I 'm enough of a Calvinist to believe that: in any walk of life Luly would have been a saint (and possibly at times being married to me was as much of a test as any, though I hope not too often), and I fear I never could have been one even if I had gone to the South Seas as a missionary, or to any of those remote inconvenient places I used to imagine I might go when I was in the seminary; if I had gone into the wilds I think I would have done fairly good work; but I probably would have got along better with the natives than with my fellow missionaries, and if there were cannibals my sympathies would probably have been

just as often with the eaters as with the eaten, which
might have put me in rather awkward situations.

"You know, Brad," he said, "if I should ever become
a chronic invalid, I hope you will devise some scheme to
get rid of me. I would n't want there to be any mess, and
I certainly would n't want you to get into trouble, but
if you could contrive to slip me an overdose of medicine
. . . or I tell you what: suppose I should arrange to
murder Ellen in some expeditious and humane fashion.
Then, you see, I 'd be killing a number of birds with
one stone: I 'd get rid of her; I 'd be hung and thus
spared years of being a burden to my family, and yet
I 'd avoid the sin of suicide. I don't see why God
should n't forgive me for making away with Ellen. It
would be partly at least an act of sacrifice for the sake
of one of my children, and that ought to rate pretty
high. I don't see how I could be damned for it, do
you?"

"Damned for it?" Brad said. "Hell no, you 'd win
a martyr's crown."

"No, I could hardly hope for that," Mark said, "because my motives would be rather mixed after all; and
it would be difficult not to get a certain element of personal satisfaction from the deed. Of course I should
dislike having a scandal connected with this lovely place,
and one disadvantage of being a clergyman is that the
most ordinary and moderate crimes make you notori-
ous."

Brad looked at his watch. "It 's after three," he said.
"We 'll have no more stalling. Hurry up. Get your
men ready."

Rather guiltily Mark began arranging his men: if Pat
arrives before Brad makes his first move, he thought,

we'll postpone the game; and just as Brad was touching his pawn, Pat appeared in the doorway.

"Ready, Grandpapa?" he asked.

Mark looked at Brad. "I'm afraid it's the Lord's will I shouldn't play," he said.

"Ridiculous!" Brad exclaimed. "It's after three. Come here, Pat. So you expect your grandfather to do stamps with you, do you? You wouldn't mind waiting for half an hour or so, I suppose?"

"I've been waiting ever since lunch," Pat said, and gazed at Mark with a look that showed more reproach than surprise.

Mark smiled at him apologetically. "I know, Lamb," he admitted. "I did say I'd do stamps with you, but your Uncle Brad is so very insistent. I don't suppose you'd consider calling it square if we did some stamps right after supper."

"Darn Brad," Pat said, scowling at his uncle.

"Don't call me Brad," Brad commanded. "Call me either Uncle Brad or Mr. Waring, do you hear?"

Pat smiled suddenly. "I will too call you Brad," he said, and reached toward the chessboard as if to sweep the men out of position.

"Don't you dare touch those men," Brad exclaimed, "or you'll wish you'd never been born."

"Is it all right for this evening, Lamb?" Mark asked.

"Oh sure," Pat said. "I suppose so. I kind of thought there wouldn't be many stamps this afternoon when I saw you starting to play chess. That's a funny-looking one. What's it called?"

"That's a knight," Mark told him.

Pat laughed. "It's a funny knight," he exclaimed, "with a horse's head; and I don't see any armor."

246

"That's so he wouldn't drown if he fell overboard," Brad said, and Pat laughed again.

"I bet you that's how they invented diving suits," he said, "sometime when a man in armor fell overboard."

Brad stared at him, frowning: "That's an intelligent remark, isn't it?" he asked. "Now you run along, and I suppose I'll have to give you something for not making a fuss. How about a twenty-cent special-delivery stamp the next time I go to the post office? You haven't one of them, have you?"

"Oh, that would be swell!" Pat exclaimed. "But you don't have to give me anything. I guess I just as lief go fishing."

Pat walked slowly to the door. "I hope Grandpapa wins," he called back, and ducked out of the room as Brad pretended to rise in pursuit.

"Now hurry up, Parson," he said. "It's your turn. Don't sit all day. It won't do you any good."

No, Mark thought, I'm afraid it won't; and if I get what I deserve this sinful game will merely increase Brad's lead by one. If only I might be allowed to catch up with Brad before I die, and keep ahead of him for perhaps an hour or two! But I'm afraid that is too much to ask; I'm afraid my humiliating score is a just chastisement for my many sins.

IV

DICKY listened at Mother's door; so that was where Linda was; that put her out of the running. He stood for a moment, doubtful, in the centre of the hall. Joel was in his room lying down; poor guy, Dicky thought, he must be pretty well shot if he has to take a nap in the afternoons. Ellen was writing letters, and Dicky knew he was supposed to be guessing whom she was writing to and worrying about it, but he'd be damned if he would; and yet he did; he could hardly keep himself from going to her door and opening it and sticking his head into the room just to hear what she would say, to see how she would look. But he knew exactly how she would look: she would be pleased to be interrupted, would act as if she were not and yet pretending that she was. Damn Ellen, he thought, and walked downstairs. In the library Father and Brad were still playing chess. "Say, you guys," Dicky said, "you'll go crazy if you don't stop that."

"Hush," Father said, and Brad scowled at him.

Dicky stepped into the room and watched Father put out his hand to touch a man, draw it back, put it out again, and at last move the man a few squares forward, cautiously and quickly, as if he hoped Brad would not see. A crazy way to be spending time, Dicky thought,

248

for two grown men; but I don't know, it may be better than most: it's not hurting anyone and it keeps your mind busy, and there are not many things in life you can say as much for.

"How about a set of tennis?" he asked Brad. "If you can tear yourself away."

"Sure," Brad said, "but not now. I have to trim the Parson a couple of more games. About five, perhaps. It will be cooler then, at any rate."

"I want to do something now," Dicky said.

He watched Brad move a man and take one of Father's. "Fool!" Father exclaimed. "I certainly am an unmitigated fool." He looked up at Dicky: "You see, Lamb," he said plaintively, "that was your fault. You disturbed my calculations."

"Like hell," Dicky said. "Well, so long, folks. Have a good time."

He walked on to the piazza and stared over the lawn. I might go sailing, he thought, or I might call up Denny and play a set or two at the Casino, but I hate to fork out the cash, and besides I don't really want to play tennis, I don't want to go sailing. He looked at his watch; it was only half past three: the rest of the afternoon stretched before him like a flat dusty field that you could not see across. If I walked around Sachuest, he thought, and stopped for a couple of cigarettes, that ought to take me until after five.

He walked down the path and out into the road. It was a beautiful day, so clear you could almost see Block Island beyond the point of Newport; you did not often have it as clear as this in July; but he felt that he could not break through to the clearness, the beauty, of the day. He walked fast as if to escape from the vacuum

that surrounded him: it's just as well I could n't dig
anybody up, he thought; why inflict my company on
others when I feel like this?

He stopped at the crossroads. Hell's bells, he exclaimed
to himself, I forgot it was Sunday! There was a line
of cars parked behind the bath houses and reaching almost
to the corner; the sand was crowded with people; even
on the point beyond he could see a dozen cars, and of
course there would be lots of them around the bend, that
you could not see; all Sachuest would be littered with
picnickers and fishermen and necking parties like flies
around a garbage can. What the hell, he thought; I
have n't the energy to walk around there anyway; I'll
keep on to the beach and then turn back along the top
of the cliffs toward the rock; I might go down there
and smoke and get a little more sunburn. Thank God the
crowd does n't seem to drift in that direction — too
much poison ivy, too many brambles, I suppose; and
what an appropriate setting for me just at present:
brambles and poison ivy! If I were in jocund mood I
might attempt a poem.

He cleared his throat and spit in the dust. "And Jesus
spat on the ground," he remembered, "and made clay of the
spittle, and anointed his eyes." I don't believe He could
have done much for me, he thought; but would n't He have
given Ellen a thrill casting devils out of her? Picture
her rolling on the ground at His feet and wiping them
with her hair, and then walking meekly after Him in
some little sackcloth creation; but He would have seen
through her right off the bat. Seen through her! Perhaps Jesus would have managed to make her snap out of
it all; perhaps He would have given the poor kid a
chance. Humph! The kind of chance she wants, if

you can take her at her word, is a couple of prize fighters for husbands, and her always making me feel like such a brute! Was I intelligent? Or I may have been, at that. If I only knew what to believe. But why care? If she is just a young degenerate, why worry about her? And if she is not there's no need for worry. O.K., Boss, that fixes it up fine! I'm all right either way. Worry? Why worry? The very idea!

Poison ivy and brambles, he thought, as he walked past the line of parked cars (and we used to stop coming up from the beach to gather blackberries where those cars are parked): poison ivy and brambles . . .

> See how he scrambles
> Through the brambles
> Getting all hivey
> From the poison ivy.

Not so bad, what? Linda's not the only one in the family with literary talent: the trouble with me is I've never been appreciated: I'm just one of the vast army of the misunderstood. Lucky for me, or I'd be in gaol.

He walked between the bath houses to the beach and, scowling, hurried along the sand to the steps that led up the bank: there may be a lone couple or two shimmying in the grass, he thought, but I doubt it; funny if sometime I should run into Linda and Joel making love; but why think of that? What's the matter with me? He remembered Ellen's faint smile at him when Linda and Joel finally arrived after they had all sat down to lunch. Anyway it's not my business, he thought; if Linda and Joel are lovers it's not my funeral; but the idea of it made him feel queer and uncomfortable: if

251

it were true it was just one of those things that you never would have thought; one of the things, like Mother's being so weak and old, that showed you how everything was changing, how you could not count on anything. And gosh, he thought, if a girl like Linda is not faithful to her husband, — a decent unobjectionable chap like Thornton, — what can you expect from Ellen? One minute I think I'm a fool to be bothered by anything she says (just as I should n't have worried when she told me she had taken poison) and the next minute there seems no earthly reason why she should n't have been sleeping with some man or perhaps more than one: but that would be just as likely if she did n't talk this way. It's like worrying and worrying, he thought, when you have a slight sore throat or a broken-out skin, and wondering whether you will have a Wassermann test: and if it should be negative you will feel like a fool for your worry. Yes, but it might be positive, and then what? You're out of luck, that's all; but there is no test for the good old-fashioned disease that worries me. Oh, Lord, why care? Why bother about trifles? What could be worse than for your wife to feel about you the way Ellen feels about me? That's quite obvious; that's one thing I know; and perhaps any girl I had married would feel just the same way: that's what I don't know, and it may be just as well I don't. "I could tell you a lot of things," she said, "and believe me, you would n't thank me if I did." I've a great mind to challenge her, just to see what she would say — but why give her that satisfaction?

He looked down the shady cliffside through the bayberry, the small twisted cedars, to the water: it was very blue, the kind of peaceful blue that you never saw ex-

cept in the afternoon; he was almost sorry that he had
not taken out the boat. On the other shore the houses
looked slightly pink; the trees were more blue than
green; there was never a place in the world, he thought,
that was half as peaceful and shipshape as Sakonnet looks
from here. He gazed northward up the passage: there
were not nearly so many nets as there used to be; he
could see only one, a half mile beyond the rock — delicate,
transparent, as if it were made of the fine-meshed skeletons
of leaves. On the rock itself there was someone fishing:
would n't you know it! He walked nearer until he
saw that it was only a child: it was Pat. That is Brad's
place he is using, Dicky thought: mine was not quite so
far out, but I think it was a little better on account of
that seaweedy rock just under the surface; there used
to be a lot of cunners around that rock. Dicky stood
watching Pat for a minute to see whether he got a bite.
Pat did not move, did not look up. I 'll smoke a cigarette
here on the grass, Dicky thought, and then I might
venture down and see if I could coax a couple of fish
for Pat.

Seated on the rim of the cliff, Dicky still watched Pat
— so intent, so patient, now and then slightly shifting his
position, but never pulling the line from the water.
What 's he thinking about? Dicky wondered. What did
I use to think of when I was fishing? I 'm darned if I
know. It 's the same water and the same fish, or their
descendants, and for anybody watching from here it
might be the same boy except that the hair is different.
I do remember, though, he thought, the time Joel and
I set fire to the bay bushes; I do sort of remember the
look of the trees with the sun behind them as we would
come back over the hill in the late afternoon; I sort of

half remember it the way you remember a page you tried to read when you were nearly asleep.

And what is on the programme next? he thought suddenly: I go back to a new job in September, selling more insurance for a change, urging men who don't want to see me (and why should they?) to protect their dear ones (and why should they do that? Let 'em starve!); I would have to go back to-morrow if I was n't sponging on Brad . . . and then what? Life with Ellen in our old apartment! Jovial thought! And this is the kind of thing I was dodging shells for, the few that came my way, and thinking I was pretty damn clever. Well, I guess they have the laugh on me after all.

It would n't be a half bad idea, he thought, to start out sometime to swim across to Sakonnet. I could n't make it, of course, never in this world, but there might be a fighting chance. He looked again straight down at the water, dark, almost purple under the cliff, but changing soon to that lovely clear blue: from here, he thought, you would say there was hardly more than a ripple all the way across, but it may be rather choppy out there; I can hear the bell buoy now and then and it must be two miles away. It 's funny, he thought, that there are some things in life that you can love so much, the smell of things, and the feel of things, and the places that you have always known, and yet you don't give shucks for life as a whole; it 's funny the ideas you get: I have a kind of hunch that if I should try to swim to Sakonnet and really made it, it would not be Sakonnet, not the place you drive to by automobile or sail to in a boat, but that kind of peaceful far-away place it looks from over here; it might have been looking at places like that, places seen from a distance, across water, that first

gave people the idea of heaven; at least that's the kind
of place I would vote for. There is no heaven, of course,
that's the bunk too; but I'm just as glad, because that
means there is no hell: it's easy enough from this life
of ours to see where men first got the idea of hell. The
hard thing, he thought, would be making up your mind
to die and then not ducking out of it at the last moment;
but if you started for Sakonnet you could always kid
yourself that you might get there until you were so far
out you could n't make it either way. There might be
a few minutes then that would be pretty bad: you would
be as scared as the devil and start cursing most likely, or
perhaps it would be praying; but the thing to do would
be to remember what you would go back to if you were
rescued, to remember that death would come in a few
years, with life getting worse and worse all the time most
likely, to dive down as deep as you could and start swal-
lowing water. It would only be for a couple of minutes,
like going under ether perhaps, the same choked feeling,
and then nothing at all. It's funny, he thought, if I
were drowning I believe I would remember Mother not
the way she is now but the way she used to be; I believe
if I drowned to-day, when it came to the last minute,
I would feel about the way I'd have felt if I had
drowned when I was a kid. During the war one of the
things I used to hate was the thought not so much of
dying as of being killed over there and shoved into one
of those big military cemeteries so far away from this
place. I used to think if I could be chucked into the
Sakonnet River or into the sea off Sachuest that I would
be satisfied. If I should slip off the rock one of these
fine days, he thought, nobody could be sure it was n't
accidental; it would be sort of low-down to pull a suicide

on your family if people could be sure it was suicide.

If Pat was not there, he thought, I'd have half a mind to go straight down the path and peel off my clothes and start across that channel: in a couple of minutes I'd be passing that red lobster buoy; in about ten minutes I'd be out there where those gulls are flapping; I'd be far enough out to see nearly all of this field if I looked back, the tall dark cliff and the sky bright and empty on top of it; but better not look back or you might weaken, and I'm a great one for weakening. Or you might imbibe a pint of whiskey before you started; then you wouldn't know what was happening, because the main thing would be to go through with it neatly once you had begun. The only thing that would excuse you would be to go through with it; otherwise you would be acting like Ellen.

Pat's bamboo was jerking up and down; he had caught something, by gosh! He raised the pole, swung it around, with a fish flapping violently on the end of the line. That's good, Dicky thought; you always felt sort of silly when you had to go home without a single fish. I might as well go down and clean it for him there on the rock.

"Hi, you," he shouted in a gruff voice, "what are you doing down there?"

Pat looked over his shoulder. As he recognized Dicky he held up his fish and waved it in the air. "Look what I caught," he shouted back. "Isn't he a great big huge one?"

"What's that on your line?" Dicky called. "A piece of bait?"

V

ON the top of his mind Brad was thinking only of what fingers, what bowing to use, recognizing themes, phrases, which he had not heard or thought of since last summer; but underneath, through all the rest of him, there was a sense of rightness and security and peace which rarely came to him except when he was playing, and not always then: it was as if a mesh of very personal, very delicate feelings that were most himself, but that had laid for months forgotten and shapeless, like a clump of seaweed left by the tide, were now little by little being floated in a clear mild stream, so that each stem and blade and fringe trembled and unfolded, took on once more its own softly waving pattern — a living submarine forest beyond the reach of all that disturbed.

Glancing over the end of the keyboard, Linda could see Mother in her big chair by the window, her head leaning back and rather to the side, her face showing only fatigue and a kind of blankness. During supper she had kept speaking of the music and asking them to be sure to play the Brahms sonata, and her favorite Mozart, and one of the Beethoven, like a hungry child imagining the dinner he thinks he could eat; but after the first few bars she had closed her eyes, and when

257

Linda looked at her again just now you could see that she had not the energy to listen. Dicky was playing solitaire, and Ellen, unless she were carried away, could not be expected to enjoy any kind of performance in which she was not taking a part. Joel? Linda wondered; Joel will be staring at my back and brooding, half-disgusted, no doubt, or at least disappointed, because I have avoided him all afternoon and because he must see that I have simply as usual let things drift in my mind and have n't faced anything squarely and show no signs of doing it.

If it were not for these people, she thought, who pretend more or less to be listening, if it were not for this kind of conspiracy that to-night is not sad and strained but intimate and jovial, I would enjoy playing this Mozart with Brad. It is like the most delicate marble wall, with a garden inside, and a palace full of clear lovely rooms; but I can only walk around and around the wall without finding the gate which I know is there, or rather I pass gate after gate but push none of them open, because I have not enough strength, enough concentration: I am hardly a person just now, but only a rather lackadaisical breeze blowing from nowhere in particular and stirring in a pettish manner the outermost leaves of things.

Joel knew that he must not stare too eagerly at the back of Linda's neck: so he looked at Brad. Of course, it 's true, he thought, as Linda said this morning, that Brad does not really like his work; when you think of all that he might have done and will never have the chance to do, it seems a damnable shame; and yet it would be absurd to pity Brad: because you feel that he is within himself so strong, with his shy generosity, his common sense, the something deep inside him stubbornly himself that no veneer of prejudices, no smoothing-down process, no amount of living in a rut, is able quite to reach. Why is it that a person's way of social living, the range of his ideas and convictions (and certainly Brad's upon many subjects — politics, economics, even to a certain extent morals — are simply those of his class and profession), sometimes have such slight effect upon what that person really is or upon your idea of that person? Brad might be stripped of all these conventional garments with which the years have covered him and you would find him intact and strong and freely himself; and what would become of me if I were denuded of the shreds and patches that rather fumblingly and fussily I have pinned together to make the inconvenient nondescript cloak over which I am always stumbling? He looked at Ellen seated demurely in a small stiff chair beside Mrs. Waring, and conveying by her silent pose the idea of daughterly solicitude. I would not be terribly surprised, he thought, at anything Ellen might do: if she stood up now, for example, and started screaming at the top of her voice, if she picked up a vase of flowers and threw it across the room. Poor Mrs. Waring, you can see how she hates to have Ellen pay her attention, how she forces herself to be kind to her for Dicky's sake; it would help her, I think, if she could see Ellen as mad, the way I do, because then she could pity her (which I cannot do and would not want to do) and now she can only distrust and perhaps hate her for what she has done to Dicky.

The music stopped. Linda got up from the piano, closed the volume, and turned out the piano lamp. Mrs. Waring moved her head, seemed to realize that she had slumped in her chair, and sat up as straight as she could.

"That was lovely," she said. "Are n't you going to play any more?"

Her voice made Joel for the first time to-day realize how very much she had aged: her question was like a ticket you were asked to show and which, wearily, mechanically, you searched for and presented because you knew it was required.

"I think we ought to be starting fairly soon," Linda said. "We don't want to be too late in getting back."

"I 've learned not to expect you till the small hours," Mrs. Waring said, "no matter when you start out. If my light is on you might look in to say good-night."

"Your light won't be on," Brad said. "We won't be back till 4.30 A.M. at the earliest, and perhaps not till day after to-morrow, if the party gets wild. But seriously, Luly, if I find you doing anything so absurd as trying deliberately to keep awake till we get back, I 'll give you the worst bawling out you 've had in a long while. I 'm telling you."

"Trying to keep awake!" Mrs. Waring exclaimed. "I wish you could give me something that would make me sleep."

"You sleep finely," Brad said. "You just imagine you don't. I come in and look at you before I go to bed at about eleven, say, and there you are snoring like an old porpoise, and then the next day you try to sling us a line that you did n't sleep a wink till after two. I tell you, Luly, that stuff does n't get by."

"I don't snore," Mrs. Waring said, livelier now, more like herself, "and you know it perfectly well. And if I 'm sleeping so soundly I wish you 'd explain how night after night I hear the clock striking regularly to the wee hours of the morning."

"Pure imagination," Brad said.

"It must be refreshing to be so very certain," Mrs. Waring said, smiling, "but I still persist in thinking that I'm in a better position to know how much I sleep than you are."

"Mother," Pat called from upstairs. "Mother, I'm ready."

Linda went to the door. "I'll only be a minute," she said, "and then I think we really ought to start, don't you, Brad?"

Dicky laid his pack down on the table. "O.K. by me," he said. "I've finished my round. If I'd been playing for money I'd be forty-three dollars to the good, but catch it turning out that way if I were playing for money."

"I don't dare play for money," Ellen said. "I get so excited I can't behave myself."

"Now I imagine we're in for a half hour's wait," Brad said. "If I had a child and I sent him to bed that would be the end for me until the morning."

"I don't suppose you remember the way you used to keep calling and calling after you went upstairs?" Mrs. Waring asked him. "You were the worst of the three, Brad. I remember once, when we had a dinner party, your father had to spank you after he had been up to see you three times. I think that was the only occasion you were ever really spanked. Sometimes I used to slap your hand."

"No," Brad said, "I don't remember that."

"Your grandmother used to tell about a little boy — " Mrs. Waring went on, smiling all through, really being happy for the first time since Joel had seen her to-day; and yet she appeared to him, strangely, at this moment

261

so touching that he avoided looking at her — "and this really happened," she said, "though you may not believe it. His parents got exasperated. They came up to see him several times and he said that something was in the room, and they said there was nothing except a little angel to watch over him; and that made him more unhappy than ever, and he said he didn't want to have an angel in his room, that it disturbed him; and the next time they came up they were very angry and he was in tears, and he said, 'That angel's been making so much noise I can't go to sleep. It's under the bed now.' And they looked under the bed and found one of those little wheezy pug dogs that had got into the house somehow . . ." Mrs. Waring paused; she had tears of laughter in her eyes . . . "And every once in a while it would give a wheeze," she said, "that scared the poor little boy out of his wits. And that was the angel."

"Well," Brad said, "I doubt very much whether there's a pug dog under Pat's bed, but I notice that Linda shows no signs of coming down. I'll start along in the Chrysler with Ellen and Joel. Dicky, you bring Linda in the Ford. We'll meet you somewhere near the merry-go-round; and don't give her more than ten minutes."

Pat was in bed when Linda went into his room, his eyes fixed brightly on the door to greet her the moment she appeared.

"Did you have a good time doing stamps with Grandpapa?" she asked.

"I'll say," he exclaimed, "and Mother, Grandpapa says he's got a lot of old envelopes somewhere in a trunk that his father wrote and his grandfather, way, way back. Some of them were during the Civil War. And he says

I can have them for my collection — is n't that fine?
But it will take hours and hours going over them and
sorting them out, and we 're going to put them in a special
book, and that 's what we 're going to do this summer —
is n't that swell, Mother? And Grandpapa says he
should n't wonder if Uncle Brad gave me his collection
sometime, if he does n't marry and get children of his
own. I hope he won't, don't you? Do you think he
will?"

Linda crossed the room and sat down on the foot of
Pat's bed, taking hold of his ankle through the covers.

"I don't think he will," she said, "but of course you
never know." When Frances broke the engagement, she
thought, I imagine she turned Brad away from marriage;
I doubt if he is still in love with her: but I think his
pride and his confidence were so deeply hurt that he
certainly would not marry if he could help it; and I
cannot picture his leaving that apartment of his, or
letting anyone loose among his things.

"And Mother," Pat said, "Merrick told me yesterday
that he had some stamps in his own collection worth one
hundred dollars apiece. I don't believe it, do you? I
think he tells lies all the time. Do you suppose I 'll
have to keep seeing him every day? I 'm very, very
tired of his face already."

Linda smiled at Pat: so he was beginning to learn that
much of your time was beset by people whom you would
rather not be seeing; and in a little while, she thought,
he may not be seeing me, he may be with Thornton: and
of course he is fond of Thornton but so shy with him;
I don't think really that he feels he knows Thornton any
more than I do; I think he respects and admires him but
is apt to be a little afraid of him, a little ashamed to be

quite natural with him. Smiling at Pat now, she felt
as if she were a traitor; she felt that her sitting here
on the bed, which should be the most natural, the happiest
thing in the world, was the most unnatural, the most
wretched.

If Pat were going to boarding school, she thought,
I would not be seeing him for eight months of the
year, and that is what Thornton would like to do
with him, I know; but somehow to be giving him up
for half the year, to feel that he is not mine but Thornton's, seems quite different: it's as if he were to come
to me, smiling, confident, and happy, to show me something he had drawn, and I should walk away without
speaking. I feel almost as if I were dreaming of him
after he is dead, loving to see him in my dreams, not
bearing to let him go, because through it all I know
really that I am dreaming, that really he is not with
me, and that I will never be seeing him again.

"And Mother," Pat said, "Merrick says he's climbed
up a mountain over a mile high all by himself. Of course
he couldn't, could he? He must think I'm a fool if
he thinks I believe him. But I'd like to climb a mountain
sometime, wouldn't you? You might find something
precious way up there above all those peaks, but I don't
suppose you would really. I bet if Merrick had thought
of that, he'd have told me he found something wonderful on top of his mountain."

Pat chuckled and moved his leg slightly so that he
could feel her hand holding him.

"Hey, Linda!" Dicky shouted. "What's eating you?"
and she got up quickly: she must go at once or next thing
she would find herself in tears, like this morning.

"But Mother, wait a second," Pat said, and she knew

that though he would not fuss he was trying to make from his voice, his smile, the long pleading look in his eyes, a chain that would hold her beside him a moment longer, "Grandpapa was telling me the most interesting things. He was telling me about what man comes from. You know those little squirmy things in mud? Well, I think they were fish first and got sort of washed out of the water, and then they got used to it in about a thousand years, I guess, and then if they wanted to be tigers they grew legs and tails, and if they wanted to be birds they grew wings, and if they wanted to stay fish they found some more water and kept swimming round not doing anything. Is that true, Mother, or was Grandpapa just fooling? — because it's hard to tell when he's fooling sometimes. And he says we came way, way, way back from the ones that got to be great huge apes, and that's why we're apt to be so silly. But I think Merrick's sillier than any monkey I ever saw. Much sillier."

"I guess it's partly true," Linda said, "or something like it; and that must be why you remind me of one of those very young little brown monkeys: you know how big their heads look when they are very small; one of those little monkeys clinging to its mother and looking backward over its shoulder at the people in the zoo with great startled eyes."

"Oh Mother," Pat exclaimed, wriggling all over under the covers, and laughing with such delight and embarrassment that he almost forgot she would be leaving him in a moment.

Linda bent quickly and kissed his mouth: he felt warm and slightly damp, like a smooth newborn animal, except that he was wriggling about in such a lively fashion; he must have been playing in the barn, for his skin smelled sweetly of hay.

"You feel hot," she said. "I think you have too many covers," and she pulled down over his feet the thin top blanket. "And now I must go really. Good night."

"What time will you be back?" he asked, a little plaintively, but still half smiling to show that if his sadness at her going was real, his showing it, his beginning to make a fuss, was only a joke.

"I 've no idea," she said. "Not late."

"But what time do you *think* you 'll be back?"

She tried to think of the evening but she could not imagine it, could not imagine its either beginning or ending. "Perhaps by half past ten," she said, "but I make no promises."

Pat suddenly stopped at the same time his smiling and his frowning, and nestled his cheek further into his pillow as if he had made up his mind definitely to face the night.

"See you in the morning," he said. "Good night, Mother."

"Yes," she said. "See you in the morning."

Luly had hated to have the children drive off to the beach (it seemed as if they could not be content nowadays to pass quiet evenings at home the way they used to do), but she had not spoken of it because she knew it would irritate Mark if he thought she was complaining; and now as she sat here on the piazza she felt no longer deserted, but peaceful and comfortably tired the way you feel after you have been riding a long time on the train, after you have twisted from one position to another, and tried to read, and tried to look out of the window, until

at last suddenly you are relaxed and drowsy, half remembering all sorts of far-away things, and not minding
any more how long the journey will be. You cannot
always capture that feeling on the train, she thought, and
if you try for it deliberately it gets more and more out
of reach; but if you do not think of it it may suddenly
come over you. I always hope it will.

Mark was walking on the drive from gate to gate,
smoking a cigar; she loved to listen to his steps as they
came nearer, to watch him as he passed the house, in the
green-gray light under the trees; but she loved, too,
watching him disappear, because she knew that he would
be returning, and passing her again, and because when
she felt this way it no longer frightened her to be alone;
she did not feel alone even when Mark was out of sight
among the trees by the north or the south gate, even with
the children gone to the beach; she felt that they all
were hers, were all a part of her, just as her father and
mother still were hers; she felt no difference between what
was near and what was far away, between the living and
the dead.

She looked over the lawn, smooth and almost endless
in the dusk. Fireflies, not many, made little green flashes
here and there, sometimes very low above the grass and
sometimes so high that they made her think of fireworks
in the distance; and away to the southeast, above the
hedge, the Sakonnet lighthouse kept flashing its white
and its pale red signals, with the sky thicker and bluer,
it seemed, after each flash, as if they were bringing on
the night.

Luly turned her head once more towards the driveway.
It may be just my imagination, she thought, but I don't
ever remember the trees being so beautiful. She looked

267

upward through the leaves, through a region of flaky shadow, to the topmost delicate branches moving to and fro in the sky. They looked smooth and soft, those little branches; they were close together and yet there was space between them, and air that seemed quite different from the air below; you could imagine the softest gray birds flying through them, their wings brushed by the leaves, and twilight spreading from their wings as they flew by and curling among the branches like fog or smoke; you could imagine that it was among those branches and leaves, untouched, so high above the ground, that all the other times you were half remembering, all the other places, had taken refuge. Luly closed her eyes. I cannot quite reach them, she thought, but they are there, around me. No, I am not afraid.

VI

As she drove with Dicky along the road behind the Second Beach Linda felt that she was embarked on a ship; she could see Pat in her mind: a small figure, waving to her from the deck, a figure to whom she kept waving, although presently she could no longer make him out across the water, could not know whether he had gone or what he was doing. Dicky was driving fast, moving the wheel casually and lightly with one hand; his eyes were bright and intent. An open car was coming towards them driven by a fat man in a brown suit, with a fat blonde woman beside him; Dicky steered straight at them until the man waved and shouted, but only at the last moment, when they were nearly off the road, did Dicky swerve to the right. He turned to Linda with a mischievous smile: "That'll teach him to drive without lights," he said. "He'll remember that."

"Dicky!" Linda exclaimed. "You scared me as much as you did him," but she rather enjoyed being scared and had perfect confidence in Dicky's driving. This was a voyage of exploration, of adventure, like their setting out from the Grove when they were children to discover new paths or new caves in the swamp and among the ledges.

"I didn't scare you? No!" Dicky said gayly, im-

pudently. "Whoa there, now! Whoa, boy!" he said
to the Ford in the soothing voice with which Robert used
to speak to horses. "He feels a bit skittish," he said.
"You notice my car's a male, or perhaps you didn't —
but he is. It's no Lizzy or anything like that. That's
the first thing I insisted on when I bought it. But how
do you like this?" He slowed down to fifteen miles an
hour.

"That's much better," Linda said.

"Now come," Dicky said. "You know you don't
really like that. You know you like to speed just as
much as I do. Why not admit it?"

"But I don't like to run over people," she said.

"Who's talking of running over people? I didn't
run over anyone, did I? Of course I didn't. You just
catch me running over someone. You don't think I'd
run over anyone, do you, Linda?"

As she watched his sharp smiling face, the bright glaze
of his eyes, she knew that he had been drinking. Already? she thought; and he was not going to drink this
summer.

"Dicky!" she exclaimed sadly.

"Linda!" he mimicked her. "But I knew it would
come, and it's better now than later. Just make up
your mind to everything you'd be saying through the
evening, and all the dirty looks and the mean glances,
and give them to me now in one dose. I reckon I can
stand it."

But seeing him so gay, for the first time really since
Ellen and he had arrived, she did not have the heart
to scold him; she could hardly even feel sorry that he
had been drinking, if only he would stop in time, if only
it would keep him gay; the trouble was it never did.

"Do you think it's polite for you to be so gay," she asked, "and not give me even a taste?"

"That's better," he said. "That's talking sense. I did you an injustice, and I apologize like a gentleman." He pulled the flask from his pocket and gave it to her. "Lucky I'm with you," he said. "It was just at the foot of this hill that a man made indecent advances to Susie Bingham one night when she ran out of gas. It must have been some poor lonely old critter, I guess, or else a pretty dark night."

"I'm past the age when men would make advances to me," she said.

"Oh I dunno," he said. "You're no longer young, but you're damn well preserved: just like me. You notice when I get to the beach how all the women can't keep their eyes off me. When I'm around, the life guards don't get a chance."

Linda smiled at him: with his short red hair curled by the dampness, his eyes this evening almost birdlike, his brown, slightly freckled features, he looked no more than twenty.

They had driven over Purgatory Hill and now, as they went through the catalpas on the other side, they could see the lights of the beach, very white and clear, with a pearly softness that would be gone in a few minutes.

"It's like going to a circus, is n't it?" she exclaimed.

"Sure," he said. "That's why I like it. What am I? Just a mad little clown. You know, it would n't be so bad, at that." Without warning he jerked the car out into the middle of the road. "Whew!" he whistled. "Did you see him? I almost did run over that gink."

But Dicky did not slow down until they had crossed

the bridge and were driving behind the huge taut curves of the roller coaster. It always looked different in the evening, and now that before long you would be riding on it, it became more than ever tense and alive. Its dark twisted track reminded her of a piece of whalebone insanely bent and scalloped, so resilient that, if its fastenings gave way, it would spring up from its scaffolding in a straight quivering strip and fall somewhere with a splash far out at sea. As she looked at it she saw a car climb slowly up the first and highest curve, pause for an instant at the top, or seem to pause, and then plunge down almost to the sand with a rumble of wheels and a screaming of women.

She put her hand on Dicky's arm as they crossed the road, as if to urge him forward. "We can go in here," she said, "between these two sheds."

As they walked through the thick sands Linda caught a smell of pop corn, and something sweetish, — perfumery, was it? — and clams, and food frying, and sawdust; there was no gunpowder certainly, and yet she kept thinking of the Fourth of July; and all these smells were floated in the smell of the sea, itself changed by this exotic cargo into something incalculable and not to be trusted.

"Look at him, will you?" Dicky said.

In the darkest place in this sandy alley, between the white wooden walls, a sailor lay sprawled on his back, dead drunk apparently and half undressed.

"Somebody's been having a good time," Dicky said.

The man looked very young but stocky, with a handsome broad face and yellow hair. Where did he come from? Linda thought; who was with him? Who took his clothes off that way? Where will he be to-morrow?

272

A strange picture, his lying there at the foot of that
wall as if he were dead, and yet so full of life: you can
feel that; and now at this moment everywhere there are
so many pictures, so many familiar ones, so many strange
ones, no two exactly alike, that you could not imagine
them all; you could not believe them all if you saw
them; they would just be pictures and you would think,
"I must not have seen them right, they can't be that
way"; and there must be so many, now, at this instant,
that any you could possibly imagine, no matter how
strange, would be there among them.

They climbed wooden steps on to the board walk,
long, dusky, and wide, with lights at intervals at the
edge, still not illumining, with the paleness of fireworks
set off too early in the evening; at this outer end, near
the roller coaster, there was no crowd, but figures in
pairs or groups sauntered by — sailors with girls, girls
laughing together on the watch for men, Armenian-
looking families with children — but all just now, except
at the instant they passed you, immaterial, semitransparent,
as if painted by Whistler against this shadowy promenade.
Linda pulled Dicky across to the railing. It was strange
to look from this walk to the quiet sand, the gray-blue
sea fading into the horizon; as the waves curled and
broke, wave after wave, always two or three deep, you
could think of them as white feather flounces on a dress
ruffled by the wind; at their edge a dog, dimly seen, was
sniffing a newspaper; and Pat is in his bed, she thought,
dreaming of what? And Mother may be going to bed or
looking sadly through the trees only half seeing them;
and Thornton, whom I can never see, is playing bridge
perhaps, in a small bright room on his boat, with Jim
Ballou and his friends; or they all may be doing some-

thing different; even little Pat may not be in his bed; I cannot know. This morning, she remembered, I sat among the dunes with Joel, looking at the waves, such different waves, such a different sea, but no more different than the I that was watching: because now Dicky and I are just another of those darkly transparent couples walking under the lights or leaning against this rail; we are part of this mixed exciting smell from the sea and from all those booths, and the sound of the cars on the roller coaster, and the faint, faint beat of the drum that must be from the dance hall and that you cannot hear except when the waves are still. "Oh, Dicky!" she exclaimed. "Isn't it beautiful? Don't you love it?"

"Uh-uh," he grunted; then, leaning towards her confidentially and speaking out of the side of his mouth, he said: "Listen, kid, how about us two having another little drink? Just you and me — what?"

"O.K. by me," she said, "but Dicky . . ."

"Now — now — now — " he patted her hand with exaggerated protectiveness. "I'm a reformed character, see? You gotta have faith in me, see? Here you are — but be discreet: *les oreilles ennemies vous écoutent.*"

Linda took another sip and returned the flask to Dicky. He drank, and wiped his mouth with the back of his hand. "Come on," he said, "we're due at the merry-go-round. I don't want to be spoiling Joel's evening."

His voice startled her. "What do you mean?" she asked.

"Nothing," he said. "You know me. I wouldn't hurt a flea. Come on, kiddo," and with shoulder slightly hunched, head thrust forward, her arm held close against him, he started with her down the board walk towards the merry-go-round, swaying his body at the hips like a young Apache.

The lights were beginning to cast a glow on the board walk. As they hurried between the strollers, rhythmically, with always a slight skating motion, Linda's glance moved along the booths, jumping from picture to picture: a row of pink and crimson bottles in an orange cave, displays of painted chinaware, of dolls, of huge beaded lamps, rows of degenerate-looking Teddy bears, a shooting gallery with a group of sailors in front of it, its walls a jungle full of pinkish-yellow tigers; and here at last was the merry-go-round; its music came out to her, pushing back the waves; and as soon as they entered the white shed that covered it they saw Joel and Brad and Ellen seated in a row and watching. Joel and Brad and Ellen! It was like discovering portraits of people you knew in a vast kaleidoscopic painting, one of those Hindu or Thibetan paintings so involved, so crowded with figures, that you could not quite see it as a whole.

Dicky put his hands on Ellen's shoulders. "Hullo, sweetheart," he said, "did you think I'd forgotten you?"

"No such luck," she answered, raising her eyes to him, but smiling, rather, at Linda; but you could not talk through the noise, and Linda was glad: she would rather simply watch.

It was as if from here, from this revolving core, all lights and mirrors and shining brass poles, with that wheezy powerful music that pushed you down in your chair like the steam from a locomotive, all the life of the beach, those garish pictures she had just been passing, the crowds, the shrieks from the roller coaster, the colored lights, the mixed unreliable smells, as if it

275

all were being unreeled from this axis persistently turning, were floating around it like the whorled streamers of a nebula extending so far its white gaseous substance and then being swallowed up by the blue night and the ocean, beyond the flounces of the waves. A bell kept striking in her ear, like a fire bell, and Linda saw in a moment that it was at a bell that the young men, sailors, half of them, were throwing the metal rings they must have reached for on the other side of the whirl; they stood by their horses, their left arms linked around the poles, growing more and more tense until suddenly they would draw back their right arms, jerk them forward and outward with a snap, with a twist of the whole body, and then relax, limp and casual, as they were swept out of sight. Beyond in the two inner circles of rising and falling animals sat girls in gay dresses, carefully nonchalant, most of them, and watchful, not so charming, she thought, as the Apsarases with their cloudlike curves, their delicate harnesses of jewels, and their spiry crowns. But these riders after all were just on the surface, they could change, they would disappear, thrown off in one or other of those whirling streams until the darkness took them; the real things were those shining rods and the strange beasts which they impaled, rising up and down, leaping forward mechanically in a smooth seasick rhythm to that stupefying music, that blunt powerful sweetish noise that even the clangor of the bell could not cut but only glance off, a noise, a music, that for all its power was somehow squashy inside, that seemed to seep into you, enfold you through every sense. It was as if you were eating on and on, not hungry, of some heavy food and you could not be sure whether it was meant to be more sweetened than salted, or being sprayed with a cloying perfume that was tainted with kerosene or tar; or it might be just the steady mad rise and fall of those galloping animals that you were hearing as music. What were they? Horses mostly, but you kept discovering new ones; bears, giraffes, pigs, lions, brown and orange and red and black, with a texture that made her think of the varnished models of internal organs, stomachs and livers and hearts, that she had once seen in some anatomical museum. Would it go on forever, this dream procession of leaping animals? But no; they were rising and falling more slowly. They were stopping. They had stopped.

"Come on," Brad shouted through the music. "I've got tickets. Linda, Dicky . . . Hurry up or you can't get an outside place."

"You go," she said. "I'm going to watch. It makes me sick to ride on them," and she saw them take their places, Brad, then Dicky, then Joel, and Ellen on a giraffe in the middle row, next to Joel's horse.

Each time they come around, she thought, gliding so smoothly past me, I recognize them, I smile at them when I catch their eyes, and yet I see them not quite as themselves; I see them each time somewhat as I saw Joel the moment he got off the train this morning, as a stranger might be seeing them; or as if, after death, I might from somewhere be seeing them still in life. Brad stood quite straight, not moving, looking out with narrowed eyes, the faintest smile about his lips, not deigning to clutch at the rings, to throw at the bell, wrapped in a mantle of his own special air that revolved with him always, unpierced by the noise and the lights; while Dicky each time threw at the bell and nearly always hit it, twisting, swaying, like the others, but fiercer, more tense, than most of them, not seeing Linda except

277

now and then when he would grin at her suddenly and call out something which she could not understand; Joel, like Brad, did not try for the bell, but that was because he was all attention for her; he was leaning back against his horse; as he came into sight he would at once try to catch her eye, would smile so quietly that no one but herself was supposed to guess that he was smiling; and Ellen, behind him, seated sidewise on her giraffe that moved up and down, Ellen, very still, did not smile at all. She looked incongruous among those bars and mirrors, like a Victorian valentine; and yet she was very much aware of Joel, Linda could feel that; perhaps silently she was willing him to turn, to look at her; but also she was aware of a young sailor behind her who stood on the outer edge between two horses, swaying slightly as if on a ship, with arms crossed, proud to be holding on to nothing, and turning his head now to look at Ellen. I can feel exactly how she is feeling, Linda thought: quite formless and uncertain within herself, with the music churning all around her, thinking of that sailor, of what he is thinking of her, of the way he must think she belongs to a different world, and that thought vaguely excites her, and she does not know whether to smile at him or perhaps to speak to Joel, longing really to make some sudden gesture that will outline and give point to all her vagueness (the way when you have a messy drawing you hope that perhaps some sharp random line somewhere may happen to bring it all together just as if you had seen that it exactly would), and slightly annoyed with herself because she cannot be sure what gesture to make. Or does she feel that way? Sometimes, looking at people, you have no idea how they are feeling, and then sometimes it seems suddenly as if you knew absolutely, so that if you glanced in the mirror your face would even be suggesting theirs; but of course it is quite different really, even if in a way you do exactly catch their feeling, because you always know that it is you that are able to be feeling like them, and that keeps you partly outside; it makes your sense of their feeling never quite the same as their own, and probably just that difference makes everything different.

But it is of Joel, she realized suddenly, that I am thinking, not of Ellen, because he is so much nearer to me now than he was a minute ago; because each time he moves past me, even when I almost do not see him, he is nearer than before: it is because he stands so still, because his smile is so quiet and confident; because his eyes look so drowsy and yet watchful; I can imagine, she thought, that it is I that am moving past him, revolving around him; that he is standing still, quiet, all-seeing, and that everything is whirling around him as he stands; he is like a god, she thought, in the midst of those lights and mirrors; and suddenly she could picture herself clinging to him, her arms about his neck, her face against his breast, clasped and clasping like Parvati in the arms of Siva, among clouds and lights and colored flames, while around them in wavy circles moved swarms of animals and people, circle beyond circle, of every kind and shape and color, doing everything you could think of and could not think of, to the sound of those bells and waves, and this loud enfolding music that was somehow empty at its core and that was really the total, brought together, of all the noises everywhere in the world.

But the merry-go-round was stopping again; and Joel,

who really was moving while she sat still, was moving more and more slowly. Dicky jumped off beside her before it stopped, running a few steps to keep his balance, and now Joel, not too eagerly, was helping Ellen down from her giraffe. Linda looked out through the open squares in the wall to the board walk, and all she could see were the pale faces and hands of the people looking in, with a screen of blackness beyond them.

"As soon as you fellows decide you can't hit anything with those rifles," Brad said, "you'll find me over there on that bench."

He left them, all four of them, at the shooting gallery and sat down with his back to the walk, his elbows on the iron rail. Those green walls with the yellow tigers are enough to make you sick, he thought, and I bet those guns don't shoot straight; I bet they are fixed somehow. He was thinking too that beaches like this, or amusement parks or county fairs, were never quite so much fun as you thought they were going to be, that everything was too much alike: you were just doing the same thing over and over again and throwing away your money. That moon is a beauty, though, he thought, so clear and yellow, like a huge fire balloon; at the Grove now it will be over Sakonnet; no — it is high enough to be further than that — somewhere between the lighthouse and Sachuest; I wonder if Mother saw it rising.

He could see her on the piazza, rather feebly, sadly waving good-bye as they drove off in the car. Of course we really should not be going out like this, he thought, when we know it makes her unhappy; we ought to have stayed at home; we could never do for her as much as she has done for us, never, and she may not live long;

but he could not imagine how he would feel, or what the Grove would be like, without her.

In a lull between waves he heard music: from the dance hall? Or was it the merry-go-round? The restaurant? I hope they don't start dancing, he thought, or I never will get them away. There's the roller coaster, that will be fun, but two or three rides, I should think, would be enough for anybody. He looked over his shoulder and saw Dicky still shooting. Come, come, he exclaimed to himself; this is getting ridiculous: I see I shall have to be firm.

"You're not paying much attention to me," Joel heard Ellen saying, and knew that she had been talking to him for a minute or more.

He looked down at her: how could she have disturbed, revolted him so in New York? Why could he not simply have laughed at her? His thoughts were now only of Linda: I will be finding her again and again, he kept thinking, as I did on the merry-go-round, and all the unreality of these pink plaster walls and the indigo sky and the unbelievable whiteness of those waves, Hollywood waves, makes that seem only the more substantial and clear.

"You love attention, don't you?" he asked.

"Of course I do," she said. "Don't most people? Oh look, Joel!" She clutched his arm and drew him to the edge of a group staring in one of the windows of the dance hall: you could hear the drums and very faintly the other instruments, but hardly enough to catch the tune. "Joel," she said coaxingly, "why are you so horrid to me? Now I'm going to make a suggestion which will probably shock you, though I don't see why it should.

Let's go in and dance, just you and I. Let's lose the others for a little just to tease them. I'd love to tease Brad, he's so bossy. Come on. Shall we?"

He smiled at her ironically: she was pressing his arm as much as she dared, he knew; this was a return to that night in New York; it's my own fault, he thought, for not telling her then what I thought of her.

"And suppose I did dance with you?" he asked. "What then?"

"What then?" she repeated. "I don't know what you mean. Nothing, I suppose. Are you afraid of me, Joel? I wish I could think so."

"I know what you want," he said suddenly. "I think I understand you, Ellen. You want to make Dicky just as wretched as you can, don't you? You get a thrill out of it. I can understand that: it might be great fun trying to torture someone. Isn't that partly it? But why choose me? He won't believe anything serious between you and me. Why not take one of those sailors?"

"Oh!" she gasped. "Joel, aren't you cruel?"

"I'm sorry," he said, rather surprised that he had spoken as he had, but not particularly caring. "I didn't mean to talk that way, but I think you rather like it, don't you?"

She gripped his arm more tightly and drew him back across the board walk to the outer railing. "If you tell me to go with a sailor, I will," she said in a low voice. "You don't believe me, I know, but you just tell me — point any one out, and I'll go up and speak to him and let him do anything he wants. Try it and see."

He looked at her curiously. "You better not make too many promises," he said. "Perhaps I will try it."

She looked white and hard and feverish in the light

from the dance-hall windows across the way. "I'm warning you," she said.

He nodded his head towards a big negro sailor who was strolling by, looking in at the dancers. "What if I signaled him?" he asked.

Ellen trembled; he could feel it through her fingers as more and more tightly they dug into his arm. "All right," she said. "If you tell me, I'll do it."

If it were not for Dicky, he thought, I'd take the chance; I think she would do it; at least she would start to; she would carry it as far as she dared, but I'm not especially curious how far: perhaps all the way.

"Why should I give you an excuse?" he said.

"Do you hate me?" she asked in the same breathless voice.

"I'm sorry," he said. "I can't give you that pleasure."

"You do hate me," she said, "or you wouldn't talk that way."

"Oh, you mustn't mind how I talk," he said. "I say anything, just the way you do."

He saw that her face was changing, growing less tense, more watchful and smooth: he looked over her shoulder along the board walk and saw that Brad and Linda and Dicky were coming after them. Dicky was carrying under his arm a mustard-colored Teddy bear.

"Hullo, sweetheart," he called. "I've got something for you. Won it throwing baseballs. Aren't you proud of your small husband?"

Linda clutched the rod in front of her as the car started with a jolt and began to move slowly along the track through the scaffolding that towered all around them. It is too late now to change, she thought; we

283

have begun and now we must keep on; I'm glad that Dicky is beside me. She looked at Joel ahead of her in the very front seat which he had bravely stepped into, and Ellen, who had followed him before anyone else had a chance; she turned to smile at Brad, who had not been allowed to come in with Dicky and her, though there was plenty of room, and Brad, as he caught her eye, expanded his nostrils and glowered, because a fattish old young woman, much painted, had taken the place beside him, asking him if she might; poor woman, of all the men on the beach, Linda thought, she picked the least likely prospect in Brad.

And now the car was starting noisily up the long slope to the top of the highest curve. Suppose, Linda thought, that I absolutely had to get out, suppose I knew that there would be an accident and we would all go crashing to the ground, what would I do? Could I call to the men below to stop the machinery and let us out? They would not hear me; they would not believe me if they did. Could I quickly warn everyone in these two cars so that the people behind could begin at once climbing carefully over the back seat and making their way down this openwork greasy track? But they would not believe me either, and if they did, it would be awful to climb across these seats as they kept rising. She looked over her shoulder and turned away half-sickened: it was so high and the track was so steep; but in that glance she saw the crescent of the beach spread out in a dust of light; she saw the people strolling where she had been strolling, and the long swaying curve of the waves, and the empty moonlight behind and above and all around. We are on the edge of the whirl, she thought;

284

we are about to be flung off into space, to be falling forever.

There were screams, but you could hardly hear them. Could you bear it? Would your heart stop beating?

You were rising again and wished that it would have the same terror as that first slow rise; you were no longer on the rim of space; that was just a trick; you were still part of that gaseous whirl moving around and around its thin outer edges.

It was Ellen that screamed so near, she thought; and she saw that Ellen's arms were flung about Joel; her head was buried against his shoulder, while Joel sat up very straight but of course did not dare to push her away; and now they were once more falling, and Linda saw Ellen's fingers clutching Joel tightly, her body shaken as if with pure terror: that might have been so at first; you could imagine doing anything through that first awful drop, but now when everything was all at once so mild, when it was just this scaffolding, not so high after all, that you were racing about, not even Ellen could be quite so scared unless she wanted to be.

But Ellen's fingers were working desperately as they clung to Joel's back and arm; and then as once more the car started climbing Dicky leaned forward, and Linda held his arm in fear that he was going to stand up. "Don't mind me," he shouted through the rumble at Ellen: "Enjoy yourself"; but she did not lift her head, did not release the grip of her fingers.

Dicky got out of his seat the first one, before the car had quite stopped. He saw Joel trying to push off Ellen; he saw Joel's face: Joel was on to her all right; he knew

285

what she was up to. I'd be sick too if I looked at her, Dicky thought; perhaps I will be anyway. Now to get out of here before the rest of them, to get lost among the folks on the board walk and slip back to the car: there is plenty of room for them in the Chrysler.

He hurried through the gate and pushed between slow-moving people. If she would hang on to Joel, he thought, my best friend, and rub against him that way until she almost passed out in public, I guess there's not much more to be said. It may not be her fault, he thought, it may be mine; it may not be anyone's — but it's too much for me. If I'm to blame, what's the difference? and if I'm not to blame, what's the difference? and if it wasn't this it might be something as bad, and who cares? And if this isn't anything and I'm all flooey, there has been plenty without, so there's no need to argue. I'm granting anybody anything they want; so everything is O.K. But things can ride you just so far and then it's up to you how much longer you will stand it. It's your own business, however people talk. Cowardly, they tell you: let them try it and see.

He walked down the steps into the path between the sheds by which Linda and he had entered, stopped in the shadow to pull out his flask and drink what was left. That's something like, he thought, and I'll get some more at home when I leave the car.

As he hurried through the sand, he saw something dark by the wall: it was that drunken sailor, still on his back, his trousers still half off him — what a treat for Ellen!

"Hullo, brother," Dicky said. "You're all right now, but what about the morning?"

"Where is Dicky?" Linda asked as they reached the board walk.

"He went that way," Joel said. "I saw him start. He was walking pretty fast."

"I suggest we go after him," Brad said, and Linda knew that he too was worried. Why should you be worried, except that he went so suddenly, ducking through the people coming in for the next ride? It was his face that made you worry, just as he was leaving: a very motionless face though the rest of him was moving so quickly, a face that appeared stripped of some layer of skin, some protecting atmosphere; you were seeing it, others were seeing it, and yet it looked like a face that was not being seen.

Joel and Brad hurried along looking to either side, and she followed them, nearly as fast, with Ellen clinging to her arm and carrying the Teddy bear that Dicky had given her.

"I don't see why he went," she said. "Do you, Linda? I don't see why he got so cross. I couldn't help it if I was scared. I was terrified. I didn't know what I was doing. I think I fainted, I'm not sure. Could you see me? Could you tell?"

"No," Linda said. "I could not."

She too was looking from side to side; of course he might have gone into one of those rooms, but that was not likely. She lingered for a moment to peer into some little red automobiles run like trolleys on electric poles, beneath festoons of lights, — blue, cherry, amber, — paused simply because Brad and Joel had not; but Dicky would not go in one of those absurd little cars unless he thought that would be a way to lose them, which seemed to be what he wanted. Once she thought she saw him far

287

ahead slipping between two couples, and started to run,
but when she saw the figure again she knew it was much
heavier than Dicky's. Brad and Joel were waiting by
the merry-go-round; that music was still going, the
animals were turning; there were sailors balancing beauti-
fully on the edge or throwing their rings at the bell.

"He isn't in there," Brad said. "I bet he's gone home,
and I think we might as well go too, if no one has any
objections."

They walked out past the merry-go-round, crossed the
road, and hurried along in front of the parked cars looking
for theirs.

"The Ford is gone," Brad called. "That's what I
thought."

Joel opened the rumble seat of the Chrysler: Linda
stepped in; he followed her, leaving Ellen to sit in front
with Brad. For a moment Linda could hear shouts from
the roller coaster; then as they crossed the bridge over
the creek the beach fell behind them with its lights and
noises, and you saw simply the moon over the fields and
the car's headlights bringing out tree after tree. They
were going faster than Brad usually drove.

"Do you think he did go home?" Linda asked Joel.

"I guess so," he said. "Where else could he go?" But
she knew he did not feel certain.

"He must have gone home," she said, "and Joel, we
better not let him know we followed him this way. He
wouldn't like it."

"We won't," Joel said, "unless Ellen should make a
story of it."

"I don't think she will, if I speak to her," Linda said.

"I don't blame him for running off," Joel said after
a pause. "I'd have done the same thing."

288

"I think you were right," Linda said after another pause. "She is mad, Joel. At least she's not sane: there may be a difference."

"I'd like to take that neck of hers," he said, "and squeeze it very slowly till her eyes and her tongue popped out."

"Joel!" she exclaimed with a laugh. "Do you think that sounds very sane?"

"I wish all my remarks were as much so," he said. "They used to think the mad were possessed by devils. They knew what they were talking about."

"But this is foolish," Linda said. "Of course she's not really mad, Joel. . . . You can't call a person mad just because she's silly."

"She has a mad smell," Joel said. "I've noticed it often."

Linda laughed again. "That's just the perfume she uses."

"Not what I mean," he said. "But let's not talk about her."

It does seem a waste, Linda thought, when the night is so beautiful, with this soft sky full of light; but if I do not talk of something I keep thinking of Dicky, and wondering about him, and it scares me that I should be so scared of thinking of him just because I saw that look on his face; but really it makes no difference, she thought, because whether I talk or not I think of him, and now we are almost at the Grove. The question is, will Dicky be there?

Brad turned so sharply into the drive that Linda bent towards Joel to escape being brushed by some leaves. In a minute, she thought, we will be knowing about Dicky; we may find him peacefully talking with Father — or he may be upstairs in his room, drinking.

They got out of the car very quietly in order not to waken Mother.

"I'll see if he's with Father," Brad said; and Linda watched the lighthouse as they waited, not speaking, until he returned.

"Father says he stopped in a few minutes ago and said he was going over to the rock for a swim. Joel, let's you and I go along, shall we?"

"I want to go," Linda said.

"You better wait here," Brad said. "He may be around the place somewhere drinking. He may come back any time, and you don't want him breezing in there with the Parson if he's too drunk, or perhaps waking Mother."

"All right," she said, but she could not bear not to be going.

Ellen came close beside her as she still watched the lighthouse. "Linda," she said, "I'm afraid."

"What of?" Linda asked.

"I'm afraid that Dicky's done something awful."

Linda felt for a moment as if she would laugh: to hear Ellen talk in this dramatic way made everything seem absurd; perhaps, she thought, when we left the beach so suddenly and drove back here in such a tense mysterious fashion we were all of us behaving like Ellen; perhaps any minute Dicky will open the door and ask what's the matter.

"Why should he do anything awful?" she asked.

"Because he was so angry," Ellen said. "I'm afraid he may kill himself."

"People don't kill themselves because they are angry," Linda said impatiently.

"It's not only that," Ellen said. "Oh Linda, you

understand perfectly well. I know you do from the way you were talking the other night. If I were Dicky I 'd kill myself, I really would; because I know what I 'm like. And you don't; you never have."

Linda could not bear to answer her.

"I 'm telling you this," Ellen said, "because I love you. I always have, but you never believed me. You would n't believe I could, but I do, and I know you don't believe me now. But this is the kind of person I am, Linda: I 'm really hoping that Dicky will drown himself. You don't believe me, but I really am. I don't know why. I am fond of Dicky, I suppose, but I 'm hoping that he will kill himself because it would be so awful and so exciting, and because I 'm trying so hard not to hope for it and trying to pretend that I 'm not hoping, but that only makes me keep hoping more and more. Now what do you think of me, Linda?"

Linda turned sharply to look at her. There was a quality in Ellen's voice, a mixture of excitement and misery and even a kind of triumph, that she had not heard before. This all may be true, she thought: Ellen may be as wretched as anyone, as even Dicky; there may be dark chasms inside her that she is always walking round and peering into, hypnotized by a kind of terror and re-pulsion; she may feel other people's feeling about her, and never for a minute be able to escape from it, and that may be what drives her crazily on, as the gadfly sent by Hera to torment poor Io drove her in a wild gallop all over the world; but I cannot think of her now as in any way important; I can only think of her voice going on indefinitely.

"Ellen," she exclaimed, "do stop talking. No one can help the way they are made, I suppose, if that's any

291

consolation. But if you love me, do leave me in peace."

"Look out!" Brad called from below, but Joel needed no warning: this path down the cliff was treacherous after dark, even by moonlight. If Dicky came down here in a hurry, he thought, especially if he had had something to drink, it would be the easiest thing in the world for him to stumble, or step off the edge; and Joel stood still for a minute at the curve to peer down at the stony beach, half expecting to see Dicky fallen. There was a dark splotch on the stones that gave him a start, but he saw that it was only a bunch of kelp.

By the time he had scrambled down, Brad was climbing over the slippery end of the rock. If we see no trace of him, Joel thought, what then? What can we do? Is this a fool's errand, or is it something awful that you can hardly believe?

He joined Brad, who was standing on the ledge where they always undressed.

"His clothes are here," Brad said. "He's in swimming. He can't have been here more than five or ten minutes."

They clambered to the edge and looked across the water: southward it was so bright that you would think anything within two or three hundred yards would stand out clearly, and yet as you stared at that blinking dancing whiteness you could see it filled with innumerable black holes blurred by the glitter all around them; as you let your eyes move over the moon path you could imagine any number of people swimming, though if you kept your gaze fixed on one special place you could see that those dark moving holes were only the shadows of ripples; and then the very texture and pattern of the moon path would blur and change, and you could not be sure of anything. Eastward, towards Sakonnet, you saw only the vague water and the black line of the reef, for it was low tide, and then beyond that you could see nothing but emptiness until the row of lights on the other shore.

"We might try shouting," Brad said. "He'll hear us if he's anywhere around"; and one after the other and then both together they shouted his name: it seemed as if their voices were traveling on indefinitely over that black and that shining water, but Dicky did not answer them. We might as well be dogs, Joel thought, howling at the moon.

"If he dived almost anywhere to-night," Brad said, "and wasn't pretty careful he might have hit his head on a rock."

"What do you think we better do?" Joel asked.

"We might go in ourselves," Brad said, "and swim around a bit. I don't know much else we can do. Of course he may be swimming quite far out, but he wouldn't stay in very long at night, I should think."

They took off their clothes, dropping them beside Dicky's. Joel shivered as the air blew along his naked body, but when he dove he found that the water was not so cold as he had feared: it felt very salty and smelled nicely of seaweed.

"Why don't you swim along by the cliff," he said, "and I'll go out around the reef."

As he swam straight out he turned his head now and then to look after Brad in the midst of the moon's glitter; but in a few yards he lost sight of him; and now while he swam on, moving easily so as not to grow tired, he kept peering to either side for a trace of Dicky: but how can you hope to find him, he thought, if he does not want to be found? Brad and I are swimming here off Castle Rock by moonlight looking for Dicky, and perhaps he is not alive. It does not seem possible, when we all have swum here so often; it seems if he were to be drowned off this rock that somehow we would have felt it, felt something strange and wrong; how could we always have been swimming here, before breakfast sometimes, and all through the morning, and often late in the afternoon when the rock was covered entirely by the cliff's shadow, and sometimes, but not often, like this, at night; how could we always have been doing it, not suspecting, and then be swimming here now, Brad and I, Brad swimming down the moon path towards the Third Beach and I swimming through this dark water towards Sakonnet looking for Dicky, who probably is drowned, who probably wanted to be drowned?

He thought he heard Brad call, but he was not sure. Turning on his back, he shouted with all his strength; and suddenly he felt that it could not be borne that this was happening: it's the hellishness in life, he thought, that you may find yourself in the midst of at any time, and always you feel that it cannot be borne, and yet of all things you know it cannot be escaped; you may not be remembering there is such a thing and then, as you turn your head, it is upon you. He could see the sky full of its drifting light extending forever above him, and the water through which he swam seemed to have no bottom. Perhaps that is what turned men to their Gods, he thought, the hope to escape what they felt, being man, must be there waiting for them, even those who as yet had not felt it actually; perhaps some never feel it; but surely at some time or other everyone must feel that it is there, that sometime he may be feeling it. The Peace that passeth understanding, he thought, would be the peace that it could not enter or disturb, and it was from this hellishness that Buddha offered mankind an escape into Nirvana.

Joel heard Brad calling, this time surely; and the voice, as far as he could tell, seemed to come from the rock. He turned around: it's no good swimming on like this, he thought; it is just wasting time; perhaps the thing to do would be to get a boat, or perhaps Brad has found Dicky — but no, I am sure not that.

He stared along the water to see if he could make out any figure or figures on the rock; but in the moonlight the rock itself became part of the cliff; you could tell nothing: the cliff might be a smooth mountain barrier a mile high seen from far out in the ocean.

Mark, rubbing the end of his cigar round and round in the ash tray, stared upward almost sharply at Brad.

"You say you've been all about in Manuel's launch?" he asked. "Did you look along the edge of the cliff?"

"We looked everywhere," Brad told him. "We've been cruising back and forth for the last couple of hours."

"There's not a chance that he's alive," Mark said.

"If he got too far out," Brad said, "there's always a chance that some boat might have picked him up."

"A chance, yes," Mark exclaimed dryly. "About one in ten thousand, I should say."

"It was very low tide," Brad said; "he may have hurt himself diving and not been able to land."

"Possibly," Mark said. "My opinion is we'll never know."

Brad went to the door. "I guess I'll go back," he said, and couldn't keep himself from yawning. "Joel's still cruising around, and he's going to pick me up at the mooring. I thought I'd better let you know how things were. Mother won't have to know anything till to-morrow, but I thought you should hear about it to-night."

"Yes," Mark said, "I'm glad you came back. I don't suppose it will do a particle of good for you and Joel to keep on, but perhaps you better. You might find . . ." and Mark closed his lips tightly together, knowing that he could not make himself say the words: *his body.* "Have you told Linda?" he then asked.

"Yes," Brad said.

"And Ellen?"

"Linda will do that."

"I don't envy her her job," Mark said. "Good night."

"Good night. You better go to bed, I should think."

"I may presently," Mark said.

But he still kept rubbing the end of his cigar in the ashes, pushing on it harder and harder until the tobacco crumbled into pieces; then he moved the ash tray to the other side of the table, put his hands on the arms of the chair as if to get up, and sat there poised for almost a minute, a slight scowl on his face. Then he leaned back again, his arms tightly folded.

"There's not a chance," he muttered to himself; "of course there's not a chance, but I suppose it does no harm to keep looking."

This will kill his mother, he thought; or perhaps in her condition the shock will be dulled; let us hope so. Of course Dicky knew what he was doing, but she need never be told that.

Suicide, he thought; it is called a sin, but I do not blame Dicky; I defy anyone to blame Dicky. The sins of others, he thought, oh, the sins of others, how good they make us feel!

If he had been killed in the war, Mark thought, I was prepared for that, at least I think I was; and now it is much better that he should die than it seemed then; so I should be able to face this: but then I would have thought of his life as being happy. I suppose, he thought, the thing you keep wishing more than anything else, really, is that your children should be happy. . . . The greatest sacrifice that could be made would be to send your son to be crucified.

I must go to my room and lie down, he thought, and if I can get some sleep, all the better; I'm glad Luly is sleeping because it would be hard just now to talk to any-one. In my work I have talked to many in deep afflic-tion; I have grown familiar with death. Now let me profit, if I can, by my own counsel.

VII

LINDA walked through the hall, between the rows of white doors with their black iron knobs, and very carefully opened the door of Pat's room. It was just beginning to be light and she could hear the crowing of cocks from around the fields: cockcrow, she thought, the symbol of another day. Always the first morning after we arrived they would wake me, and if I was not too excited at the thought of being here I would go to sleep again; and sometimes they would wake me the second morning, and then I would not hear them again all summer.

Pat lay on his side, his head bent far back so that his throat made a smoothly swelling curve that did not look very comfortable; but she hesitated to lift his head for fear it would waken him. For Pat sleeping, she thought, none of this has happened; it has not happened for Mother; if Joel had died in Persia there might have been days and days when for me he would have been living: but everything must happen, she thought, on some day or other, even if it has been preparing for years, and that day, as you look ahead, seems no different from all the rest; it is just next Wednesday or next Thursday, and yet hiding somewhere among its hours is the thing that when it happens you cannot believe, that sets it apart forever. It seems that if the day could have been skipped that special

298

thing might have been avoided; perhaps sometimes it could, but often, I'm sure, it would simply be passed on to the next. She remembered Pat asking her once if you would have a birthday every year if it came on the twenty-ninth of February: "I don't see how you could," he had said; and, smiling, with wide-open eyes, not quite believing himself, he had moved his hand slowly along the tablecloth. "I should think it would come along like this to your birthday, and then I should think it would leap right over it," and his curved hand made a dolphin-like leap from the table and came down a foot further on. If to-day, or rather yesterday, could have been jumped, she thought, would Dicky not have done this? But what does it matter now? If you were given two or three days in your life that you would be allowed to skip, the way you were given just so many steps to take in blind-man's buff, you would never know in advance what ones to choose; and if from the start you could see them all, every one, perhaps you could never choose enough to be able to go on living.

Mother, she thought, who now is sleeping, must often have looked at Dicky asleep, when he was small like Pat, as I am looking at Pat now; she must often have wondered; and when she was most filled with love for him she must sometimes have been filled with dread as she thought of all the days of his life; but luckily she could not see this; and if you are sometimes filled with dread you are sometimes filled with such hope, such yearning and joy, that it more than strikes a balance. It is strange, she thought, that if I could be seeing enough, I might at this very moment wish more than anything that Pat would die before he wakes, that Joel would die; I might wish for my own death, but that is not so strange.

299

Since I am to go on living, she thought, living, as far as I know, for many years, I know at last what I must do: of course I knew it from the first, knew it so well that it is strange to remember how I wavered. Dicky, she thought (and how simple it is now to see you, even the parts of you that were most deeply hidden, because now all parts of you are equally near to me, and all your different times), when you fled last night so swiftly, so quietly, escaped once and for all from what you could not bear, you made me realize that I too cannot bear not to escape: you made things that had seemed too intricate ever to disentangle suddenly quite clear. You were caught and perhaps your flight was the best you could have chosen; Brad in a way is caught, though not so desperately, and there is something in Brad, which is not in you or me, that is able to trick what has captured him, to let him keep escaping without its knowing, without his knowing, and so to prevent its secretly destroying him; but for me, if I let myself go on living the strange half-life the days have drawn me into, or I, through many days, have drawn myself into more and more deeply, among the multitude of dead or half-dead things that I cannot see over, with Pat the one thing, for me, truly living and yet myself so doubtfully at all times living that some of that deadness comes even between me and Pat; if I let myself go on I would simply grow thinner and thinner inside myself, and what is outside would be more and more un-meaning; and when anything in me moved it would simply be blowing here and there, quickly, in this or that direction, and have nothing really to do with my outer movements. Now at last with Joel it seems that gradually I can break through into life, Joel, who happens to be near me, who happens to be living out of all possible time at the time that I am living; and dear little Pat, she thought, I know now that this is the best thing for you as much as for me, and I know that my thinking this is not just one of the excuses that I am so skillful at making; because in that kind of life, always among those things, there was every chance that you too would be caught; and I who might have seen it happening, and now and then have rushed quite desperately about inside myself, I could not have helped you much, I'm afraid, because my own life would have been so nervous and brittle; but now at the worst you will have two kinds of life, two ways of living, and I hope your own life may become free and strong, more and more a part of all life, so that if I could see it now I would not dread or despair, I would only be glad.

Dicky, she thought suddenly, you must not mind (and this is one of the things that, smiling, you would never have minded) that thinking of you and of your death makes me think and keep thinking of Pat's life and my own; because it is only by feeling death that you can begin at all clearly to see life: how it always matters and always does not matter.

PART V

September 1931

September 1931

O F course," Mark said, "if your mother were living it would have been out of the question; but I believe now that it 's the only thing to do — that is, if you don't object."

"I 've told you," Linda said, as she looked through the foggy trees, and made her steps once more a little slower so that she would not hurry him, "I 've told you a dozen times that I don't object. Why won't you believe me?"

"Because I 've put you in a difficult position," Mark said; "I 've tried not to but I have — but I don't see exactly how I could have avoided it. I 'm afraid without meaning to I 've been using a sort of polite blackmail: because you probably feel that any objection on your part will seem selfish and greedy. Of course it won't. It will be quite reasonable."

"Father, what shall I tell you?" Linda said with a laugh, but feeling a little impatient. "Even if it was n't for Brad I think it would be the best thing to do, and Joel agrees absolutely. We have talked it over."

"I know I 'll have a time with Brad," Mark said. "He will think I 'm cheating you and Pat out of your birthright, but I know, too, what it will mean to him. Captain Bigelow, even now, I think, would give forty or fifty thousand. Of course that 's dirt cheap for the house

305

and the trees and the fifty-odd acres, but I think we can count ourselves lucky at this particular time to sell it at all. As Brad says, when you 're rich one thousand dollars is n't much, but when you 're poor one thousand is an awful lot; and forty thousand will be enough, I 'm sure, to carry Brad along. Of course, if he did fail now, it would not be dishonorable; men are doing it right and left; but I think it 's something that Brad would n't get over. He 'd always feel responsible."

"I should think the best way," Linda said, "would be not to consult Brad until it 's all arranged."

"I don't know but what you 're right," Mark said.

Linda kept staring at the trees with the fog drifting among them: how soft they looked, as if the fog were their own damp essence slowly seeping out of them, out of their trunks and their branches and their leaves, all now the same color, the color of wet gray lichens; as if the darkness that would be hiding them completely in a few moments, by the time Father and she had walked from gate to gate once or twice more, were simply the shadow, the dark-saturated air, into which they had dissolved. She listened vaguely to the foghorns, far-away, persistent, that you kept forgetting and then kept hearing: you could not think of their coming from any particular direction, from any lighthouse or ship; their sound must be simply this darkening air drifting through coils of fog or moving heavily along the rough tops of the waves.

"Of course," Father said, "possibly Pat could buy it again when he grows up, if he really wanted to."

"I hope not," Linda said. "It would not be the same."

If Mother were alive, she thought, we could not think of it, as Father was saying — but now that Mother is dead

306

paressed

. . . This place belongs to the past, she thought, this place
and its way of life are going surely, as the life in the South
before the Civil War has gone, the life of which Mother
caught echoes from her mother, when she was a girl in
Savannah: and of course it is right that it should go, and
whether it goes by the kind of violence that destroyed the
old South, the upheaval that changed Russia, or whether
it goes gently, little by little, with each of the next few
generations, does not in the long run make very much
difference; but I am glad Mother will not be able to see
its going, because she belonged to it entirely, to all that
was finest and most beautiful (among so much that was
anything but beautiful, and surely always there will be
enough of that) in the generation that is disappearing.
Suppose that Mother were a young girl to-day . . . Then
Linda thought of something that Mother had told her
years after it happened: of how a colored girl who was
working in the Rectory became involved with some men
and contracted syphilis; and how Mother, though Brad
and Dicky and she were children in the house, had kept
her as a second maid during the years of her treatment.
"The doctor said there was practically no risk," she explained, "if certain precautions were taken, and I knew
that if I let her go in that state her life would have been
ruined"; and Linda remembered all that Mother had done,
for so many people, through years and years, and thought
of all she must have done that no one knew of, unless
perhaps Father.   It is easy to sneer at that way of helping,
she thought, as bourgeois charity, as hopelessly out of
date, but for Mother it was devotion always, in the way
she knew, to the people around her, her struggle always
to lighten the sum of human suffering; and if she were
a young girl now she would be giving herself for others, in

the new ways, with the same devotion, looking forward perhaps as ardently, as confidently, to a future heaven on earth as she believed always, during her life, in a heaven after death.

Linda thought of the bureau drawers she had been going through all day, and the desk and the wardrobe and the closets: because in March when they opened the house for the funeral there had been no thought of selling. There were letters that Mother had tied in bundles, dated some of them from the years when Mother was a girl in the South, some from the years in New York, and some from North Chester, with Mother's request that they were to be burned at her death; and Linda had burned them in the open fire in the dining room, knowing that they contained, some of them, things about Mother, parts of Mother, that she had never known, some of them that Father had never known, and that now were gone forever. She had found here and there many photographs of Mother at all ages, and of Brad and Dicky and herself when they were babies, when they were growing older, photographs some of which she remembered and some of which she did not; she had come across quantities of old programmes of recitals in which they had played; and all the old reports of their years in school and college. Apparently Mother had kept them all, everything that had to do with her children. And Linda now in the darkness, as she walked with Father, who perhaps was thinking also of Mother and of his own life, and his summers here at the Grove since he was a young man, felt a ghostly sense, as you might catch an echo of sound, a reflection of light, from the far side of a hill, of all the years that Mother had been living: of Mother as a child, in a plaid dress, with a round comb in her hair, and pouting lips, with her father reading to her,

a very wise little girl who loved history as much as stories
but had trouble with her spelling; of Mother as a young
girl dancing to Strauss waltzes (and as Linda this afternoon had played one of those waltzes that she came across
while going through Mother's music, she had had for a
moment a sense of Mother, slim and passionate and dark,
graciously dancing and dancing: such a sharp sense that
she almost had to stop playing); as a young woman in
Switzerland, with her alpenstock, her tight shirtwaist,
her neat little hat, standing on a glacier with Father (it
was before they were engaged and Father looked young
and pale and wore a drooping moustache like the guide's);
of Mother looking at the sea, listening to the wind, filled
with life, all the life that was afterwards to come out of
her; a young woman breathing the air of the mountains or
the sea, or the close air of tenements and prisons, but always the air that belonged in a different region from the
air you breathed, the air of another time, another generation, the air that little by little loses its power to keep
alive all the people, girls and boys, young men and young
women, climbing mountains, making love, having children,
all the men and women who breathed it, who perhaps
had created it, unless it created them, old men and women
now, those that were left, breathing the remnants of that
thin air: thin compared with the air I breathe, she thought,
because they have strayed into our region, but in itself
behind that hill (which I can just peer over, just cannot
peer over) life-giving and indestructible.

Then she thought of Mother in those last pitiful months:
asking sometimes for Dicky, remembering and forgetting,
sometimes thinking of Brad and Dicky and her as children, thinking of herself sometimes as a child. She remembered the way Mother's eyes would follow her as she

left the room (and how often she had left it) and how
they would turn towards her (with such an effort in those
last few weeks) as she came in the door. I would sit by
your bed, she thought, until you went to sleep, watching
your face, holding your hand, just as you sat by my bed
when I was a child, there in that room where I was born.
Oh, Mother, did you know how much I loved you, how
much we all loved you, though we did not always say it,
were not always able to show it completely? Now you
are dead; you are no longer the helpless body that I
watched, while you slept or lay half-conscious with neck
and mouth distorted and a sad dull look in your eyes that
had been so beautiful; but always, even now, you will
be giving me more than I could give: because through
you, through your being, I cannot help having still faith
in life; and without the sense of you, of what you always
were, my happiness with Joel might seem, I am afraid,
simply an island that I had found by chance, that I did
not deserve to find and might not have found, in the
midst of the uncertainty that is almost everywhere.
Perhaps you did not always understand the selves that
we became, because the air we breathed was different;
possibly among much good you worked us some harm
in your devotion to our happiness, seeing us always as
your children: but perhaps the way you saw us, different
as it was from the way we came to see ourselves and each
other, from the way other people came to be seeing us,
perhaps your Brad and Dicky and Linda caught and
preserved in us something that came to exist only in your
vision and yet of all the pictures of ourselves was the one,
if there can be one, that had the most truth, because it
was created by the deepest love (just as, whatever he
becomes, my own vision of Pat may always be the truest);

and in your Brad and Dicky and Linda there was something young and fresh and loving which if it ever existed
in us at all makes it surely better that we have lived: yes,
even better for poor Dicky, better for Brad and me in
spite of all that may happen.

Through the drifting darkness of the fog and the
sounds that you kept hearing and not hearing of the foghorns somewhere at sea, there came the long deep whistle
of a boat, muffled like all the rest but more powerful, a
sound that made you think of lights looming high above
you and the churning, through the dark, of dim white
water.

"That must be the Fall River boat," Father said, "just
coming in to Long Wharf.   Or is it too early?"

And Linda remembered how they used to hate leaving
the Grove each September, Brad and Dicky and she,
leaving each autumn by the Fall River boat as they arrived
each June by the train; how during the last few days they
would slink apart from each other and sometimes be
found with signs of tears on their faces; and sometimes
she used to dream in midsummer that the summer was
over and wake up from her dream so happy to know that
they still had several weeks that she could not go to sleep
for an hour; and she remembered the awful feeling of
climbing into the surrey or the carriole after dark and
driving through the trees not bearing to look back at the
house, not bearing to speak to each other, and the coldness,
the scariness of the wharf, the lights from the boat as it
swiftly came through the harbor, the tiny white state-
rooms, and the miniature cakes of soap neatly wrapped
that they loved to divide between them; and then the
red plush and gold and white of the saloon where the
orchestra was playing, and the huge mirrors on the stairs,

and the windy darkness of the upper deck where they would stand, side by side, holding firmly to the railing until they were out of the harbor, and the last lights from the shore were gone, and from the mastheads of the yachts — and their summer at the Grove was ended.